# Bougainvillea along the Bosporus

## City of Love

# Bougainvillea along the Bosporus

## City of Love

### Alex J. Owen

Winchester, UK
Washington, USA

First published by Roundfire Books, 2013
Roundfire Books is an imprint of John Hunt Publishing Ltd., Laurel House, Station Approach,
Alresford, Hants, SO24 9JH, UK
office1@jhpbooks.net
www.johnhuntpublishing.com
www.roundfire-books.com

For distributor details and how to order please visit the 'Ordering' section on our website.

Text copyright: Alex J. Owen 2012

ISBN: 978 1 78099 931 9

A CIP catalogue record for this book is available from the British Library.

Design: Lee Nash

Printed and bound by CPI Group (UK) Ltd, Croydon, CR0 4YY

We operate a distinctive and ethical publishing philosophy in all
areas of our business, from our global network of authors to
production and worldwide distribution.

# Chapter One

JJ gently put down his empty beer glass, the froth still hanging on the inside like small white clouds, the dew on the outside reminded him of how cold it had been to drink. He looked across at the reception desk and foyer. It was quiet, the group of Japanese tourists having left a few moments before. It seemed the ideal time to start his journey. Standing, he walked briskly to the main street door, pushing his way through as another party of Japanese tourists entered bedecked with cameras, guidebooks, sunhats and reflector sunglasses – or was it the same group coming back? It was the sixth day he'd made the journey but on no occasion had he been able to prepare himself for the thud of heat and noise that greeted him as he reached the street. He stood and spent a moment adjusting his hat – a Panama he had decided gave him an easily identifiable image with his light summer suit, together with a pair of Ray Bans and a light cane. Turning right on leaving the hotel, the heat was stifling in the narrow streets as he made his way down the hill, with each step resisting the temptation to turn and check whether he was being followed.

Being followed was, of course, the purpose of his daily walk, the sixth consecutive time he had made the trip. He was trying to create a routine, a pattern. If he wasn't being followed today or any other day it was over before it began and no amount of planning would allow their escape.

He paid no attention to the sights that were thrilling groups of tourists, all the time getting closer to the water, sensing the mingling smells of cooking as the street traders came into sight. By the time he reached the first of them he could see the bridge, the water and his destination. This was the part of the journey he feared the most, fearing he would lose his followers, but fearing most of all the noise; that was now very loud and would become even louder as he crossed to the other side of the bridge, crossing the river as it entered a larger expanse of water, a small sea in fact.

Crossing the bridge on the lower pedestrian level to avoid the chaotic traffic, he took time to dawdle, looking at the goods outside the little shops and, as usual, resisting the temptation to stop at a cafe and have a drink. He was starting to need one not only to quench his thirst but also to steady his nerves.

By the time he reached the other side of the bridge the noise was so intense it hurt, the heat of the day containing the noise, forcing it down, like a giant weight. The pressure on his hearing had increased since he had started to cross the bridge. The noise from a mass of people all appearing to be going in different directions, all talking at once, seeming to shout as though trying to communicate with other planets. The endless flow of traffic all trying to reach some unknown destination, cars, lorries, tractors and mopeds each making their own contribution to the sounds of the city. The water that had to be crossed to go to work, return home, and back to work again. Crossing back and forth all day and most of the night the ferry boats added their contribution to the noise. The thrashing of the propellers in the water, the shrill blast of the ship's whistle as it announced its arrival, the hoot, hoot as it prepared to depart, and the more strident blast as it tried to avoid small boats being crushed under its bow. The small boats selling supposedly freshly-caught fish which was being fried in oil over open charcoal fires and served as sandwiches, the hot oil in the pans sloshing back and forth with the rocking of the boat in water, the charcoal flaring with every drop of oil that spilt.

The ferries unloading people, cars, lorries, tractors and even an occasional donkey cart. The vehicles were all impatient to join the thousands of others already clogging the roads. A blast from a horn as a driver tries to persuade those on foot and on bicycles to move out of his way. There were people rushing, the ferryboats rushing, the vehicles attempting to rush. Everything and everyone was rushing.

This was a city with a prized heritage in railways; the main station just across the road, the thud and the roar as mighty diesel locomotives hauled a huge array of carriages, clanking over the ancient track into the station. His timing was again perfect for he needed to be on the platform when the train was about to reload for its return journey to distant shores.

Steeling himself for the ordeal, he crossed the road at a set of traffic lights on red, knowing well that if the lights turned to green the drivers would show him little mercy, not run him down but trap him in the middle of the road; surrounded by noise.

Trains only arrived and departed from this station, they didn't pass through. It was the end of the line. No provision had ever been made for trains to cross the waterway behind him; passengers wishing to continue their journey to other parts of this huge country and the continent beyond took a ferry and caught another train on the opposite side of the waterway.

He entered the station at the closed end, relieved to have some respite from the noise and the blazing sun, walking down the platform as the train was drawing to a stop. The huge diesel locomotives, once stopped, shut down their engines. The concourse area of this magnificent station, more a monument to the Architects and Builders of the bygone age of steam, the magnificent moldings and ornate columns, complex cast iron roof supports holding in place the glass, colored brown from the years of steam, dust and the humid city air. Small shops, car hire firms and cafes lined the concourse like the bridge he had just crossed with the railway offices above them. He could now see his goal, the last café on the left.

As he walked tentatively towards the cafe, panic started inside him. The person he expected to see was not sitting at the table by the door. Instead, there sat a policeman looking intimidating in green uniform complete with its black belt and its holstered pistol and those silver reflector sunglasses. Unsure of what to do next he said to himself, 'Don't panic, sunglasses don't shoot you, guns do and his is in its holster.' He started to tremble with fear; having been unable to convince himself of his safety.

At that moment a slim, cool hand slipped into his, he turned and looked down into her smiling face. The feeling of relief was almost as painful as his fear had been. Francine was here with him holding his hand, smiling, lips slightly apart, fresh and looking perfectly calm and relaxed, not locked up in some prison cell or worse. He tried to compose himself and relax to rid himself of the fear and panic that had gripped him since seeing that policeman sitting there at the café. She sensed how tense and afraid he was and to relax and comfort him she reached up, put a hand on his shoulder, pulled him down to her level cupping his face between her hands, kissing him briefly on the lips said, 'Sorry darling, both you and the train are five minutes early today; I was in that shop over there.'

Walking with her hand holding his arm, they started for the café. As if on cue the policeman stood up as they approached and started walking towards them. She gripped his arm, trying to relax him. He was level with them now. As he walked past them his radio crackled giving him a message as he continued his journey down the concourse towards the closed end. Shaking with a mixture of fear and relief as the adrenalin rush subsided they collapsed at the café table and ordered coffee and brandy; the local, not imported, both needing the stiff hit as the harsh spirit burnt their throats. He downed his brandy in two gulps, but after the first sip she put down her glass and concentrated on her coffee. Pushing her part – empty glass towards him saying, 'Drink the rest of that and for goodness sake relax, I'm going to the little girls' room.'

Leaning back in his chair, clutching the glass she had given him, he closed his eyes and tried to relax. Suddenly remembering the little chap in the stiff dark blue suite, he started forward in his chair and looked around the platform, finally spotting him trying to look inconspicuous. He had also sought refuge in a café, looking very out of place with that ridicules suite he had worn every day!

He sensed, rather than heard, her behind him, Francine had always had had that effect on him. She caressed the back of his neck. Then as she started to knead her thumbs into the muscles at the base of his neck she said in a soft voice, not a whisper but a soft, gentle caring voice, 'When you answered that stupid advert six months ago I bet you never expected all the trouble we are in now?'

'We are not exactly in trouble at the moment are we? We haven't really done anything wrong.'

'No,' she said. 'Nothing really apart from planning a major terrorist attack against the State, having a store of high explosives and automatic firearms, consorting with known criminals and worst of all committing adultery with the wife of a Muslim. If my husband's brothers ever find out they will cut of all those important pieces of you that I love.' At that point she kissed him on the back his neck and pushed him up.

'Come on let's go, we have served our function today,' she said.

The stupid advert she had referred to was the one that had brought him to this city.

# Chapter Two

John Jamison, JJ to anyone who had met him once, was sitting at his office desk; he always liked to be in early. It gave him time to recover from the train journey into London. How he hated the commuter train, it was always overcrowded and noisy; he was halfway through his coffee and Danish pastry and had just turned to the appointments section of his newspaper when he spotted a perfect opening for him to escape the humdrum life that he'd created for himself.

*Are you one of those who can do and teach?*
*We are looking for an experienced Civil Engineer to be a mentor to students; you will be working in an overseas environment. A military background would be an advantage. Phone for an application form.*
*Etc.*

Without further thought he picked up the phone and rang the number listed in the advert.

The following day, Saturday, the post arrived containing the application form.

'Why can't you have a job like other men?' His wife Elizabeth shouted. 'It's always the same, we get settled and you get bored. When you get bored you start looking for another job.'

What she really meant was *she* had got settled!

'Darling,' he said as calmly as he could, 'it's not that at all. You don't understand – you never have. I've been doing the same job for nearly thirty years, all I do is change where I'm doing it and who pays me. I don't want a new job. What I want is a new career, to start something new, something different!'

'You're thirty-nine for Heaven's sake,' she snapped back, 'you'll be forty in two weeks' time. Why can't you accept what you are and what you have? You've got a good income, a lovely home, an exotic car, the twins adore you, the dogs worship you and I love you. Isn't it enough that I don't want you to go away again?' She had lowered her voice to a faint tremble and was looking at the floor, a sure sign tears were on the way.

'Look what happened when you were working in Rhodesia, you joined the army and got shot. You could have been killed, not just left with a big hole in your leg.'

JJ thought back:

*Always on the lookout for 'adventure' he called it. Elizabeth called it many other things, JJ joined the part-time Police Anti-Terrorist Unit. His reputation with explosives, (his party piece was to blow a door knob from a door without scorching the paint or damaging the lock) soon came to the attention of the Commander of the Selous Scouts, the finest, toughest and roughest bush troops in the world, and he was persuaded to try for a transfer to that unit as a regular soldier. Military service was compulsory at that time for all adult, white Rhodesian, male residents. As JJ was a new immigrant, he was allowed a twelve-month period free of conscription. JJ was happy with the prospect of being a regular and his employer could not object as it was for the security of the Country. Being a regular meant that he would do three months in the army and three months at his normal work.*

*The training was both grueling and vicious, the food a joke, with the occasional luxury of a Kudu steak but mainly a diet of raw baboon or snake which made him think fondly of the shortages in the shops of Rhodesia and Zambia, those wonderful toilet rolls, oh so much better than a leaf, unless you could find a fresh one on a banana plant, which were rare in the bush. After three months, JJ won his place in the Scouts, taking with him his rank of captain which he had previously enjoyed in the Police Anti-Terrorist Unit. His function in the Scouts was the demolition of enemy installations and the line of escape into their strongholds in the neighboring countries. Occasionally his special talents were called upon to open a safe in the office or bedroom of some Communist commander or instructor. This he enjoyed; his comrades* suggesting that if a bank safe was ever blown after the war the police would know who to look for.

He was sitting, taking a few minutes' rest in the right-hand, co-pilot's seat of the helicopter that had picked his unit up from a PV 'Protected Village' outside Fort Victoria where they'd had been on patrol for the last 10 days, one of the least liked duties that the Selous Scouts got involved in. A 'PV' is a new village created to house people from the surrounding area and provide a secure environment for them to live as normal a life as possible, ensuring that they are free from infiltration by insurgents. As he'd sat in the seat, he had automatically put on the headset, and now wished he hadn't. A very excited male voice came over the headphones.

'We are under attack. Someone please help us'

The caller gave his location, which JJ knew was close by. He told the panicking voice to hold and asked the pilot to confirm their flying time to the location. He confirmed, four minutes. Getting back to the radio he told the voice that help was only minutes away, trying to calm him down at the same time giving orders to his unit to be ready to drop into a fire-fight in under five minutes, switching the radio onto the rear-cabin PA system in order that they all could hear the details as they came in.

The voice identified itself as Frank who, with his wife Kate, farmed a small dairy herd. The attack had started a few minutes before with a burst of tracers into the thatched roof of the homestead. Frank and his wife were so far unhurt but they were badly shaken up. They could see the farm now. The thatch was glowing as brightly as the floodlights that illuminated the cleared killing area around the homestead. The killing area, as recommended by the army, was an area of about one hundred meters, around the house, cleared of all vegetation and other objects that could hide a terrorist and illuminated by floodlights. The only recommendation they and so many other farmers ignored, was to replace the thatch on the roof with corrugated iron to prevent just this.

JJ joined his unit, getting into his kit for the rope drop into the thick of the battle as the exchange of fire could now heard over the clatter of *the rotors. The pilot's voice came over the PA.*

*'Over target; now, go. Go...'*

*As they swung out through the large doorways on both sides of the helicopter and started the descent, JJ looked down. They were over a nest of Terrs. The farmer had been sloppy with where he had stored the detritus from the ground clearance, forming a perfect lair from which to launch the attack. JJ looked down, surprised to see a group of five youths, the oldest; about fifteen, was holding an AK47 and aiming it straight at him. The youth pulled the trigger but held it too long; the recoil of the sustained burst spoilt his aim, sending most of the burst wild. JJ however caught a couple of rounds in the thigh, the impact sending him spinning round and round on the rope. Then, to his delight, one of his unit sent an RPG round into the group, for a moment, lighting up a whole vista of flying limbs and blood, then silence; the gunfire had stopped. At that moment he passed out.*

*When he came to, the unit's medic was bending over his leg, emptying a syringe of morphine into him. As he put a field dressing around the wound, he sensed that JJ had regained consciousness and, rising, he smiled and said,*

*'Hi, Captain, you're fine. You caught two slugs in the thigh inches from any bone or other important part. You'll be playing cricket again tomorrow.' With that, he went in search of his next patient but fortunately not finding any he returned five minutes later and updated JJ on the battle that never was. The group of five had been the entire terrorist force, taken out with one RPG.*

*'The farmer is waiting to see you, if you're up to it.'*

*'OK, send him over.'*

*It took the farmer and his wife about half an hour to finish thanking JJ for saving them from a fate worse than death. Pleading a painful leg, he finally managed to persuade them to let him rest.*

*The army medic was right about one thing the 7.62 mm bullets from the AK 47 had missed bone and other important areas but what he hadn't seen was the damage those bullets had done to the muscle on their way through. After weeks of pain and treatment JJ was transferred from active duty with the Scouts to a training unit. Amongst other things before joining the Rhodesian Army he had been a civil engineer and explosives expert, now the army was using his engineering expertise to train the Scouts in how to blow up buildings, roads and bridges, taking the weak spots and using that to the demolition's advantage. He spent the next nine months on this assignment but it hadn't been as rewarding as being in the thick of the fighting. Eventually he managed to resign his commission, left the army; Rhodesia, and returned to England.*

He shook his head to clear his thoughts,

'I know. I love you too and it's not a very big hole, you can hardly see it now and a Porsche 911 is hardly exotic.' JJ sighed, putting his arms around her and pulling her to him, nuzzling his face into her hair. 'I always miss you when we are away from each other, you know that. It's just that I can't stop thinking there is something more exciting out there than doing the same thing year after year. Despite being shot at I really enjoyed my time in the army, there was always something different happening. There's a whole world I've hardly explored.' The front of his shirt started to feel wet – the tears had arrived.

Over the years JJ had become totally disenchanted with his job, his career, and had been constantly trying to think of something exciting, something different, some new and alternative way to make money, a deal, a scam, anything, anything for a change, for some excitement. He knew she was right of course, she always was, and he had no right to feel so fed up with things. He'd always had a good life and income and they had lived in many countries around the world in a fair amount of luxury. His stint in the Rhodesian army was probably the most exciting and certainly the least luxurious. He worked on contract, changing employer when he got bored or was offered more money by another company. It was surprising what a few extra pounds on the hourly rate could do for the morale. JJ worked in the oil industry. He was an expert, a true professional – a mercenary!

He was between overseas contracts at the time, due to the price of crude oil being down and when that happened investment in new oil related projects ceased. It had been so for one and a half years, which was why Elizabeth had complained about being settled. She didn't mind the short visits he made overseas, he would phone on his way home. 'I'm going to Italy tomorrow for two days or a week in Abu Dhabi.' It was, she knew, a way that his boredom, to some extent was kept in check.

He'd decided not to drive into London as the Hotel in Kensington had no car park and he didn't want to use his office parking space, as he'd phoned in sick that morning. He drove to the station and parked the Porsche in a space as near to the ticket office and security cameras as possible, hoping that it wouldn't be vandalized before his return. The journey to Kensington was quick and uneventful and he arrived at the hotel five minutes early, announcing himself to the incredibly attractive receptionist and taking a seat as requested. He began trying to plan the impending interview. He couldn't plan anything; the receptionist was holding all his attention, hotels of this type don't have large reception desks, just normal desk like tables. She was tall, with long dark brown hair falling thickly to her shoulders framing her very pretty face, a very shapely figure and the most magnificent legs he had ever seen. Sitting behind her desk, ankles demurely crossed, she was a sight so wonderful that time should not to be wasted on thinking about interviews and jobs. JJ was immediately filled with guilt, what would Elizabeth think? She wasn't English but he couldn't place her accent. She spoke with a trace of American but looked more as if she was from a country around the Mediterranean. He couldn't get the guilty feeling out of his head, about staring at her, as well as surprised by his thoughts.

'Hello. Captain John Jamison? I'm Conrad, Conrad

Mackenzie.' He spoke with a deep southern American drawl. JJ was a little taken aback by the use of his old army rank.

They entered a room, a typical central London hotel meeting room. Conrad went straight to the table he was using as a desk and started shuffling papers about in an effort, JJ thought, to hide his nervousness. Looking over he indicated the other table saying

'Well, Captain, help yourself to coffee and tell me why you're here.'

'Can we please drop the Captain bit? That was nearly twenty years ago. Please call me JJ everyone does.'

Resisting the "You invited me" response, JJ launched into the "I have always had an ambition to teach" routine and how rewarding he had found the training post with the Rhodesian army. It appeared to go down well.

Conrad nodded in what appeared to be the appropriate places and said 'mm' a lot. He then outlined the job he had on offer, that the successful applicant would teach mature students who could already speak, read and write English, not to teach grammar and punctuation, but to provide an engineering slant on the language. To assist the students pass their engineering exams. JJ thought back to his time at university and started to feel sorry for those wretched students trying to understand textbooks that he, a native English speaker, had had trouble understanding without guidance. They continued to talk for about an hour, Conrad asking about the various places where JJ had lived, were there any places he wouldn't, or couldn't, return to? Places that he loved, places that he hated. If he had a choice where would he like to return to? He seemed particularly interested in his army experiences, saying, 'You didn't have to join the army, did you?'

'No I didn't have to join the army; I just wanted to do something for a bit of adventure.'

'What about your expertise with explosives?'

JJ was surprised by the question; he had only added the bit about his explosive experience to fill up space on the application form. He launched into a recount of his mining and army experience, finishing with a thrilling tale of demolishing a series of bridges that crossed the Zambezi:

*'The river in that area of the jungle was infested with crocodiles, the surrounding bush with snakes and armed insurgents. Everything and everyone trying to eat or kill you! I had to gain access to the bridge supports to plant the explosives, normally I would have just swam out but the wild life put me off that idea, instead I and my African sergeant found a native canoe and decided to use that, Sergeant Maputo assured me that he knew how to paddle it?*

*"Yes, sir, no problems, easy."*

*'Well, on a Sunday afternoon on a boating lake it may have been easy but on an African river in pitch darkness with only the occasional gleam from the star studded sky to guide them. The light not only guided them but made the eyes of the floating crocodiles shine red. We arrived at the last of the bridge supports and leaning over the side attached the explosives.*

*'I never knew what happened; Sergeant Maputo had let out a faint gurgle and disappeared over the side of the canoe. I'd heard nothing to indicate the cause; my only thought was a poison dart from a Blowpipe! Within seconds the water started to boil as two huge crocs fought over the body of my friend and fellow solider. They appeared to agree on half each; with a final flick of a tail the river once again resumed its quiet journey to the sea. The whole event had taken less than a minute; I paddled back to shore where the rest of my unit was waiting, when I explained what had happened they wailed their traditional goodbyes. My tears had stopped, my hands and body still shaking, I was violently sick. I then started to feel a little calmer.*

*'It wasn't the death that had caused me distress as much as the manner of his final moment being savaged by leftovers from the prehistoric age.'*

JJ answered the rest of Conrad's questions as frankly as he could;

Conrad started to smile a little, looking less nervous and seeming to relax.

*Maybe it's my interview technique that is relaxing him,* JJ thought. *I'd always understood it was supposed to be the other way round.* By asking whether he had any questions, Conrad was indicating the interview was coming to an end. He had nothing to ask except, how much, where and when? Now just didn't seem the appropriate time to ask. So, not wishing to appear uninterested, he asked. 'When could I expect a decision on my suitability for this vacancy?'

Conrad smiled, replying, 'Soon, very soon.' With that, he stood up saying, 'I'll walk you down. I'll introduce you to my wife, Ayşe the young lady on the reception desk.'

# Chapter Three

As he stepped through the plane door he felt engulfed in a cocoon of cold damp mist. It was a month since he had had a call from Conrad to offer him a job in Istanbul. JJ had accepted immediately; he had never before been to the city, which had at one time been the capital of Turkey and the whole of the Ottoman Empire before the creation of the new capital of Ankara. He'd been prepared for damp and chilly weather but with the combination of rain, wind and cold he was forced to stand for a moment to catch his breath and to hold on to his hat. He had rather foolishly worn a Panama hat and a long trench coat. The coat was to keep him dry on the journey to the airport and the hat because he didn't know what else to do with it. This had certainly got him plenty of attention at Heathrow before he boarded the plane, now he was getting more attention as he fought to keep it on his head in the insipid, damp weather. He gave in, removed the Panama and stuffed it in a pocket of his coat. As he did, he thought for a moment that it would be OK because a Panama hat was supposed to pass through a napkin ring unharmed. Trouble was he couldn't remember where he had heard that fact – he was having enough trouble keeping his balance in the weather.

He was pleased he'd worn the coat as he staggered down the plane steps to the warmth of the waiting coach that would whisk him and the other passengers to the terminal building but was wishing he hadn't worn the hat that was now stuffed roughly into his pocket. It was making his coat feel bulky and awkward.

Immigration and Customs formalities were a simple and speedy process. Pushing an overloaded trolley out of the terminal building was, however, a more complicated process. Trying to navigate an unwilling trolley around the masses of people who didn't care whether your trolley had wheels that all wanted to go in any direction other than the one preferred.

Having finally reached the outside and found the taxi area, he contemplated the prospect of finding a ride into the city. As if on cue, a bright yellow car drew up at the curb beside his unwilling trolley. A cheerful face, resplendent with a huge black moustache, appeared in the car window, looked at JJ's luggage and said, 'Are you Professor JJ? I am your taksi, sir.'

'Yes, I am JJ but no, I am not a professor.'

'You are new teacher for Mr. Conrad?'

'Yes.'

'OK so you are Professor JJ.' At that, JJ nodded and opened a door to get in.

The driver hurried round to put the luggage from the trolley into the trunk and, failing to get the entire luggage in, he tied the lid down with string, passing a number of the smaller packages to JJ who was sitting on the back seat trying to remove his coat. A hotel had been booked for him and he had no sooner given the address to the taxi driver than they were zooming out of the airport. As JJ was regaining his composure after having been thrown back into his seat when the vehicle set off, the driver declared, 'My name is Abdul and I always collect Mr. Conrad's new professors from the airport to take care of them and to see that they get safely to hotel.' He continued, 'I have bestest taksi in Istanbul.' JJ had noticed the sign on the roof when he got into the car which confirmed that he was indeed in a "taksi". JJ managed to get a word in, 'Please call me JJ, everyone does.'

Abdul continued as if he had never been interrupted, continuing in a mixture of English, French, German and Turkish, which appeared to change with every pothole the taxi hit, which was often. JJ was beginning to wonder about Abdul's early comment that he was to see that people got safely to their hotel as once again; the taksi hit a spine-shattering pothole.

Continuing to chatter away without pausing to find out whether JJ understood what he was saying, JJ suddenly understood the subject of Abdul's remarks, he was saying, 'You are a lucky professor to be staying at Pera Palace Hotel. Mr. Conrad usually makes new professors stay in tourist hotels near bazaar. Maybe all full.' JJ had wondered at the choice of hotel thinking that it was a bit on the luxurious side. Perhaps Abdul was right and all the cheaper hotels were full.

JJ leant back in his seat and contemplated his new job and surroundings, his mind on the reason he was staying in the luxury of the Pera Palace Hotel. Had Conrad an ulterior motive for his choice of hotel? JJ returned to the present with Abdul's shouting excitedly.

'Professor JJ, we go round next corner you can see Topkapi Palace on left.'

'Good,' said JJ, trying to show enthusiasm he didn't feel his mind was still on what he could expect at the school the following day and the prospect of a luxury hotel.

Abdul was shouting again. 'We very soon pass Sirkeci train station – end of line for Orient Express train, all rich people in olden times, from train used to stay in Pera Palace Hotel – then we go over Galata Bridge and we are at hotel two kilometers maybe fifteen minutes – traffic OK at this time of day.' JJ wondered why it would take so long to cover two kilometers if the traffic was OK, almost immediately finding out. They screeched to a halt as they reached the tail end of a traffic jam. JJ couldn't resist saying to Abdul, 'Thought you said traffic OK at this time of day?'

'Sure, traffic fine, you should try this journey in rush hour, then traffic slow, lot of traffic coming off the ferry boats at Eminonu we'll be moving in two minutes.' Sure enough, as if by magic, the vehicles in front started to clear allowing them to become free of the traffic that had been restraining them. As they moved forward JJ caught a glimpse of the Bosporus and the white painted villas dressed in the vibrant hues of the bougainvillea that lined the water's edge.

Abdul was delighted and started to sing; the song had no meaning for JJ and in his opinion sounded more like a cat in pain! They arrived at the hotel and stopped with a jolt. A hotel porter rushed to the taksi and, opening the trunk by cutting the retaining string with a knife that seemed to appear from nowhere; amid Abdul's protests about being an almost new piece with lots of life left in it, piled all JJ's luggage onto a handcart and disappeared into a side door of the hotel. Meanwhile, Abdul was exercising his arms by windmilling them around and JJ thought he would either take off or dislocate one or both arms. In an attempt to save Abdul from permanently damaging himself, JJ enquired, 'Do I pay you?'

At the mention of money Abdul stopped gyrating saying, 'No need, Mr. Conrad pays me; but tip OK for bringing you on tourist route.'

JJ gave him a $5 note saying. 'Thanks for the tour. I'm sorry no Turkish money yet.'

This didn't seem to matter. He nodded and smiled grateful thanks. 'Jolly good, Professor JJ, I collect you at 8:30 in the morning and take you to see Mr. Conrad. OK yes?' With that he got into his taksi and with a cheerful wave and a blast on the horn almost leapt away from the pavement, leaving JJ in a cloud of spray from a puddle.

He entered the hotel foyer and stopped to admire the old world charm, pleased it was still probably as it had been when seen by people like Mata Hare, Agatha Christie, Kim Philby and Jacqueline Kennedy as well as umpteen Heads of State over the years. Reaching the reception desk he announced himself, saying, 'Good morning. I'm John Jamison. I believe you are expecting me.'

The desk clerk smiled. 'We are pleased to welcome you to the Pera Palace, sir, your luggage has already been sent up to your suite.

'A suite, are you sure?' JJ enquired. The clerk checked the pile of papers in front of him and nodded saying,

'Yes, sir, that is what we were instructed to reserve for you.'

JJ was bewildered. A room in this hotel was more than he expected, but a suite? His bewilderment turned to astonishment when he entered. It was opulent to say the least although a little over furnished for his modern taste. He walked quickly over to the window and, looking out, gazed at the spectacular view of the Golden Horn, the narrow strip of water that separates the European part of Istanbul, the ancient from the modern. He stood for some time admiring the view and wondering what had possessed Conrad to spend this sort of money to provide him with accommodation. Giving up on both, he decided to take it up with Conrad in the morning. He turned and went into the bedroom to unpack his cases, again astonished to find his clothes all neatly either hanging up or folded in the drawers. A little card was on the bedside table saying that, should he require any further valet service he should pull the adjacent bell cord. Sitting on the edge of the bed he picked up the phone and dialed his home number.

An evidently tearful Elizabeth answered. 'JJ is that you?'

'Yes darling it's me, I promised to phone as soon as I got to the hotel. It's a beautiful place, shame you didn't come.'

'Let's not go through all that again, you know I don't want to leave England again and I've just got the house how I want it. When you get over your midlife crisis hopefully you will come to your senses.'

'Ok. Let's not argue again, so long as you are ok? I will phone again in a day or two, love you, bye.'

'Bye darling, take care. No more bullet holes, please,' she added lightly.

JJ gave up and decided to take a walk, the weather having improved considerably since he had landed. It was now a pleasant spring day.

On leaving the hotel he paused, unsure which direction to

take. The porter, seeing him hesitating, approached him enquiring whether he could be of assistance. JJ told him he would like a short walk to see the area. The porter suggested he turn to the right and go down to the Halic (the Golden Horn). As JJ made his way down towards the water he began to smell both the water and food. Although he had driven up this street earlier in the taksi, he hadn't heard the noise of the throngs of people, the chaotic traffic or the mixed smells of the water and cooking, the combination of which he was finding overwhelming. He stopped at a pavement café and ordered a cold beer, using some of the few Turkish Lira that he had manage to get from the hotel reception, the tangy bite as the beer went down his throat, to some extent relieving his discomfort. He was sitting contemplating another but decided against it thinking that he was glad it was not midsummer, when he knew that the temperature could be in the mid-thirties with high humidity. He continued his stroll down towards the noise and smells, arriving at the water's edge; he saw the bridge ahead had two levels – the top for traffic and the lower for pedestrians. Taking the lower level reduced somewhat the traffic noise but increased the smells of the water and cooking. Continuing he soon arrived at the other shore, emerging into the traffic noise once more.

Seeing the railway station Abdul had pointed out on the other side of the road JJ decided to investigate further. On entering the station he was treated to the spectacle of the passengers alighting from the Orient Express train. At the end of a short red carpet there was a group of four people, three men and one young woman, all dressed in traditional Turkish costume! The men were playing musical instruments and the young woman was handing out pieces of the local sweet delicacy, Turkish Delight, and what a delight she was!

As JJ took a seat at a café at the end of the platform to watch the free show, the young woman, dressed as a belly dancer, came over to his table and leaning over towards him said in sultry

English, 'Can I interest you in a piece?' Offering JJ the plate. He took a piece with a smile and a nod of thanks. She smiled radiantly at him as she turned away and said, 'See you soon,' and danced away wiggling her bottom as she went. JJ was bewildered by her comment but couldn't think of a rational explanation he shrugged and ordered a beer from a passing waiter, settling back to watch the show.

With the show and his beer finished – Efes again, he was starting to enjoy the local brew – he left some money on the table for his drink, rose and left the station. Not fancying the prospect of the walk back through the noise and the smell, he flagged down a passing taksi, returning to the Pera Palace some twenty minutes later as they had caught the start of the evening rush hour.

Entering the hotel, JJ stopped at the reception desk, reserved a table for dinner in the main restaurant then took the lift to his floor. Opening the door of his suite he walked over to the window and gazed at the spectacular view, remembering dinner he undressed and had a hot shower, then, finding he still had three hours until dinner, lay on his bed and went straight to sleep. He awoke in confusion, his body covered in perspiration. He had dreamt of the girl belly dancer at the station, mixed with Conrad as a benevolent uncle, Abdul, the taksi driver, a Peter Pan style tour guide, Ayşe, Conrad's wife with those amazingly long legs strutting around like an Amazonian warrior and his wife Elizabeth crying at his graveside. He took another hot shower finally finishing with a cold burst! Feeling revived and forgetting his dream he dressed in cream linen slacks and a maroon silk shirt. Picking up his navy blue blazer he went down to dinner. He was seated at a table adjacent the dance floor, the head waiter assuring him that he needed to be close to the cabaret if he was to enjoy it. He placed his order for dinner – sirloin steak, medium-rare, with sauté potatoes, a Turkish salad, and a bottle of red wine as recommended by the waiter. He was part way through his dinner when the lights dimmed and a curtain at the back of the dance floor drew back revealing a small Turkish band playing the tune he had heard earlier that day. He recognized it as the one on the taksi radio that Abdul was singing along to, also the one that the band had been playing at the railway station that afternoon. Smoke started to rise at the right hand side of the band, illuminated from above by colored lights, first red, and then yellow, blue and finally green. The smoke cleared to reveal a Turkish belly dancer, her body shuddering from head to foot in time with the music. She started her dance, the different parts of her body moving in different directions, in time to the music. She shimmered and shook; her stomach muscles doing the most amazing things to his imagination, as she got closer JJ recognized her as the girl at the railway station that afternoon. She was tantalizing, a fantastic, breathtakingly beautiful young woman who looked so sensuous now she was dancing. This afternoon she was just beautiful; now it was if the music was controlling her every breath. She was wearing a short skirt version of the traditional belly dance costume which she had worn that afternoon. It revealed superbly shaped legs and thighs, leaving even less to the imagination than before. With every movement of her body the coins on her costume jingled in time with the rhythm she was beating with the little cymbals she had on finger and thumb of both hands. As she danced her way across the floor it seemed at one time she was coming straight towards him. She was in the middle of the floor when the music stopped. Sinking to the floor in a form of curtsy, receiving a rapturous roar of approval from the diners and springing to her feet, she ran from the room. JJ, along with his fellow diners, resumed eating. He had finished his salad, not enjoying it, although the steak was delicious and went down well with the wine, the bottle now half empty. The waiter came to clear the table gave JJ a wink and said, 'You like dancer, yes?'

JJ nodded, saying nothing. He was thinking again about the

coincidences of the day when the music started again, the room lights dimmed, more smoke mixed with colored lights. There she was again, wearing a differently colored costume still with a short skirt this time she made no immediate movement towards JJ, keeping to the edge of the dance floor with the same lithe movements as before, pausing for a brief moment before each table. By the time she reached his table she appeared to be dancing just for him. She wiggled and moved her body in such a way that it appeared she was in the throes of passion. The music stopped whilst she was still in front of JJ's table and, as she sank to the floor, the applause this time was even louder and lasted longer than last time. JJ, like most of the other men, was on his feet cheering and clapping her talented display. Looking up at him she held up her arm for him to assist her to rise, putting her tiny hand in his, she paused for a moment before moving then with almost effortless ease she rose to her feet and smiling him a "thank you", turned and ran once more from the room.

The waiters appeared with coffee cups and pots at the ready. JJ declined coffee but ordered a brandy to which the waiter enquired whether he would like Turkish or French? JJ, who had enjoyed the Turkish wine that the waiter had recommended, elected to try the Turkish brandy. With the clientele now contented with coffee and liqueurs, the lights again dimmed and the band started to play once more the tune of that afternoon. This time she ran to the center of the floor before starting her dance, looking straight at JJ. He was shaken. She was dancing for him – never diverting her gaze from him, continuing to dance like this for some five minutes before sinking to the floor coinciding with the end of the tune. Without any apparent need of assistance to rise this time she jumped to her feet. The band started to play again and this time she moved around the tables, stopping whilst eager hands were thrusting notes into the waistband of her skirt or under the straps that held the top half of her costume. She finally reached JJ and, without thinking, he pushed a fifty US dollar note down the top of her skirt. She looked down, smiled and said, 'I know you don't have any Turkish lira yet,' turned, and with a definite wiggle of her bottom, looked back over her shoulder smiling radiantly whispering, 'See you again soon,' then danced from sight.

With the floorshow over, JJ, along with most of the diners, left the room. He took what was left of his brandy onto the terrace to admire the view. Sipping his brandy again, he thought to himself, 'Not a wise choice, a bit rough.' Still unable to comprehend what was going on he decided to forget about it until morning. Conrad had a lot to explain.

JJ had slept well with the combination of wine and brandy to assist. Thinking of Conrad's comments when they had last met, he dressed in jeans and polo shirt and, picking up his brief case, went down for breakfast. The day was bright and pleasantly warm. They were serving breakfast on the terrace. He ordered orange juice, coffee and toast from a passing waiter. Before he had had time to finish his coffee, Abdul arrived to collect him and take him to what he couldn't think. Did people in his new profession go to work, go to school, or just go to the office? JJ had always previously gone to the office! He must ask Conrad. *Yes*, he thought, *I must ask Conrad a lot of things.*

It took about twenty minutes to drive the short distance to the school, JJ was too preoccupied with his thoughts to listen to Abdul's chatter, and he just leant back in his seat, closed his eyes and thought about last night's dancer, he felt embarrassed and guilty by the thoughts he had had and was still having, it was the first time he'd had thoughts like that about another woman since he'd married Elizabeth, was it all a midlife crisis. He suddenly sensed the taksi had stopped as he heard Abdul's excited voice, 'Professor JJ, we are here, pretty quick eh?'

JJ looked around him. He was outside one of the most dilapidated buildings he had ever seen, the paint peeling off the door and windows, the window boxes containing the remnants of plants that had either given up the battle with the exhaust fumes from the passing traffic or the lack of water or more probably both. Abdul had rushed around the car to open the door for JJ. He paused for a moment before he got out, wondering if he should forget the whole thing and go back home to England and Elizabeth. Before he had come time to come to a decision Conrad was beside the open door taking the briefcase from his grasp and welcoming him to Istanbul, with a hearty, over-the-top, force-ten, American handshake.

# Chapter Four

Conrad almost pulled JJ out of the taksi, escorting him into the building, not letting go of his hand.

'Well how do you like our little place? Good, yes?'

JJ had to agree that once inside the place did look much better.

'Come on I'll show you around, you'll meet lots of real nice people.' Still holding JJ by the hand Conrad took him on a tour, stopping first at the reception office.

'You remember Ayşe I suppose?'

'Yes,' JJ said too quickly, 'but we were never introduced.'

'Well,' he said, letting go of JJ's hand, 'let's remedy that right now. Captain John Jamison, late of the Rhodesian Army, meet my wife, Ayşe,' somehow managing to emphasize "my wife". JJ took the proffered hand and said how pleased he was to meet her. Conrad continued. 'I've tried to keep this as much a family business as possible. Ayşe looks after the administration and the finances. Come on, let's get on, lots to see yet.' He quickly escorted JJ out of Ayşe's office. They made a whirlwind tour. He was introduced to Tony, Charles, Tom, Richard or was it Dick; it was always the same on the first day of any new job so many new faces. With each new face pleasantries were exchanged. JJ had decided that he didn't particularly like any of them very much; they all seemed a bit wet. Conrad then said, opening yet another door,

'I've been leaving the best part till last.'

JJ walked in behind Conrad.

She looked up and smiled sweetly. 'Good morning Mr. Jamison, I said I would see you again soon.' JJ did a double take – it was the belly dancer from yesterday, dressed this morning in a navy blue cotton dress with a white collar. Sitting behind her desk she looked so very different from last night but unmistakable. She still had the beauty and grace, applying it so differently to the computer keyboard in front of her. Her fingers glided across the keys with the symmetry and grace she had applied to the little cymbals last night. As if dumb struck he just stood and stared at her. Conrad slapped him on the shoulder, saying, 'You liked our little surprise?' JJ nodded. Conrad continued, 'Meet my sister-in-law, Francine.'

JJ finally regained the use of his voice. 'I am very pleased to meet you at last,' he said, a little breathlessly. 'You are Ayşe's little sister?'

'No, her big sister, I am almost one year older; she said you would like my little dance but we didn't expect you at the station. I just help at the Pera Palace if a dancer is sick or we plan a surprise.'

'I just needed a walk. I don't know why I ended up at the station and you certainly were a lovely surprise,' JJ said lamely.

Conrad continued, 'As I said, we keep as much of the business in the family that we can. You remember Abdul? He's Francine's husband's father. You shouldn't spoil him by giving him tips.' He continued without a pause for anyone else to get a word in, 'Francine looks after all of our accounts and legal stuff.'

At this JJ managed to get in quickly, 'Beauty, grace and brains as well!' It was JJ's turn to continue without hesitation. 'Does your husband also work here?' He was dreading that she would say yes.

'No,' she said, 'he's with the army.'

JJ felt relieved. At least that was not going to be a complication. Again he felt embarrassed by his thoughts. Without thinking he asked, 'Maybe we could do lunch or something sometime. Don't you get lonely?'

'I am a married Turkish woman and that would be most improper, it's improper that you should even suggest it,' she said sharply. JJ took the rebuff well. He had been stupid to make the suggestion in front of Conrad.

Conrad, taking him once more by the hand, led him out of the room saying as they went, 'Let's go and see your office now.'

It was about the same size as the others he had seen that day and he was pleased that it looked out over the rear garden away from the immense traffic noise outside the front rooms of the building. The rear garden was a joke; a wilderness, overgrown with weeds and brambles, but at least green. 'What would it be like in the summer?' he thought.

'I'll let you get on then,' said Conrad and, replacing his hand with JJ's briefcase that he had been carrying from the taksi, he strode off. JJ sat at his desk and wondered what he was supposed to be getting on with? One thing he had noticed was the lack of students and he hadn't asked Conrad why he had had special treatment in the good hotel and about Francine's dance. He decided to go and find him and get some answers. He suddenly realized he didn't know where to find Conrad's office but he could remember the way to Francine's so he decided to go there – it gave him a reason to see her on his own!

Knocking gently on her door he waited for her to say 'Come in,' before opening the door, not wanting to get her angry at him again. 'Oh! It's you; you mustn't be seen in here very often, particularly by Abdul.'

'I came to apologize for embarrassing you before and to ask how to find Conrad?'

'OK, you don't know our tradition, but you must be careful. Conrad has an office next to Ayşe's by the front door.'

'Thanks,' he said, closing the door behind him as he left. *God, she's beautiful*, he thought as he made for the front door. He thought the same thing as he entered Ayşe's office, without knocking as the sign on the door said "Reception", but Francine and Ayşe could not have been more different. Ayşe, tall, long-legged, and with dark brown hair, her face a little long with strong high cheek bones, Francine on the other hand, was petite by comparison. The most striking difference was her thick blonde hair, her face rounded with delicate features.

Conrad was standing by her desk reading the sheaf of papers he was holding but when he saw JJ standing inside the doorway he smiled and said, 'Come right on in, JJ, what can we do for you?'

'Well,' said JJ rather hesitantly, 'may I have a word?'

'Any time – let's go through to my office.' Conrad opened a door in the far wall and entered in front of JJ, and sat behind his imposing desk. 'Sit yourself down and shoot.'

JJ sat in one of the low chairs in front of the desk. They were arranged around an equally low coffee table and sitting in the chair made Conrad appear to tower over him, which he later was told was the purpose to show who the boss was. He started, 'A number of things concern me. Firstly, why are there no students? Why am I staying at the Pera Palace when you normally use cheap tourist hotels around the bazaar? And what am I supposed to do?'

Conrad laughed, saying, 'It's the end of the winter holiday, and all schools are closed until Monday. I booked the Pera Palace because your lifestyle in your previous job means you are not used to cheap hotels. I don't want to lose you for the sake of a few dollars on the cost of a hotel and you will find plenty to do on Monday after I confirm to the students that you are to be their engineering tutor. You'll find you don't have enough hours in the working day. OK?'

'Ye...yes, thank you,' said JJ. 'Oh yes, while I'm here do you say "I'm going to work/ school or the office" in the mornings?'

Conrad roared, 'That's a new one on me. Try what you said in the army – "I'm going to war". It will certainly feel like it for the first few weeks.' He was still laughing as JJ left his office.

Returning to his own office took JJ past Francine's door so he just couldn't resist knocking hoping that sweet voice would again say, "Come!" – it did.

'You again! Are you still lost'? she asked, sounding a little prickly.

'No, I just wanted to thank you for the directions and to see if you would like to go for coffee?'

She stood up, placing her hands on her hips as if to emphasize her reply. 'I have told you, I am married, my husband is with the army, and I was with him yesterday.'

Not being put off completely JJ persisted. 'I have never had coffee with a beautiful young lady – in fact I've never seen such a beautiful person.'

'You have seen my sister. She tells me that when you first met you just stared at her. Don't you think she is very beautiful? Did you ask her out for coffee?'

'No I didn't. Yes she is beautiful but you are more attractive, if that makes sense.'

'Thank you for the compliment.' As she said it she did a little curtsy. 'Now please go before somebody comes.'

JJ smiled, waved and leaving the room saying, 'See you soon.'

'Not too soon – unless it's work.'

The pattern was set and so it continued over the next few weeks. JJ did discover that he had plenty to occupy his time, he seemed to have an endless stream of students at his door, all with questions of the "How can I?" "How do you do this?" variety. His attempts at the seduction of Francine had failed dismally. He had fallen into the habit of walking past her office in the morning and evening and saying, 'Good morning, gorgeous' or 'Goodnight, beautiful' but she always made some reference to her husband. The most crippling of them all was, 'Good morning Mr. Jamison, I won't need you this week. I went to my husband at the weekend.' Or the more kindly, 'I'm going to my husband at the weekend. He is with the army you know.'

# Chapter Five

Abdul was becoming very friendly, calling at the hotel in the mornings to take JJ to work. It was quicker to walk but it seemed he wanted to be of use? He never mentioned his family. JJ always expected he would at least pass some comment about Francine's husband. He invited JJ to go to drink tea with him; to go and eat fresh fish and drink raki; something that all Turkish men seem to adore. If they could play tavla (backgammon) as well, that was even more preferable. When they went anywhere JJ always ended up paying. He didn't mind, Abdul was good company and a mine of information on Istanbul and Turkey. He had rather outspoken views on the country's politics. He was never outrightly rebellious in his remarks, though, he always just stopped short as if he wanted to say more, but wasn't sure if he could be open with JJ. Abdul was also helping JJ to find a home of his own; he was hoping that if he could offer Elizabeth a house rather than a hotel room she would be more likely to agree to be in Istanbul with him.

He had always been careful not to be seen by Abdul on his visits to Francine's office. He had once been caught by Ayşe, and as he had hastily left the office. She and Francine had laughed together at something Ayşe had said, no doubt, he thought, at his expense.

Life was starting to take on a set pattern of events. JJ would get up in the mornings, shower, shave and dress, going onto the terrace for breakfast and indulging in good-humored banter with the waiters. Abdul would arrive to transport him to work. It would take about twenty minutes to cover the journey which he could walk in ten. He'd arrive at the school feeling frustrated with the wasted time spent in the taksi, enter the dilapidated building, wish Ayşe a jovial 'Good morning!' as he passed her open door, then make the circuitous route to his own office via that of Francine's. She had started to leave her door open for JJ's morning and evening ritual. At other times of the day the door was firmly shut and visitors discouraged, although JJ managed to find a reason at least once a day to visit her. The evening was a reversal of the morning ritual with the exception of Abdul, who had normally got work of his own to complete. JJ then made the journey back to his hotel on foot, which he preferred.

Despite the crowds, he felt it gave him time to unwind from the constant stream of students who appeared endlessly at his door from eight-thirty in the morning until six in the evening. There was a slight lull between twelve and one when it appeared that even students take time off to eat. The evenings were normally spent either with Abdul or Conrad. Ayşe never accompanied Conrad, much to JJ's disgust as maybe Francine could have been persuaded to have joined them.

When they were out they seemed to enjoy hearing JJ recount some of his Rhodesian army exploits.

They particularly liked the one about breaking into the bank in Mozambique.

*The Rhodesian army had got wind of a large amount of money being held for the terrorists given to them by the Chine's communists. JJ and his platoon had been ordered to break into the bank, open the safe deposit boxes and capture the money. After an uneventful journey to Tete in northern Mozambique that had taken three days as they could only travel at night to avoid the national army, they arrived at their destination just after midnight, the town was quiet, the usual army guard outside the bank, the post office and town hall. They all appeared to be sleeping. JJ and two of his troopers killed the guard to prevent him from waking and raising the alarm, the bank door had been an easy object to open; the vault, a lot more difficult. JJ stood and look in amazement that something so massive had been built in this small town. He packed the explosives with care and he hoped that they would be effective and not cause damage to the contents. Knowing that they would have only minutes after the explosion before the local army and police would arrive he stationed the rest of his troops outside equipped with M60 light machine guns, they had a clear line of sight both ways on the street. The noise from the explosion was deafening even though they had retreated outside before JJ had pressed the detonator trigger. Wearing gas masks because of the fumes and dust the three of them changed down to inspect their handiwork. The vault was open the door a twisted mas of steel, they entered shinning their torches to try to see through the gloom. The safety deposit boxes were lined on the opposite wall JJ had prepared for this each of his men had a haversack containing explosive charges, all they had to do was to fix them to the boxes how they had been taught. JJ didn't need to check their work, he trusted their professionalism, he merely said ok out quick. Another explosion took place, in fact twenty but with their simultaneous detonation it was if it was just one. Rushing back with their now empty haversacks, they set about emptying the open boxes. It soon became evident that the stash was greater than expected. JJ said just take the cash and the diamonds the gold would be heavy and might slow them down, they could already hear the clatter of machine-gun fire and the occasional clump of a grenade. Mounting the top of the stairs he realized that his men were winning the fire-fight. 'OK!' he shouted, 'let's pull back and get out of here.' Not needing to be told more than once his men started to move out the way they had come, their exit went well the local forces did not have the appetite for more fighting, knowing they were outclassed and outnumbered by a superior force. They of set at a fast run, they could keep that speed up for twelve hours with little more than comfort stops. They reached Mazoe some fifty kilometers from Tete before daybreak; their luck was still with them, they spotted an army truck, after a swift check on fuel JJ ordered his men to clamber on board, his friend and number two took the driving seat and soon they were speeding out of town. JJ couldn't believe his luck was still running high; he blessed the slackness of the Mozambique army with a more efficient local force they would never have got away. Their journey to the border was as uneventful as the rest of their trip. They ran the border at Cochemane* then immediately halted at the Rhodesian border post. The border guards had been alerted to expect a Selous Scout commando unit, the post commander greeted them like royalty, he radioed to Salisbury with the news of their safe arrival. JJ requested transport back to his unit, it wasn't until they were safely on their journey that he got the opportunity to inspect their haul, in JJ's opinion the diamonds and other gem stones were worth at least ten million sterling; the cash must amount to another two million.

'Not a bad few days' work,' Abdul sighed, 'if only you were my son.'

They would also ask his opinion on the current Turkish political events, as if trying to ascertain where his sympathies lay. Francine never reappeared as the Pera Palace belly dancer. JJ had promised the waiters fifty dollars to tip him off on any forthcoming performance she was to give. In fact, JJ never saw Francine socially until one day she visited him in his office and, closing the door behind her, walked up to his desk like some naughty child and said,

'Mr. Jamison, I am leaving my job here at the end of next week. Will you please come to my farewell party?'

JJ was amazed – he had assumed she was happy working with Conrad and the rest of her family and said, 'Why are you leaving? Not because of me I hope?'

'You are conceited aren't you?' she snapped at him. 'Do you really think that you could chase me away if I didn't want to go? No.' She added more softly, 'I have had the offer of another job which involves a lot of outdoor activities, which will be better for me than being stuck inside in the city all of the time.'

JJ asked a little hesitantly, 'When exactly is your party to be?'

'Why, on the day I leave of course.'

JJ's worst fears had suddenly been realized, it was the day he had promised to fly home for the long UK Easter weekend. Over the weeks he had been in Istanbul he had been dutifully phoning

Elizabeth. She was still annoyed with him for taking the job. As a peace offering he had suggested it only the evening before, saying, 'Let's discuss it calmly over a nice quiet weekend at home. It will be Easter in just under two weeks and I could fly back first thing on Good Friday. It's not a holiday in Turkey, but Conrad will be OK about it. If you meet me at the airport we could be home in time for lunch.' In fact he had a surprise for her that he wanted to tell her face to face; he had found an absolutely idyllic house in the little fishing village of Yesilcoy, thirty minutes' drive from the school. It overlooked the sea, had its own little garden, a wonderful kitchen, stunning decoration and furniture. So no more living in hotels which was one of Elizabeth's major gripes about moving to Istanbul, that and the fact that she was settled and didn't particularly want to move anywhere, ever!

He had in fact seen Conrad when he had first got to work that morning and, as JJ had surmised, he'd agreed without any problems. The next two things he had done were to book his flight and phone Elizabeth to confirm. She had agreed to drive up to Heathrow in the Porsche to meet the plane at ten-thirty.

JJ really hated the idea of turning down Francine's invitation, suggesting that instead maybe they could have dinner before he left for the UK. She turned his invitation down flat saying,

'I wouldn't dream of detaining you. I would hate you not to go to your wife.' With that she turned and marched out of his office slamming the door behind her. JJ was surprised at her reaction; did she not go to see her husband every other week? Why should she be so upset about him going to the UK? He took one of his business cards from his pocket, wrote the address of his new home in Yesilcoy on the back, phoned the agent and got the house phone number, saying he would be in at lunchtime to sign the lease. He added the phone number to the address he had already written on the card, slipped it into his shirt pocket and set of in search of Francine. It was a quick search as he found her sitting behind her desk and she'd obviously been crying. He said in as kindly a voice as possible, 'Hi gorgeous, what did I do wrong now?'

'After all the weeks of telling me how much you want to go out with me I give you the perfect reason and you say you can't. If you don't understand what's wrong, you are not the person I thought you were.'

JJ felt like a naughty boy. Shuffling his feet he mumbled, 'I'm sorry; I only made the final arrangements about half an hour ago. If only I'd known. You never hinted anything about leaving your job or that you were unhappy.'

'I'm sorry as well. I was just disappointed that's all.'

JJ smiled and, taking the card from his shirt pocket, he laid it on her desk in front of her saying, 'If you can, please phone me when I get back from the UK. Maybe we could have a belated party?'

'You'll probably not want me after you've been to your wife for the weekend.' JJ couldn't resist replying a little tersely. 'Like you when you've been to your husband?' It was his turn to march out slamming her door. Had he looked back he would have seen her pick up his card, smiling as she put it carefully in her purse.

# Chapter Six

The fog over London had settled in overnight and was causing the arrivals at Heathrow to be about an hour late as the first arrivals of the day had been stacked for some hours earlier. JJ had only brought hand luggage with him so didn't have to wait to collect his baggage. As he entered the public area at Terminal Three he had to hunt around to find Elizabeth, who had got fed up with the delay and had gone shopping. By the time JJ finally found her neither of them were in the best of moods. With no other greeting than a grumpy 'You're late!', the relaxing weekend that JJ had planned had begun with the same acrimony as had been exchanged when they had parted in early January.

The drive home down the M4 had done nothing to cheer JJ up. Normally the exhilaration of the speed of the Porsche would have lightened his spirit. Under his breath he was cursing the fog that was making him keep his speed down and the champagne that he had had with his breakfast that was doing nothing to improve his vision. Elizabeth said nothing on the journey that had taken the best part of two hours, other than that the fog had been far worse when she had driven to the airport five hours earlier.

As they drove up to the house they were greeted by the dogs who at least seemed pleased to see JJ. They jumped around barking and wagging their tails in pure delight. JJ hugged them, patting them on the head, calling each by name. Elizabeth stormed off throwing a rebuke to him over her shoulder as she slammed into the house. 'You're more pleased to see them than you are me!'

JJ thought about that comment often over the next few days and finally decided she was right. Lunch had been a disaster. Not the food – it was cooked with Elizabeth's usual talent, it was the atmosphere which hissed and crackled like a tropical storm that was about to break; after several attempts at conversation JJ went into the garden to play with the dogs. After about half an hour he re-entered the house to find Elizabeth had cheered up considerably, suggesting a walk down to the pub, 'Like we used to?'

By this time the fog had lifted and the sun was shining in a brilliantly blue spring sky. As they strolled down to the village she slipped her hand under his elbow and pulled him closer. He looked down into her face and realized why he had married her. She was a handsome woman, dressed well, cooked like an angel. It was also at that moment that he decided he wasn't in love with her anymore!

The pub was, as usual, busy, but they managed to get a table on the terrace and JJ went to get the drinks. Elizabeth was chatting with friends who were also their nearest neighbors, living only a few hundred yards away from them down the lane. They seemed surprised by JJ's arrival. It appeared that Elizabeth hadn't told them of his planned journey home. They drifted away as others they knew arrived, leaving JJ and Elizabeth on their own again. JJ was mildly surprised that she hadn't told them that he was coming home, he said, 'It's not like you, not to tell people that I am coming home.'

As she answered him she looked down into her drink, saying, 'I haven't seen you for weeks and we have so much to talk about I didn't want people dropping in to see you, we need all the time together without interruptions.' JJ sensed that tears were not far away. At the thought of tears he was taken back to the last time he had seen Francine, wishing he was going to her party that night not sitting arguing with Elizabeth. As it turned out the evening was quietly convivial. Elizabeth had exceeded herself in the kitchen, producing a splendid dinner of prawns that was both light and tasty with a bottle of JJ's favorite wine and a beautiful apple pie with a crisp crust that was cooked to a delicate shade of brown, to finish. As she cleared away the dirty plates she said, almost as an afterthought, 'There is nothing much on TV tonight, why don't we have an early night? We were both up early this morning.' Their attempt at lovemaking was a disaster to say the least. They were both asleep, back to back, in about twenty minutes. The following morning JJ felt guilty about the night before. Taking the blame on himself; he got up without waking Elizabeth, showered and shaved went down to the kitchen to make breakfast to take her up to bed. To the tray with tea and toast he added two lightly boiled eggs. Taking the tray he climbed the stairs. She was still sleeping when he entered the room. Crossing to the bed he must have made some sound for she stirred opened her eyes and seeing him with the tray, immediately said, 'I hope you haven't made a mess in my kitchen?'

Without a word JJ placed the tray on a low coffee table, picked up his clothes, and went into the bathroom to dress. When he came out the breakfast tray was untouched and no sign of Elizabeth! He went downstairs, picked up his car keys, logbook and insurance documents and, after patting the dogs, got into the Porsche and drove towards the coast with a trace of an idea forming in his mind.

He was unsure how to set his plans into action. He drove to Portsmouth, checked in at the ferry terminal, and asked how close they could take him to Istanbul. The booking clerk looked amused, thinking JJ was trying to pull his leg, but replying that the best he could offer was Le Havre in France, not Turkey.

JJ accepted his offer and bought his ticket. Still feeling guilty about Elizabeth, he went to a payphone on the quay before boarding the boat. He dialed his home number and was greeted by his own voice on the answering machine. He left a message to say that he was driving the car to Istanbul and would phone when he got there and, driving up the ramp to board the ferry, felt freer than he could ever remember.

'Elizabeth will be OK,' he said to himself. She had her own car, a 3 series BMW he had bought for her last Christmas, there was plenty of money in her bank account that he kept regularly topped up; she needed nothing.

JJ joined the other passengers as they filed up the stairs from the car deck to the comfort of the upper levels with their restaurant areas and duty free shop. He was feeling on top of the world as he walked out onto the aft deck and watched England fall away behind him as the boat set its course to France. Walking around the shops he selected a bottle of scotch and some after-shave and, as a complete impulse, he added a bottle of perfume to his purchases, hoping that Francine would like his choice. Taking his purchases in their plastic carrier bag he went to the restaurant and joined the queue for lunch.

France at last, after a splendid lunch he was still feeling buoyant. Whilst waiting his turn to disembark, he took a few minutes to set the Porsche's GPS satellite navigation system to Istanbul and, starting the engine, began to edge his way into the stream of traffic leaving the ship. Following the instructions issued by the GPS he drove over the two elegant bridges that take traffic across the river Seine near the giant oil refinery and petro-chemical works, part designed by a company that JJ had worked for previously.

The drive to Turkey was pleasant and uneventful, through France, Italy, Yugoslavia and finally Greece. The car drove like a dream and the traffic on the main motorways was light, only beginning to get busy about twenty kilometers out of Istanbul. JJ was pleased he had judged the time to arrive as the mid-afternoon traffic was, as usual, heavy but at least moving. He headed straight to the school, looking forward to seeing Francine and even, to some extent, Abdul and Conrad. Parking the Porsche was difficult and he eventually left it half on the pavement outside the building, hurrying into the building with a shouted 'Hello!' to Ayşe as he passed, heading straight to Francine's office. The door was wide open and the room empty. He suddenly remembered with dismay that she no longer worked there.

Feeling lost and suddenly lonely he pushed the bottle of perfume into his pocket and retraced his steps to the front office, this time going into Ayşe saying, 'Sorry I rushed by just now but I'm parked on the sidewalk.'

'Welcome back. I'm afraid Conrad is out this afternoon. Did you want to see him?'

'Not particularly, just confirming that I'm back and to give you a little present,' he said, handing her the perfume that he had bought for Francine.

She took it saying, 'Are you sure this was for me?'

'Who else is there? I'm going home now because tomorrow is Saturday and I'm moving into my new house!'

She smiled up at him and, seeing the unhappy look on his face, rubbed the back of his hand that was resting on her desk, saying, 'Cheer up, things can't be that bad.'

Without replying he walked out into the street, got into his car and drove the short distance to the Pera Palace.

It wasn't until he was sitting on the edge of the bed that he realized how tired he was. He hadn't slept properly for three nights – the bucket seats of a Porsche, whilst being superbly comfortable for driving, were not the best for sleeping on. He looked around the room trying to remember where he'd put things. His eyes came to rest on the phone, suddenly remembering that he had promised to phone Elizabeth when he arrived. It was a call he was not looking forward to making. He, however, picked up the receiver and dialed his number; it was answered almost at once.

'Hello?'

'It's me. I'm here, OK.'

The tearful response came more suddenly than JJ had expected. 'I'm sorry,' she sobbed into the phone. 'It's just that I hadn't expected to see you with a breakfast tray for me and sometimes you do make a bit of a mess in the kitchen.'

'I'm sorry too, I shouldn't have just walked out like I did, but

I didn't want to have another row.'

'OK,' she replied 'Let's forget about it.'

'I'm a bit tired at the moment. I've only just arrived. I'm moving tomorrow to a beautiful place up the coast. I was saving the news as a surprise. I'll phone you on Sunday when I'm settled in.'

'OK then. Goodnight, love you.'

'Goodnight, love you too.'

With that JJ lay back on the bed and went to sleep. He awoke after about an hour, feeling drained as he'd had another nightmare. This time Ayşe and Conrad were both chasing him with huge perfume bottles in their hands as if trying to attack him. Francine came into the picture then, huge tears running down her face shouting after them, 'The perfume is for me, it's OK, it's OK.'

JJ had a long hot shower and, dressing in clean clothes, he went down for his farewell dinner at the Pera Palace. He was again seated next to the dance floor and ordered the dinner that he had had on the first night he had arrived, He began to hope that Francine would appear out of the smoke next to the bandstand. Instead, an overweight, over aged, dancer appeared. As she went through her routine he saw a similarity in the moves but none of the sensuousness of the performance that Francine had displayed. He was disappointed in the cabaret and left for bed before the final show!

He slept without dreaming and woke feeling refreshed. With the help of a number of porters he squeezed all his belongings into the Porsche and set off to his new home in Yesilcoy. It was not quite as peaceful and tranquil as he had imagined it would be. Being a Saturday, many visitors had descended on the village, but the noise was only good-humored fun, from happy people.

Sunday evening had arrived and time to phone Elizabeth again. Again he was greeted by an obviously tearful, 'Hello?'

'Hi! It's me again. How are you now, cheered up any?'

knowing the answer would be accompanied by more tears. It was. He finished the brief conversation by telling her to cheer up and he would phone again later in the week.

The beginning of a new week dawned, He looked out of the window, half expecting to see Abdul's yellow taksi waiting to whisk him of to work but there was no sign of him. JJ had decided to use the train into town rather go through the problems of parking. As he walked out of the door, as if on cue, Abdul's taksi drew up. Jumping from the vehicle smiles all over his swarthy face he shouted, 'Sorry late, damn traffic, roads out here are all full of taksi's'!'

The comment amazed JJ as much as Abdul's sudden arrival.

'I didn't expect to see you.'

'OK, so I hear you have fancy sports car now, but, no damn good in Istanbul rush-hour traffic!'

'I was going to take the train.'

'Better not, too many people, not good! Use Abdul's taksi, much safer.'

With that they almost took off as they screeched away. As they wove in and out of the traffic Abdul continued to curse the other drivers he thought had driven badly but always had a friendly wave for those he annoyed.

The day passed fairly smoothly. Conrad came to enquire how the journey had been etc., not expressing any emotion as JJ told him about the row with Elizabeth.

# Chapter Seven

It was five days after JJ's return to Istanbul. He was working his way through a stack of paperwork, at his dining room table, still trying to catch up from having taken unofficial holiday when the phone rang. He assumed it was Elizabeth – he had promised to phone but couldn't summon up the necessary enthusiasm. The voice was unmistakable.

'Hello, JJ. This is Francine.'

'Hello,' JJ said a little lamely.

'Is it OK? You said to phone.'

'Yes, sorry. It's great to hear your voice. I just didn't expect to ever hear from you again.'

'I said I would.'

'I know.'

'This conversation is going nowhere,' Francine said a little stiffly. 'The reason I phoned is to invite you to lunch on Saturday is that OK?'

'Yes, I would love to see you again.'

'Good. Get the ferry from Eminonu, opposite Sirkeci Station, to Kadikoy at 1130. I will meet the ferry in Kadikoy at twelve noon. Don't bring your flash car – we don't want to be too conspicuous, do we?'

'No OK, I mean yes, OK, see you on Saturday at twelve.' JJ was still in a mild state of shock; Francine had always refused to call him JJ saying it was too familiar and that she preferred Mr. Jamison.

Now she had actually phoned him and given him instructions on where and how to meet, telling him his car was too flash and calling him JJ! Obviously Abdul and Ayşe had been gossiping. Women! She sounded like Elizabeth who had criticized his purchase of the Porsche as "flash".

Over the next few days he displayed all the signs of happiness causing everyone at school to comment on his light and cheerful attitude. He had taken to whistling in the corridors, something he had positively deplored previously. Despite his happiness at the prospect of lunch with Francine he was suffering inner turmoil over deceiving Elizabeth, not knowing what the outcome of lunch would be. He knew what he wanted but he was torn between his desire for her and his love for Elizabeth.

Conrad had taken him to lunch on Thursday and commented on his happy behavior, enquiring whether everything was now OK between him and Elizabeth? JJ had replied that things were looking up and refused to say more. Even his phone call with Elizabeth on Friday evening, which would normally have had him reaching for the whisky bottle, left him feeling, if anything, sad!

Saturday dawned, a wonderful spring morning, blue skies, warm breeze, and the birds in his little garden singing as if they were as happy for JJ as he felt. He was determined that today everything would be wonderful. He took the train into the city. Being Saturday it was not crowded. The crowds and noise at Eminonu however were as bad as any weekday. This would have normally have been an oppressive force that would have made JJ want to scream but today he hardly noticed it. Catching the 11:30 ferry and securing a seat outside on the upper deck, he enjoyed the warm spring-like sunshine, happily watching the boat man oeuvre out of its berth on its short voyage across the water.

JJ had never been to the Asian side of Istanbul, never having had reason to do so. He watched in fascination as his ferry just missed colliding with other boats that appeared to be going in every other direction but towards Kadikoy. One of the sights that always had drawn his attention in Istanbul was when a warship of the American, Russian or English Navies sailed through the Bosporus on its journey to or from the Black Sea. Seeing the giant ships gliding past his little ferry boat made him feel very small and vulnerable. Shaking his head to clear his thoughts he reminded himself of the reason he was on this frail little ferry crossing in the wake of a warship that was on its own clandestine journey. As the ferry boat bobbed its way across the water he got his first real look at the magnificent villas that he had seen the first day in the city when Abdul's taksi had caught the tail end of a traffic jam. The villas mainly painted white, all covered in gaily colored bougainvillea lined the Bosporus, they made a spectacular display.

Still feeling bright and happy as they docked in Kadikoy, he looked down onto the dock and saw Francine searching the ferry for him, then the look of pleasure as she saw him and waved. He waved back!

As he hurried down the gangway towards her she was standing by a taksi, the doors open in invitation. Offering him her hand as he rushed towards her, gone was the Francine of the telephone call. The demure, correct, Francine was again in control. It suddenly occurred to JJ – the willpower it must have taken to have made that phone call and to be meeting him like this. The generations of training that had had to be overcome. He felt very guilty, like being in a sweet factory and not able to resist the temptation of helping himself to one of the delights, despite knowing that it was against the rules.

An image of Elizabeth's face flashed through his mind, as he took the proffered hand, surprised to note that it was covered in a black lace glove. Her fabulous blond hair tied in a ponytail by a long length of matching black lace, the free ends of which reached to the tip of her hair. She was wearing a bright blue dress, which emphasized her blonde hair in the sparkling sunlight. The dress had a loose skirt which was displaying a billowing tendency in the gusty breeze coming from the Bosporus; she constantly pushed it down with her hands as each gust rushed in. It was obviously causing her some discomfort, although to JJ it was pure delight as, unlike her sister Ayşe, Francine had worn to the office nothing but blue denim jeans and tee shirts; except on his first day, then she had remained seated. The one and only time had she displayed her legs was when she had appeared in her belly dancer costume.

Her outfit was finished off with black flat shoes on her bare brown feet. She was carrying a small black shoulder bag with its long strap dangling, threatening to trip her over with every step she took! Her clothing was simple but only added to her outstanding natural beauty.

Trying to keep her skirt in place, she quickly withdrew her hand saying,

'Sorry, I didn't think it would be so windy this early in the day.'

'Don't be, you look fantastic and what's a bit of wind between friends?'

JJ helped Francine into the waiting taksi. She gave the driver the address of the restaurant and, as they set off, JJ noticed his surroundings and how much quieter and more peaceful it was than the constant hustle of the opposite side of the Bosporus he had just left. The streets were wider, the buildings cleaner, the pace of life so much more relaxed. She gained his attention by taking one of his hands and holding it between her demure gloved hands as she said to him, 'Now I need you to listen to me, today is my treat I am paying for everything, do you understand? I will not allow any attempt on your part to take over today, if you can't let me treat you, you can go back home now.' JJ attempted to hold one of her hands. But she pulled quickly away. 'And none of that either! I only held your hand to make you listen to me, OK?'

JJ nodded. With that she seemed content, leaning forward in her seat and starting to point out the landmarks as they sped through the streets.

They arrived shortly afterwards at the restaurant where they were greeted by everyone, staff as well as other diners. Francine, JJ thought, is well known in this part of town. They were shown onto a small terrace that overlooked the Bosporus and were seated at a corner table that afforded a distant view of one of the two massive bridges that connect the European and Asia areas of Istanbul. The terrace was surrounded on three sides by crumbling walls covered in bougainvillea and jasmine giving a heady combination of color and perfume; Francine spoke first after the waiter had departed with their drinks order.

'I love this place. On a warm summer night you get the smell of the water, with the perfume of the jasmine mixed with the smell of the charcoal from the kitchens.' JJ interrupted,

'And don't forget the smell of drains!' They both laughed the initial tension of their meeting broken. Now relaxed, they ordered lunch, JJ agreeing to Francine's suggestion of fish with a salad but preferring a rosé wine instead of her suggestion of a dry white, saying, 'At the correct temperature it's fantastic.'

She smiled her acceptance.

They settled down to their lunch with enthusiasm, the salad crisp and sweet, the fish a little oily which the sharp wine cut through. He asked how she had become a belly dancer and why she was not dancing full time as she obviously had the talent.

She started to tell him what had brought on the belly dancing. 'It's quite simple really. I was trained to be a ballet dancer then failed my audition with the National Ballet Company. I didn't want to teach; which is the obvious choice of those who can't make the big time. Could you see me with a shawl, my grey hair in a bun and beating time with my walking stick? I needed to keep fit so I took up belly dancing and discovered that I had more talent for that than the ballet. After failing my audition with the ballet I was so disappointed and wasn't interested in a dancing career anymore.' JJ couldn't imagine her with a shawl. 'When Conrad married my sister, Ayşe, he offered me a job, so here I am. Now you tell me about you?'

JJ started, 'When I came down from Manchester University, I went to Africa.'

'No, no,' she declared. I have read all that in your CV that you sent in. Tell me about you.'

'Ah, that's a bit more difficult.'

'What were you like as a little boy? What did you want to be when you grew up? Engine driver? Astronaut? Soldier? Sailor?'

'I don't think I had any of those glamorous ambitions, I hated school, but got by. I seemed to drift to university, All my friends were going up, and I suppose I thought I would. I was a horrible little boy; you wouldn't have liked me then, even I didn't. I would have pulled your hair and put frogs down your blouse. I suppose I just couldn't commit to anything in the long term. Then when we moved to Rhodesia during the bush war; again I joined the army because all my friends and colleagues did. That's when I think I found my true calling in life. When I got transferred to the Scouts; the Selous Scouts, like the Special Forces, the SAS,' he added, seeing a puzzled look on her face. 'It wasn't just the combat or anything like that. It was the planning and carrying out that plan. You knew that if your plan failed, you and probably a lot of your friends would die. The Geneva Convention wasn't being observed in my war! I also enjoy blowing things up.'

She smiled at him happily, patting him on the back of his hand that was resting on the table but moving her hand back quickly to avoid JJ's hand as it turned palm up in an attempt to catch her fingers.

'Do you want to go home now?' she asked with humor in her voice. 'We have not had dessert yet and they do a wonderful Crème Brule here.'

JJ felt silly, he wasn't a teenager anymore he must not make a grab for her. To cover his embarrassment he laughed an apologetic, 'Sorry.'

The Crème Brulée arrived with a bottle of sweet white dessert wine. As JJ busied himself pouring the wine into fresh glasses he noticed Francine had become quiet and in deep thought. She noticed the wine and smiled again with a slight sigh and launched into the most extraordinary story JJ had ever heard.

# Chapter Eight

The story she told him had left JJ with a feeling of both sadness and excitement.

'When I used to tell you that I had been to my husband, it was true, but I only ever saw him on the opposite side of a razor wire fence with armed soldiers watching us, and I was always with his mother.'

'I don't understand,' JJ said in amazement.

'It's all very simple really. He is in a military prison. He's a convicted terrorist – well, an anarchist really, he was caught when he tried to blow up the Turkish Parliament building. They sentenced him to ten years' imprisonment. I was jailed for six months for being associated with him.'

JJ said nothing, he couldn't, he was too stunned.

'It all started when I went to university. After the failure of my ballet career I was determined to do more than be just a belly dancer so I decided to study law – my mother is a lawyer. I started at university later than my old friends, I was twenty-five at the time. I had a lot of catching up to do first as my studies had been let slip to concentrate on the ballet. So being more or less on my own I started meeting new people and that was when I met my husband. He knew lots of people; was involved and inter-ested in politics. I met his brothers and his father. We used to go to political rallies usually held at night in some old warehouse in the city or a derelict barn in the country. They had formed some fringe cell of the anarchist movement. It was all very exciting!'

JJ was still unable to speak. Francine continued, 'The author-ities were determined to get me on some charge, I was lucky only to get six months. The prison they sent me to wasn't that bad, I was lucky they treated me well, it could have been a lot worse.' She gave a little shrug, as if to say "that's life". She paused for a sip of wine, and shuddered. JJ was unsure what the shudder was for, was it the wine or the memory of her time in prison?

Earlier, during her account, JJ had started to feel uncomfortable. Sitting in public with a convicted terrorist, he had started looking around him every time new people arrived or others who had finished their lunch left. He was checking trying to see if they were being watched. Francine patted his hand that was lying on the table in an attempt to relax him,

In near panic and utter disbelief JJ got up from the table saying, 'Please excuse me, I don't feel well.' With that he staggered from the restaurant and onto the pavement. He felt nervous, frightened, and apprehensive of what would happen next.

'Don't worry; I haven't been under observation for months,' he heard her behind him just as he was violently sick. Propping himself against the wall of the restaurant all he could think of was that time in Rhodesia when he had watched his friend Sergeant Maputo being torn in half by crocodiles, he was immediately sick again!

Once again Francine appeared by his side with a glass of water, 'Drink this and please come back inside, we are perfectly safe here.'

Taking him by the hand she led him back to their table, 'A raki could help settle your stomach.'

'I'd sooner have a brandy rather than something I have never tried before.'

She signaled to the waiter and ordered two brandies, the waiter concerned that maybe the food had caused the sickness. She obviously explained to the waiter in Turkish, the cause of JJ's discomfort. He smiled at JJ, Saying to Francine, which she translated for his benefit, 'You must not fear the secret police in this restaurant, here we are all friends of the movement, and you can speak freely on any subject.'

'I think you had better make that a very large brandy for me.'

They sipped their drinks, Francine trying to reassure JJ that they were not being watched or spied on,

'How about dinner on my side of the Bosporus – and it's my turn to pay?'

'Don't worry; we are safer on this side and in particular in this restaurant. It's run by one of my husband's friends. All of the customers that have been here today are people from the organization. I took my husband's permission to have lunch with you today.'

JJ was amazed. He said, a little frostily, 'Did he choose the menu as well?'

'Don't be petty. If I was your wife and you were in prison, how would you feel if I asked you whether I could have lunch with a good-looking Englishman and asked you to get word out that you approved of the meeting?' JJ felt guilty, not for the first time that day, still feeling guilty about the possible betrayal of his wife.

'Why did you ask him?'

'So you didn't end up with a knife or a bullet in your back. That's why.' JJ again felt guilty; but couldn't resist.

'Did you also tell him that I've been trying to date you for the past two months?'

'Of course, you were not very discreet at school so everyone knows. My husband would have also been told; you can't keep a secret like that in Istanbul.'

'What else did you tell him?'

'There is nothing more to tell. Now, about this dinner you offered me?'

'Don't forget, dinner is my treat.'

'When my money runs out you can pay!' she replied simply.

She used the last of her money to buy tickets for the ferry.

Landing back in Eminonu JJ explained that he had come down by train from Yesilcoy, not trusting the locals with his flash car; he emphasized the word "flash". But Francine didn't rise to the bait.

They boarded the dingy local train as the glistening blue and gold carriages of the Orient Express pulled out of the station, being towed by mighty diesel locomotives. JJ looked at his watch. It was 5pm.

'No belly dancers today?'

'No normally only to greet a train. When you saw me here before it was about half past three.'

The journey to Yesilcoy was swift and they soon arrived at JJ's house. Francine mumbled appreciative noises about the Porsche standing in the car port saying openly, 'Do you know what the price of that car could buy in Africa or India?'

'I paid for that car with money that I made working in Africa and India and similar places around the world. It's nothing compared with the cars that the local politicians and businessmen drive in those places,' JJ replied a little crossly 'Why don't you lecture them?'

'That is what we are all about, we want to change everything; everywhere.'

JJ was again feeling guilty. 'Let's go inside then you can freshen up before we go for dinner.'

'Dinner at five-thirty? I know the English are strange.'

'Only a bit early.'

'OK, let's freshen up.'

Francine made a tour of inspection, freshened up in the bathroom on the way round then proclaimed.

'I will use your telephone? Yes?'

Francine was obviously talking to a friend. The conversation was too fast and furious for JJ to follow, at one point becoming very heated, until with a final 'thank you' to the person on the other end she hung up, turned and looked up at JJ with a radiant smile on her face, saying in a low voice. 'It's OK. It's all fixed.'

'What is?' JJ asked.

'I will stay the weekend. Yes?' She gave a little squeal of pleasure with a little jump before she ran across the room throwing her arms around his neck, kissing him with such force that she almost knocked him over. When she finally broke off for air she held him at arm's length and in a husky voice, almost a whisper, said, 'All those times I used to say I was going to see my husband or that I didn't want you because I had been to him? Yes, I had been to him with his mother and armed guards and razor wire. Oh! I did want you so very much; in fact I still do want you so very much. Please?'

JJ pulled her to him and very gently kissed her whispering, 'Your every wish is my command!' He tried to blot out his guilt over cheating on his wife!

They never had dinner or supper that night. JJ visited the kitchen on one occasion for a bottle of champagne and 2 glasses which he took back to the bedroom. Francine spent the few minutes that JJ took to open the bottle and pour out two glasses of the fizzy liquid to lecture him further about waste and what the money that he had spent on that bottle of champagne could do in the Third World! JJ handed her a glass, which she sipped appreciatively. JJ decided it was wiser to be quiet rather than argue with her. She had stopped her lecture and was contentedly drinking from her glass. He offered her a top-up which she refused smiling with a shake of her blonde hair, rearranged the bedding and with a gesture suggested JJ put down his glass and return to her!

The morning dawned, the sound of the mosque calling the faithful to prayer, the traffic on the road outside, the sun starting to stream in through the bedroom window, a train, seagulls shouting, and all the things that made living interesting. JJ was awake first. He turned to look at Francine, with her blonde hair fanned out on the pillow under her head. Having decided not to waken her just yet, he slipped out of bed and made his way to the kitchen to make breakfast. As the microwave pinged announcing that the croissants were warmed, he heard her in the bathroom. Putting the cups of hot chocolate, croissants, butter and jam onto a tray, he carried it through into the bedroom. Francine had used her time in the bathroom thoughtfully, had brushed her hair, removing the ravages of the night, washed her face and cleaned her teeth. Now, sitting upright in the big bed, she took the tray from JJ, allowing him to disappear to the bathroom. When he returned to the bedroom she was sipping her chocolate, smiling as he entered the room, 'Thank you for making me breakfast, it was a lovely surprise to wake up to.'

What a different reaction to the last time he had made breakfast, when Elizabeth had complained about him possibly having made a mess in the kitchen, JJ thought.

Allowing her to finish her breakfast he took the tray from the bed and slipped back under the covers, they dozed. JJ was woken by urgent shaking from Francine, 'Wake up,' she was insisting. 'You must take me into town quickly.'

'What's the panic? It's Sunday.'

'I forgot, I'm meeting my husband's mother to go for a prison visit!'

'Not today,' JJ said lazily and a little annoyed.

'Do you want to spoil everything? I must do everything as usual,' she continued a little coyly. 'You had me all last night and this morning and I can be here again tonight if you would like me to. But you must get me to Buyuk Ologar, the main bus station near to Bayrampasa. It will only take ten minutes in that flash car of yours.' She again seemed to emphasis the word "flash". JJ was far from happy but got out of bed and made a dash to the bathroom, just beating Francine.

'That,' she exclaimed, 'was not fair.'

He chided, 'All is fair in love and war.'

'Please hurry I must do my hair and face, I haven't time to shower.'

He shouted back through the closed door, 'Got to make yourself pretty for little hubby?'

'No, just his mother!'

JJ got the car onto the road before Francine closed the front door to the house. To JJ's delight she showed her thighs as she wriggled into the car, she had put on the blue dress of yesterday. He looked at her with a smile, saying, 'It takes a bit of getting used to.'

'If you don't get a move on I will never get used to anything of yours.'

They arrived with five minutes to spare. JJ said, 'I would have had time for another kiss.'

'Well you will have to wait for it. I'll catch the train up this evening, be there about seven, OK?'

JJ drove away with a roar from the big twin exhausts as the Porsche scattered the few pigeons that had settled near to the parked car. He drove more sedately once he had exited the bus station, not wanting to draw more attention to himself and the car than was absolutely necessary. Once he was back on the coast road he settled back in his seat and started to relax. The past twenty hours since he had met Francine in Kadikoy had completely sapped both his emotion and energy. He stopped at a roadside bar, parked in the shade of a large sprawling tree and ordered a beer and a snack. He hadn't eaten his breakfast and remembering why he'd missed dinner, he smiled. God; she is beautiful, he thought. Once again as he thought about Francine he immediately felt guilty about Elizabeth. If he was having a mid-life crisis he was certainly enjoying it!

The beer and his breakfast arrived, something in a fluffy filo pastry coating that was supposed to be prawn, with a chilly dip. Whatever it was it tasted wonderful. While he ate JJ reflected on those past twenty hours. Why had it happened? From his point of view he knew why, but why had she almost thrown herself at him? In fact, she had literally thrown herself at him, with that rush across the room, the thing that confused him most was, why him?

She is young, incredibly beautiful, talented…why him?

The story about the anarchist cell, blowing up buildings, military prison, all seemed very farfetched. He was determined to find out more. Getting back into his car he drove to the city. JJ found Abdul in a cafe in Yenikapi. As he walked over to Abdul's pavement table he ordered two beers from a passing waiter, and slumping into the vacant chair he was about to speak. Abdul raised his finger to his lips, indicating JJ should say nothing. The waiter left, having deposited the beers on the table in front of them. Abdul spoke first.

'Sorry, you don't know who people are. Just because he is wearing a white apron doesn't mean he is not a police spy. Anyway, did you enjoy your lunch yesterday?'

JJ was astonished that Abdul had heard so quickly and asked, 'How did you hear?'

'My son, Francine's husband asked me to put the word out that it was OK for you to see her.'

JJ wondered what else Abdul knew. He asked, 'Does she always visit her husband with your wife?'

'Generally, yes. I go sometimes but it makes me sad to see him like that, with his head shaved and in prison uniform. Dogs get treated better.' To JJ he looked about to cry. 'Tell me,' he said 'what did you two talk about?'

JJ knew that Abdul was just fishing. So he replied, 'She told me about how you all met, how her husband got caught and what happened afterwards and that she was also sent to prison.'

'Did she tell you why he was caught?'

'No.'

'Well I will. Francine was the planner in our little group and that day she hadn't planned very well!' He sounded bitter, JJ thought. It was obvious that Abdul knew nothing of what had happened last night. JJ was relieved, as he didn't need Abdul as an enemy.

Abdul declared, 'Let's go for lunch, I'm starving. I bet you didn't eat again yesterday after that enormous meal you both had.' Still fishing, JJ thought. However, it must all be true. But still the big question, why him?

# Chapter Nine

JJ had left the Porsche in an underground car park when he had gone in search of Abdul. So rather than risk the traffic he left it there, going to lunch in Abdul's taksi. They headed up the Bosporus to a restaurant that Abdul had declared, 'Sells the best octopus salad in town, with a bottle of cold dry white wine; what could be better?'

JJ agreed that the wine was excellent but refused to comment on the octopus salad, apart from, 'A little chewy.'

Abdul asked, 'What was the wine like yesterday?'

'Not as good as this,' replied JJ. He continued, 'Is it OK to talk here?' Abdul nodded.

'Tell me more about your little group.'

'It will be better to ask Francine, she is better with English than me.'

'Francine? I thought you were its leader and we speak English together without problems.'

'Francine is better.'

JJ persisted, 'Can you at least tell me if you have still been active after your son was caught?'

'Yes, I am the leader; but we have agreed that Francine is our spokesperson. Please don't ask me anymore. Anyway, we are wasting this salad and the wine is getting warm.' JJ took the hint and ordered another cold bottle. He was quite pleased that he had left the Porsche behind. It appeared that no matter what Abdul drank it didn't affect his driving, which at best could be described as competitive and worst downright dangerous. He fitted in perfectly with the rest of Istanbul's drivers.

Abdul took JJ back to Yesilcoy. He entered the house as a train went past and looking up and was surprised to see the blue and gold of the Orient Express glide passed. He looked at the clock on the kitchen wall it was five past five. Damn, he thought, Abdul and his long lunches. He had wanted to prepare a meal for Francine so that they wouldn't have to eat in a restaurant that evening. He wanted to be alone with her; he didn't want to share her and he had a lot of questions to ask. Running a hot bath he wished that she was there now, it was a long time since he had had someone to wash his back. The excesses of the past day and night had started to tell. He lingered in the bath, letting the hot water soothe his aches and pains. Feeling a little light headed from the combined effects of the lunchtime wine plus the hot bath, he dressed in linen slacks and an old silk shirt, made a strong coffee which he drank hot and black. Now feeling better he started to think of food for dinner. Picking up his keys and money he hurried to the little supermarket close by. He bought some steak, potatoes and the makings of a salad. As he left the shop he saw Francine coming down the road from the station. He was delighted – she was early!

JJ waited for her but could see she was agitated. She asked excitedly, 'Why are you standing there like that? Do you want everyone to know that I'm visiting you or are you waiting for me to give you a big hug and kisses? I keep telling you that this is Turkey and we can't be seen like that!'

JJ was embarrassed.

'Sorry,' he mumbled, 'I was just pleased to see you.'

'You go in. I will follow in a few minutes.'

She came into the house by the back door; put her arms around his neck and kissed him briefly before stepping back saying, 'I need a bath, I always feel dirty when I get home from that dreadful place. I can still smell it.'

'I'll do dinner while you bath then.'

'Don't you dare? I keep telling you, this is Turkey. You go watch TV while I bath then you can sit in the kitchen and talk to me while I make dinner.'

'Do I get to do your back?'

She wrinkled her nose at him and said, 'Would be nice, but

only if you behave.'

The bathroom was full of steam and smelt like a perfume shop. JJ took a glass of cold white wine into her. As he entered, she covered herself coyly with a towel.

'I'm sorry my husband would never have come into the bathroom while I was in the bath. I've got a lot to get used to being with you being English. I suppose you do it all the time with your wife?'

JJ prickled, 'I have come to do your back and bring you a drink.'

'Thank you, old customs are hard to break.'

'That's OK.' He placed the glass on the wash stand and turning, he bent down, kissed her lightly and putting a hand on the top of her head ducked her under the water, he hurried to the door to escape, she was so angry that she threw the bar of soap at him and ordered him out. He was laughing as he left. She smiled at him, no longer cross.

'Please pass my wine before you go?'

When she came out of the bathroom she had her hair wrapped turban style in a small towel and wearing a large bath towel as a sarong she stood in the doorway to the lounge looking radiant and a little flushed carrying the empty wine glass in her hand. She said holding out the glass, 'I am destitute. No wine, no clothes, please you help me?'

JJ didn't accept the obvious invitation, saying, 'Go into the bedroom and have a look, I'm sure you will find something to put on. Leave me your glass and I'll fill it for you.'

She pouted her full red lips and disappeared taking her empty glass with her. JJ let her get something to wear, resisting the temptation to follow her into the bedroom. She reappeared after about five minutes dressed in one of his cotton short-sleeved shirts which covered her modesty, but, if anything enhanced her sexuality. The top two buttons were undone, revealing her slender neck and amazing cleavage, the shirt was short enough to expose her thighs.

JJ said, 'You can get arrested wearing clothes like that.'

'Even in England?'

'Especially in England.'

'I've heard your prisons are better than ours, but I don't wish to try them, thank you. I had better take it off.' She started to lift the shirt as if to remove it.

JJ had to hold her arms down to stop her actually taking it off saying, 'Later.'

'Oh! Will you want me later?'

'If I had accepted your offer earlier we wouldn't get dinner. Now be a good little Turkish wife and go make my dinner.'

She gave a little curtsy, 'Yes master,' and disappeared into the kitchen taking her wine glass with her. After the curtsy JJ had begun to wish he had accepted her offer, but resisting the temptation to follow, he remembered she had to answer a lot of questions later and bed was not the place to ask them.

Francine called from the kitchen. 'JJ please set the table and sort out a bottle of decent red wine. I can't drink this white stuff with steak.' It was like the Francine of those few days before, giving him orders on where and how they should meet, not the simpering obedient Turkish girl that she had been masquerading as since they had first made love.

'Turkish or French?'

'Turkish of course! It's a waste of money to buy French wine if you live in Turkey.'

She appeared from the kitchen five minutes later with a bowl of salad asking, 'Did you get bread?'

JJ headed for the door, 'Be right back.'

By the time he returned with the bread the smell of steak and frying onions was in the air as he hurried up the path. 'I'm back.'

'Sit down. Dinner's ready.'

She bustled into the dining room with two plates of steak and onions. The steak was juicy and rare, the onions a golden brown.

'That, my angel, was the best meal I think I have ever had; apart from last night.'

'But we didn't have dinner last night.'

'That's what I meant,' JJ said. Francine blushed.

'Now,' she said, 'you have the choice between ice cream and me.'

'You, but first we need to talk.'

'OK,' she sighed reluctantly.

'I met Abdul this afternoon; he wouldn't tell me anything about your little group saying you were its spokesperson. He also implied that you were responsible for the failure of the group's last mission and because of that your husband was captured.'

She looked devastated. 'I knew he didn't like me but that's stupid, how could he even suggest such a thing? I don't understand.'

'Can you tell me about it?' JJ asked.

'Well, we all discussed and agreed the plan, yes. I made the plan at first. I was to carry out the mission on my own but I came down with a heavy cold the afternoon of the attack so my husband volunteered to carry and plant the explosives. No-one knew of the change of plans, there wasn't enough time to tell anybody. It was a very simple plan, but, when he got to the parliament building the army was there as if they knew and were waiting for him. He wasn't carrying a gun – it was only a simple job and there should have only been a single guard on duty. He had no chance of escape if he had tried they would have gunned him down.' With that last statement the tears came. 'I'm sorry JJ, it's the first time I've cried since I got news of his capture. I suppose it's talking to the new love in my life about him. To a certain extent I feel a little guilty about you. That I am so happy and contented I have just had a good meal and nice wine with a handsome man and my husband has a shaved head, a nasty dirty prison uniform and gets the food that the pigs won't eat.'

JJ still hadn't found out, why him?

Francine continued, 'I'm so sorry but I can't talk about it anymore at the moment, give me a little time and I will try again.'

With that JJ knew that it was pointless to pursue his quest for the moment. Trying to comfort her, he got up from his seat at the table and walked around to her putting his hands on her shoulders gently as if expecting them to be shrugged away. He said, 'It's me that should be sorry. I shouldn't have asked about things like that.'

'It's OK. Just give me a little more time, please? You have a right to know. Don't forget I was there this afternoon.'

With that, she turned her head and kissed JJ's wrist, the only part of him that was within kissing range. She gave her nose one last blow and declared, 'I think ice cream could be in order, don't you?'

'Yes, and a nice brandy?'

'Please.'

'Turkish or French?'

'Definitely French, I need to be soothed and decadent.'

They had their ice-cream dessert with their brandy on the terrace overlooking the little garden. Francine yawned, saying, 'I'm not sure if it's the combination of wine, food and brandy, or the lack of sleep last night, but I am very tired.'

'Very tired?' asked JJ.

'Well a little bit tired. I think an early night, don't you?'

She said a little later, looking at the clock. 'You must set the alarm; I must be gone before Abdul comes to collect you.'

'Damn! I forgot it's Monday tomorrow,' JJ replied.

# Chapter Ten

Over the next few weeks they settled into a happy routine. JJ went to school Monday to Friday. Francine was there when he arrived home on Friday evening and they had decided it was better to wait for Abdul to collect JJ on Monday, before she left the house. They had no contact all through the week with the exception that Francine phoned him on Thursday evening to confirm that JJ still wanted her to be there on Friday. JJ phoned his wife Elizabeth on Monday and Thursday evenings, always waiting for Francine to call before he dialed his UK home number, not wanting the phone to be engaged when Francine's call came through. Since JJ and Francine had been together, his relationship with Elizabeth had improved. It was as if by being with Francine he had become more tolerant towards his wife. Strange, he thought. Deep down he loved her, it was as if the sex with Francine made up for the short comings in his married life? It hadn't stopped him feeling guilty every time he phoned home and heard her voice.

JJ had usually got sufficient food in for the entire weekend, but had taken to insisting that on the Saturday evening before her fortnightly prison visit they go to a restaurant to eat. They would drive well out of Istanbul to be sure that they were not recognized. JJ considered that it was his way of saying "she's mine" so she had the evening to remember on her visit to her husband. He always drove her to the bus terminal in the morning to meet her husband's mother. He had also started to resent her going to visit him. He assumed that he was jealous and didn't know why.

It was six weeks since he had tried questioning Francine about the anarchist group she was with, or had been with. JJ knew nothing of Francine's life during the time they were apart. He decided that the next Saturday when they had dinner at home he would again broach the subject.

'Francine, I wish you would let me cook dinner for you tonight.'

'JJ, my darling, if I ever come to England then you can.'

He had never considered the possibility before and said, 'You're on.'

'Just one small problem, I don't have a passport. I can't leave the country. In Turkey it is considered a privilege to have one and having been in prison I don't qualify.'

'I suppose that's one of the things you would change?' JJ said, realizing that she had given him the opening he needed to continue. 'You were going to tell me about your group of friends?'

'Let me do dinner then we can talk I promise.'

'OK. I'll sort out some wine and soft music.'

'Not too soft and nothing romantic otherwise I will not be able to answer your questions.'

'Right I'll see what I can find.'

He could hear her in the kitchen. He put on some music and pulled the cork from the bottle of the most expensive bottle of Turkish wine he had been able to find, hoping that it would be as good as the price said it should be. Sniffing the cork, it smelt fruity and heady. Pouring two glasses he took them into the kitchen. 'I've come to seduce the cook,' he joked lightly.

'Put mine on the worktop please and if you're staying, sit down and keep your hands in your pockets. I'm busy.'

'Yes, madam.' He walked up behind her lifting the back of her hair and kissed her neck below her right ear. She sighed contentedly. Letting the hair fall back into place he sat down with his glass in one hand the other in his jacket pocket. She turned and looked at him and said simply, 'Seni seviyorum, Jamison Bey. I Love you, Mr. Jamison.'

'And I should hope you do after the things I let you do to me.'

She threw a partly peeled potato at him and sternly ordered him out of the kitchen. He was content that she had missed him.

He felt certain that if she had really wanted to she could have easily hit him.

She called at his retreating back. 'First course will be ready in five.'

As she came into the dining room with a large plate of mixed Turkish meze, she asked, 'Why don't you drink raki with the meze like Turkish men?'

'It may have the reputation for being lion's milk but it just makes me feel sick!'

She pouted and made cow eyes at him and said, 'Let's wait until the main course before you start with the questions.'

The main course, when she served it, was a salad with huge prawns and crabmeat still in its shell, the bread still hot straight from the oven. JJ said, 'Would you prefer a white wine?'

'No, this is fine thanks. Now, question one?'

'Would you prefer to tell it rather than me ask you things?'

'I think that would be perfect.'

She took a deep breath and launched into another amazing story, more fantastic than the one she had told him before. 'I never knew my real parents. I was adopted as a baby. When I was eighteen, my parents explained that they had adopted me in Germany – they had wanted a baby but couldn't – so they adopted me. They told me that my real parents were dead. Soon after they had me, my new mother had become pregnant and then Ayşe was born. We were brought up together, neither of us knowing that we were not real sisters. They all encouraged my ballet career and were upset for me when I failed. I had a very happy childhood. Just before I went to university, both my adopted parents were killed in a road accident. Ayşe and I were going through the family paper work and we found a letter from an adoption agency in Germany which stated they had available for immediate adoption, a baby girl whose parents had both died in a German prison in mid-October 1977.' Francine paused to chew on a crab claw.

JJ asked, 'Did you find out who your real parents were?'

'Let me finish please.'

JJ could see that the emotion of telling him the story was liable to end in tears. 'I'm sorry, please go on.'

'Naturally, we checked all the rest of the papers very carefully. I tried the adoption agency but they would tell me nothing. The German government was a little more helpful. They confirmed that on the 18<sup>th</sup> October 1977 a man and woman had died in prison. The two were Andreas Baader and Gudrun Ensslin. They refused to confirm or deny that they had had a baby girl. The most startling thing for me was that they were the leaders of a Red Army Faction – the Baader Meinof gang.' She paused again to chew on the other crab claw. JJ was drawn to her mouth with its set of perfect white teeth normally hidden behind full red lips and remembered the pleasure those teeth and lips had given him.

'Go on' he encouraged.

'I remember the press coverage at the time. I thought the leaders were Baader and a woman called Meinof.'

'That's a popular misconception. Ulrike Meinof helped Andreas Baader to escape from police custody in May 1970 and afterwards the press nicknamed them the Baader Meinof gang. Well, I never did find out if they were my real parents or not, but I felt that they were. I had always had an interest in socialism and politics. It seemed logical somehow. When I went up to university I met my husband. You know the rest.'

'Not all,' JJ said.

'It was because of who I believed were my real parents that I happily joined in with the ideologies of the man who was to become my husband and with his family and friends. Well, we decided that we should strike a blow for freedom, a little like your Guy Fawkes. In a way that's where we got the idea from. What we intended to do was create a huge explosion and do some damage to a high-profile building then our group would claim the credit and get loads of publicity and hopefully new members who could see that we meant what we said in our little pamphlets. We don't know how, but they seem to have been tipped off about what we were going to do. They were waiting. It's a good job my husband was not carrying a gun that night, if he was he would have tried to shoot his way out and been shot down. It may have been better if he had been killed than for him to spend ten years in that filthy prison. I know that I would have been happier for him.'

'Just relax for a little while. Would you like some water?'

'No I'm OK. It's that I hate him being in that place.'

'Just relax.'

She took a gulp of her wine and continued. 'Shortly after I came out of prison, my sister Ayşe married Conrad. They had waited for me to be released before marrying. I'm her only living relation and they wanted me to be there. Ayşe had been a member of our group since before our disaster. After the wedding we enlisted the support of Conrad and he brought with him a much-needed influx of money. We decided not to let the previous disaster stop us so we started to plan the next attack. We decided to blow up one of the Bosporus bridges; it would be high profile and cause the maximum amount of chaos. It very soon became obvious that we didn't have the skills or experience. Most of our knowledge came from the "Anarchist Cookbook" nothing to do with cooking but it has great recipes for just about any bomb you can think of!

'Conrad suggested that we try and recruit an army expert. It was no good looking for somebody inside Turkey; we wouldn't know if they were police informers or not. Then Conrad suggested we look in Western Europe i.e. the UK. We thought maybe an ex-mercenary or maybe ex-IRA and that, my darling, is where you come in. The ex-soldier that we hoped to recruit was to plan, train and lead our next raid. I was to be the bait for him to chase. Not get caught.' At that point she blushed and simpered, 'That was for me. You were my prize; my reward. I fell in love with you soon after we met. It was painful not to be able to be with you but I had to continue the masquerade until it was safe. If Abdul or Conrad had found out, everything would have been lost.'

JJ was again unsure what to say. He felt like he was back in the restaurant overlooking the Bosporus on the day that she had told him the first part of the story.

He picked up his glass of wine, sipping it thoughtfully. He looked up at her and said, 'You must be joking! You can't really expect me to believe a story like that, can you?'

She burst into tears. 'I don't know how to convince you apart from tell you the truth.' By now she was sobbing heavily.

'I tell you what,' JJ said. 'You arrange a meeting with all your people. Let me hear it from others. You must admit it does sound a bit farfetched.'

'I suppose so. If I do will you join us?'

'You wouldn't be able to stop me.' He lifted his glass in a toast. 'To the revolution!' JJ hadn't stopped to consider the consequences of that remark, what would happen if something went wrong, as it had before? Her husband was serving ten years in prison and Abdul considered that she had been responsible.

# Chapter Eleven

Francine wasted no time in organizing the meeting JJ had asked for. She spent about an hour on the phone on Sunday morning making about a dozen calls. After the last call she flopped onto the sofa looked up at JJ and said, 'Be a darling, please pour me a drink.'

She took a large swallow and nodded. 'It's all arranged, Abdul will give you the details in the morning. Be careful, he will try to trap you about when we met. I told him we had lunch in town and that we met by accident in the Grand Bazaar.'

'OK, I get the idea. What did we buy?'

'Don't get flippant, he's very good at getting information out of people!'

'Sorry.'

'Now, what would you like for lunch? No. Don't look at me like that. After all those phone calls I'm famished.'

'Can we go out and have a pizza?'

'I don't see why not; if we are seen I can always say I was still trying to convince you to join us.'

They walked to the local restaurant that cooked pizza in an old-fashioned wood-burning oven. JJ was feeling on top of the world; he was being seen out with an incredible beautiful woman. It made him feel special! They got admiring gazes from the men, the hostile look of jealousy from the women. It was that wonderful thick blonde hair that did it, for she hardly dressed well, sloppy old jeans, tee shirt and those damned old brown suede boots. To say she didn't dress well was actually wrong – whatever she wore she always looked like a fashion model showing the latest Paris collection. She had admitted to JJ over lunch. 'I have absolutely no interest in clothes, they are only to keep me warm. The two dresses you have seen me wearing were both Ayşe's.' He had just suggested that he wanted to buy her something nice to wear when they went out together.

'No please, I am happy with what I've got. Thank you for your kind offer! If you would like I could swap places with Ayşe, she would let you buy her many new clothes.'

'Don't you dare! I think I'm in love with you.'

She pouted and said, 'Only think; what is an innocent young girl supposed to do when you only think you love her. Maybe you would like to sleep alone at the weekends?'

'That's a good idea, and then I can get some sleep.'

With that, she threw her arms around him, upsetting the table, and said, 'Well I love you.'

After lunch they walked home via the water's edge. They stood side by side looking out across the water. She said, 'Please hold me and give me a kiss. Suddenly I feel very frightened.'

'What about being seen?'

'At the moment I don't care who sees us, I need to be held tight.' After a few moments she pushed him away. 'I'm OK now; let's go home.'

As they continued home JJ asked, 'What was all that about?'

'I had this vision of you being arrested and in that dreadful prison with my husband. I am not sure we should carry on with the idea anymore.'

'That's a silly notion, if the damn Terrs in Rhodesia didn't get me; you don't think your local cop stands a chance do you?'

'It was the vision of you in that place, I could see it so clearly.' With that she grabbed his arm. 'Don't get hurt JJ, I need you so much.'

He unhooked his arm and put it protectively around her shoulder. He felt her start to relax against his side. 'We'll be fine. I've no intention of meeting your husband, he might have heard about you and me. Not good for my health, I think?'

She put her arm up around his waist. Pulling tight she said, 'No stupid risks.'

'No. OK.' As they walked up the path JJ swore – he had left

the Porsche out and the top was tattooed with the pigeons' and seagulls' droppings. 'Do you think they are trying to tell me something?' he said.

Francine burst into tears and ran into the house. As she went she blurted out, 'It's an omen.'

He could hear her sobbing as he turned on the hosepipe to wash away the mess. Drying his hands, he slipped behind the wheel and drove into the carport. He locked the car and walked thoughtfully into the house not sure of her mood towards him. He called out cheerfully, 'Hi darling, you OK now?'

'Yes, I'm in the bathroom, I was just being stupid.' She appeared her hair damp around the edge of her face as if she had dunked her face in the wash basin of cold water to wash away the tears.

'Don't forget to practice your story for Abdul in the morning.'

'What about a siesta, then you can coach me?'

'Yes if it would please you but not for too long, I need to start preparing dinner.'

The toot of Abdul's taksi made JJ put his jacket on. He kissed Francine a brief goodbye and hurried outside as always worried that Abdul would come to the house to see why JJ was being so long. They roared away with more noise and speed than usual, Abdul was obviously not in a good mood. He spoke as he drove, erratically. 'OK. Now what's going on with you and my son's wife? I heard you were together Saturday in Istanbul and you had a pizza lunch together here yesterday? You better have good explanation!'

JJ had been prepared for questions but not for Abdul's ferocious outburst. 'Francine told me a story the first time we had lunch together on the Bosporus, which you know about. On Saturday she asked me to join some silly game and yesterday she was trying to convince me that you had fixed up some meeting and would tell me the details this morning. I don't know what you think I am; I don't go around seducing other men's wives. If that's what you think of me; you can find someone else to play your stupid games.' With that he smiled to himself and thought, *two can play games, Abdul.*

'OK, Professor JJ, OK. Just testing you, Francine is a beautiful young woman and I know you have always flirted with her.'

'Yes and that's all, more the pity.'

'Well you make sure nothing does happen if you want to carry on breathing.'

'Yes, I hear you. Now tell me what all this about a meeting?'

'I've arranged a special meeting with my people so you can meet them all. That's what you wanted right? I tell you some are not very happy. They want to know what we do with you if you talk.'

'Don't worry about me, I've said I'll be pleased to join your group if you prove what Francine has told me is true.'

'Why don't you believe her? She is telling you truth.'

'I'm sorry Abdul, but even you have to agree that it's a bit farfetched.'

'No. If you were Turkish you would know it was truth.'

'Well I'm not and I don't know it's true. So convince me.'

'OK. I will collect you from that bar in Yenikapi where we had beer before octopus salad. You remember?'

'Yes I remember. When?'

'At ten-thirty tonight. OK?'

'OK.'

They were just passing Sirkeci station when Abdul said, 'When are you seeing Francine again?'

'I assume at tonight's meeting.'

'Ah yes, I forgot.' JJ could see Abdul looking at him in the driving mirror. JJ said nothing.

JJ had taken the train into the city because of the constant worry about his car being damaged. He had begun to wish he hadn't brought it from the UK. He was halfway through a beer when Abdul pulled up. He declined a drink, which was a most unusual occurrence, pleading that they had a long drive ahead and a long night. 'There will be plenty of time for drinking later!' He settled back in Abdul's taksi and dozed. For once Abdul was being quiet.

It was 12:30 when the taksi came to a halt. JJ had fallen into a deep sleep, lulled by the motion of the car. They had pulled up by what looked like an abandoned warehouse. About twenty other cars were already parked in the area in front of the building, which looked more like a bomb site, the tarmac potted with holes and strewn with debris. The building they entered had no lighting so they followed the beam of Abdul's torch, climbing six flights of stairs before emerging onto the roof. JJ estimated there must be at least fifty people gathered. A barbecue was alight in a corner near the old chimney pots, a makeshift bar close to it. All the people gathered appeared to have a drink either in their hand or resting on some convenient object. Francine called over, 'You made it then?'

JJ waved in acknowledgment.

Heading towards the bar Abdul asked, 'What are you drinking tonight? I recommend the raki – we don't want everyone here to think you old woman.'

JJ replied, 'If I must.'

Abdul slapped him on the back saying, 'You must, you must!'

Francine had come over to join them. Feeling for JJ's hand in the darkness she gave it a squeeze and whispered, 'You'll be fine; don't worry.'

'I'm not.' With that she disappeared into the darkness.

JJ took his drink and walked around trying to get his bearings. A stage had been set up on the opposite side of the bar; and onto this Abdul was climbing, glass in hand. He completed the maneuver without spilling his drink; finding an empty crate to use as a table. He called out to JJ to join him. When JJ was standing at his side he started talking to the assembled group. He spoke with an authority that JJ had not known he possessed. JJ's understanding of Turkish had improved by leaps and bounds since he had been with Francine and with the help of various students at school was able to follow Abdul's speech fairly well. He was saying that they had recruited, at great expense, a mighty warrior from the UK who had fought in many battles and was going to teach them all to be warriors like he was. That he was the world's expert on how to blow things up and that they were all going to be taught those skills. They would all learn how to kill a man without noise or risking their own lives. He then said that Professor Captain JJ would say a few words.

JJ was prepared for this moment and with a well-rehearsed speech said in Turkish, 'I would like to thank Abdul for arranging this meeting and thank you all for coming.' He then went on to correct a few of Abdul's exaggerations on his past army life and his abilities to blow things up and kill people. He continued that he had been told a story and asked for help by Francine. The story was so unbelievable to his English mind to believe that he had asked for this meeting if he was to help them. He concluded, 'I am at your disposal over the next few hours for you to convince me not only that the story is true but that your cause is worth fighting for!' He stepped back from the edge of the stage to a somewhat half-hearted round of applause.

Abdul came and took him by the hand and led him off the stage down into the crowd and at once started introducing him to people. 'This is Suleiman, my eldest son, he will tell you about his brother.'

'Good to meet you, Captain sir. My brother, he in big trouble, he in very bad place, very dirty, bad food, rats. They shave his head because of the bugs. They beat him. It's a very bad place. Please, you help?'

'I'll try.'

'This is my wife, she tell you how they treat her son.'

She was a huge surprise to JJ who had expected her to be a typical Turkish woman and be dressed in the traditional dress with a black head scarf. Instead, she was tall, slim and dressed in a tight-fitting dress with high-heeled shoes, had long curly black hair, her makeup was perfect. She looked about forty but Francine told him later that she was over fifty.

'Please, sir, Captain, you must help, without you I don't know what we can do. My son is in very bad place. It's very dirty and bad food.'

'I'm sorry, I'll try to help you all,' JJ said.

Abdul added his own plea for help.

'We cannot do this alone; we need your help and guidance. If we can make a success of blowing up a bridge we can make the government understand that we are committed to our cause and hopefully we can negotiate better treatment for my son and the many others like him.'

Abdul continued his tour of introductions with JJ held firmly by the elbow. They met two other brothers, four uncles, two aunts and all the other guests who claimed to be his closest friend! JJ started to think, *It's more like a family reunion than a meeting of terrorists.*

He asked Abdul, 'Why are Conrad and Ayşe not here tonight?'

'Mr. Conrad a bit stuffy about big meetings in the open, he prefers just a few people in his office.'

'As he recruited me I thought he might have come to give his support?'

Abdul shook his head in contemplation.

JJ wondered silently about cozy meetings in Conrad's office. He thought, *I will have to be careful about what I say in his company.*

JJ continued, 'Why are there only your family and friends here? I thought I was going to meet your comrades from the anarchist movement.'

'Professor JJ, all of these people are the members of my group, they have all been involved in our fight for freedom. Making bombs, booby traps, robbery, kidnapping, arson, some have even killed for our cause.' JJ was clearly taken aback by this statement.

From the looks of any of the ladies there, they could have been his mother, not hardened terrorists. JJ said, 'Abdul let me speak to your people again. I would like to make a statement. I haven't planned this one so please ask them to excuse my lack of vocabulary.'

Abdul made the announcement and everyone settled to listen to JJ.

'People of the revolution. I am sorry, I would like to say friends but at the moment I do not know you that well. I hope that soon I can call you all my friends. I have decided to help you.' At that the roof erupted in applause. JJ held his hands up for quiet and continued his speech.

'I am not sure about your ultimate aims but I will do what I can to help you get decent civil rights for your people in prison.' Again the people all cheered not as wildly this time.

Abdul whispered, 'They're not sure about your comment of "ultimate aims".'

JJ again silenced them. 'I will help you as I've said. As I'm sure most of you know I own an expensive German sports car.' The crowd hissed and booed at that but JJ was not to be put off finishing his speech. 'I do not share your political beliefs. If anything; I am a capitalist at heart but I do believe in fair justice. And from what I have heard tonight I do not believe that your country's justice is fair.' He held his glass high and shouted, 'A toast to the revolution!' The crowd roared with approval.

'To the revolution!' People were invading the little stage, the men kissing him on the cheeks, the women shaking his hands all saying, 'Thank you.'

Francine shook his hand; squeezing it for longer than necessary, whispering, 'I'll give you a proper thank you as soon as I can.'

# Chapter Twelve

Abdul dropped JJ off at home just as the sun was beginning to rise. As he entered the house he heard water running in the bathroom. Not sure what to expect he opened the bathroom door to find a very beautiful, and very naked, Francine about to get into the shower. She was as surprised as JJ; and said, 'I hope you don't mind?'

'Not at all, that's why I gave you a key and told you to come and go as you wish.' That had been a month earlier when he had been delayed getting home on a Friday night. Conrad had been inconsiderate and called a staff meeting at the last minute and Francine had been soaked by a rain storm as she had waited for JJ. He was upset that he had caused her discomfort. Francine's only comment was that it was her fault she should have brought an umbrella. He had immediately given her a back-door key; which she preferred to use rather than the front. Until now she had never used it.

'I've come to thank you properly as I promised. You make some coffee and let me finish in here then I'll make breakfast.' JJ would have liked to have joined her in the shower. Apart from finding her almost irresistible he also needed to shower to wash away the ravages of the night spent on an Istanbul rooftop.

'OK.' She joined him in the kitchen in less than the promised five minutes. She smelt clean – that lovely smell of a warm body mingled with the scent of soap and shampoo.

'You were quick.'

'I was, but only for you. What would you like for breakfast?' She moved quickly out of his reach.

'If we are going to have lunch, maybe just toast, if not, maybe some sausages and egg please.'

'No lunch for me.'

'Sausage and egg it is then.'

'Would you also like some toast? You go and shower.'

'Yes please.' JJ was delighted at the prospect of missing lunch.

It was dusk by the time they had showered again; and had strolled hand in hand to the pizza restaurant where they had enjoyed lunch on the Sunday before.

'Did I say thank you for agreeing to help my husband?'

'Not quite but you thanked me for just about everything else.' He bent and whispered in her ear.

'Did I say thank you for doing that?'

'You certainly did,' he said smugly.

'Anyway I'm not doing it for him, I'm doing it for you, well, us really. If he is treated better you won't be so sad on Sunday evening when you have visited him.'

'I try not to let it show. Thank you anyway.'

'My reward will be seeing you happy.'

'If you had said that this morning we could have had lunch.'

'Would you have been as happy now if we had had lunch?'

'Why do you always have to be so smug?'

'Are you forgetting what you thanked me for?' They arrived at the pizza restaurant in time to prevent an argument breaking out, although it would have been a good-natured one.

As JJ got into Abdul's taksi the following morning, he said, 'Before you say anything Abdul, yes, Francine came to see me yesterday evening and yes we did have pizza together. We talked about when we should start training and what we will need to get in the way of equipment. I agreed to make a list over the next few days. OK?'

'OK. Fine; Professor JJ.'

JJ thought, *That's the way to treat you my friend.*

'JJ?' Ayşe called from her office. 'Conrad wants to see you as soon as you are in.'

'Be there in about five minutes.' He wondered what he wanted.

'Come in, JJ, have a seat, tell me how did it go last night?' JJ decided that this was not the time and certainly not the place for a chat. He remembered Abdul's comment about Conrad always preferring to have small meetings in his office, and Francine's premonition. He didn't like the idea of ten years in a Turkish prison or worse. He was also beginning to have other doubts about Conrad like, where did he get all his money from? It couldn't be from the school. Schools like this only made enough to survive so Conrad must have another source of income. From where, was he spying for the government?

'Can we meet and talk at lunchtime? I've got a backlog on my desk to clear.'

'OK. I would prefer to talk here, though, it's more private.'

'See you at one then,' JJ said, making for the door before Conrad had time to object. He decided to tell Francine about his concerns when they next met, which unfortunately wasn't to be until Friday.

'Come on, JJ. I've got Abdul waiting to take us to lunch. I thought we could go over to Kadikoy get away for a couple of hours. You don't have anything desperate on this afternoon do you?'

'Nothing that can't wait, I did all the urgent stuff this morning. Somewhere with a nice view would be nice.'

'We know just the place, let's go Abdul.'

'Sure do, Mr. Conrad.' The longest part of the journey was getting onto the ferry boat.

They drew up at the little restaurant where he'd had lunch with Francine on their first date. They were greeted as if they were royalty. Handshakes and kisses were exchanged, together with happy smiles and enthusiastic comments regarding the quality of the fish they were going enjoy. JJ realized that most of the staff had been at the meeting the other night. Then he remembered Francine had told him that this was a safe place because that day they had had lunch there she had said the staff and customers were all part of Abdul's anarchist group, and the owner was a friend of her husband.

They were seated at the same quiet corner table where JJ had the view up the Bosporus looking towards the bridge. They didn't actually order lunch it just seemed to appear and when a dish was emptied it was replaced by another. The only thing JJ insisted on was no raki for himself. He would have a cold beer with the meze, and chilled rose wine with the main course if it was fish if not he would drink red wine. Conrad was getting impatient for news of Monday night's meeting. JJ and Abdul told him the story. Abdul finished with a pat on JJ's shoulder and said, 'Professor JJ charmed them. At one point I thought he would be murdered when he stood there and said, "I don't share your political views, I'm a capitalist and I own an expensive German sports car".'

Conrad looked astonished. 'You didn't?'

Abdul continued, 'He did, then he carried on with, "I do, however, believe in free justice" and that they had convinced him that the justice in Turkey is not fair or free, and they loved it, then he proposed a toast to the revolution. I am surprised you didn't hear the applause over there. He will have no problem after that little speech; they will do anything he asks of them.'

Conrad said, 'I wish I'd been there.' JJ resisted asking him why he hadn't.

Lunch continued in a good-humored manner for the next hour or so. JJ was gazing up the Bosporus at the bridge. Then he said excitedly, 'Why stick at one?' Conrad and Abdul looked at him as he continued, 'If we blow them both, Istanbul comes to a complete standstill.'

Conrad sounded agitated as he said, 'You mean blow both bridges?'

'That's great, trust Professor JJ to come up with a big bang solution,' Abdul added.

Conrad and Abdul called excitedly to Ishmael the owner of the restaurant. 'Come, we have wonderful idea. JJ, you tell

Ishmael, it's your idea.'

JJ thought for a moment then started to outline his idea. 'Instead of blowing just one of the bridges we blow them both. We will need twice as many men to carry and set the explosives and of course twice the amount of explosives which means twice the cost, but, just think; twice the damage.'

At that point Abdul couldn't resist chipping in with, 'And just think, also twice the chaos. Istanbul gridlocked.'

'Yes,' said JJ, 'all the taksi's will be jammed up as well.'

Abdul cried, 'No money, I'll starve.'

Conrad intervened by adding, 'You'll have to start spending some of the money you have hidden away; won't you, you old miser?'

'I can get you the men,' said Ishmael, 'but do we have enough money to buy the explosives?'

'Don't worry about the money,' Conrad added, 'I can arrange that. Have you any idea how much yet JJ?'

'You originally budgeted to blow up one bridge, just double it then add about fifty per cent.' Conrad didn't look pleased. JJ was happy with Conrad's unease over the money and started wondering if there was a percentage in it for him.

Abdul came to the rescue, 'Come on, be happy,' he shouted, 'we have something to celebrate.' Ishmael summoned more wine and raki for Abdul and himself as he had pulled up a chair to join them. That was the nice thing about Turkey, JJ thought, everyone joined in, invited or not. He was very pleased with himself and he wished he could tell Francine but today was only Wednesday!

At seven that evening they left the restaurant and JJ was home by eight-thirty. The phone rang while he was making himself a coffee – he knew he was in for a hangover.

'JJ,' Francine's voice sounded excited. 'I've just heard about your plan, can I please come over and talk about it? Please say yes.'

'How long will you be?'

'About an hour; is that OK?'

'If you're much longer than that I will be asleep, too much wine.'

'Don't you dare be asleep? Make yourself some black coffee, I'm on my way.' The phone went dead.

JJ was amazed how quickly the news had got around and delighted that Francine was coming over for the night. At least he hoped she was staying; she hadn't said. He started to consider the task he had given himself, wondering if he had proposed too big a task; all he had to work with was an enthusiastic band of amateurs. He would need to get Francine to get them together so he could see what, if anything, they could do.

He watched TV while he drank his coffee. Just flicking through the channels, not really watching any of the programs in particular, he caught the tail end of a documentary about the Orient Express train. He started to consider how he and Francine were going to get out of the country after the explosions. He heard the back door open and close. He had just put down his empty coffee cup as Francine launched herself into the room, landing on his lap with her arms around his neck. She felt vibrant, as if she was trembling all over. He asked, 'Are you OK?'

'Yes, fine thanks, just so excited about your idea and pleased to see you. Can I have a bath before we go to bed tonight please? It is OK for me to stay? Would it please you?'

'If you are a good girl.'

'I'm sure I can be very good.'

JJ didn't have his predicted hangover but he felt very tired. He looked at the bedside clock, swore under his breath, slid out of bed and went to have a shower. He only had thirty minutes before Abdul would arrive. Feeling revived, he made Francine a hot chocolate, and coffee for himself. Taking both cups he went back into the bedroom. Setting them onto the bedside table, he bent over and kissed the still sleeping Francine. She opened her eyes wide and, putting her arms around his neck, pulled him towards her. JJ pulled away pleading the shortage of time.

'Do you know I didn't tell me about my plan for the bridges, would you like me to tell you tonight?'

'Oh! Yes please.' He bent down and kissed her again, freeing himself just as he heard Abdul's taksi pulling up outside. 'Will you be here when I get home?'

'Like a good Turkish wife I will have your dinner ready and waiting for your pleasure.' She made it sound like an indecent proposal.

# Chapter Thirteen

As JJ walked up the path to his house he could hear raised voices as if an argument was taking place. His first thought was that somehow Elizabeth had flown over and found his house with Francine in residence. The argument that was going on was in Turkish between a man and a woman. He opened the door to see Abdul and Francine, both with flushed faces.

'Hello, what's going on?' said JJ.

Abdul immediately started to shout again, this time at JJ. 'Professor JJ, how could you take advantage of our hospitality like this? I thought we were friends. My son, Francine's husband, is shut away in prison and I find that you are having an affair with his wife. It's very bad. What do you have to say?'

JJ looked across at Francine who was standing behind Abdul. She shook her head as if to say "He doesn't know anything".

JJ immediately went on the attack. 'Abdul, I also thought we were friends, you come here accusing us of having an affair when you have no justification. Francine had offered to cook me a meal and do a bit around the house and in return, if you remember, I am going to blow up your bridges for you in the hope that you can negotiate a better deal for your son.' JJ paused to check the effect on Abdul. He was standing shuffling his feet like a little boy being told off. JJ continued, 'I am fed up with your continual mistrust of anything that Francine and I do, you have hinted before that you don't trust us together or you just don't trust me. Well, if that's what you think, I will pack up and leave Istanbul today.'

Francine looked horrified and Abdul had gone bright red in the face – his embarrassment was very obvious. He said hesitantly, 'Professor JJ, I apologize; it's that you seem to spend so much time together. What am I to think?'

JJ, still on the attack, retorted, 'It was your devious little plan to throw us together in the beginning. If Francine wasn't so devoted to her husband things may have been different. I think you owe your daughter-in-law an apology?'

With that Abdul was defeated but it was so against his nature to apologize to anyone, particularly a woman. He turned to Francine, his head bent, cupping his face in his hands. He stuttered a few words.

'It's OK,' she said. 'Let's all be friends again.' With that she kissed him on the forehead, looked at JJ and winked, mouthing a silent 'well done' over Abdul's still bowed head.

Abdul turned again to JJ. 'Professor JJ, what can I do to regain your friendship and help? We need your help to assist us in our fight against the government.'

JJ was unable to resist saying, 'Don't be so suspicious in the future. My association with Francine is to help in the fight, nothing more.'

He walked towards JJ, clutching his arms around his shoulders, and kissed him on both cheeks, saying, 'I thank you for your understanding. My wife thanks you, my sons thank you, and Francine's husband thanks you.'

JJ pulled away quickly before the rest of Abdul's family wanted to kiss him as well. Abdul, still full of embarrassment quickly said, 'OK, lots to do, can't spend all evening talking. I know that Francine has prepared you a wonderful dinner you had better start it before it gets cold.' With that he waved a cheerful goodbye as he headed for the door.

Francine and JJ didn't move until they heard Abdul's taksi pull away from the back of the house. She ran to him saying, 'You were so clever to make him think it was entirely his fault, hopefully he will leave us alone now.'

JJ doubted that it would not be long before his suspicions were again raised. He didn't voice his thoughts, instead, kissing her and saying, 'I thought you had made me dinner?'

'You had better start on the list of stuff we will need for the job.'

'I have already started. How many people can we rely on being available on the night?'

'So far thirty-six have said they will be available to help.'

'That's not enough to do both bridges. Out of that thirty-six we will probably see only thirty. We will need at least forty that we can rely on. Can you rustle up some more?' JJ continued.

'I'm not sure, but I'll try.'

'Good girl, I will go through the list with you after we have had dinner.'

They ate, both in a somber mood. Saying little, eating and drinking with reserve, both thinking about the future.

JJ pushed away his empty coffee cup and half-full glass, picked up his briefcase from the side of his chair and pulled out a sheaf of papers from within. 'OK, let's start,' he said. Francine moved her chair to read the paperwork more easily. She was immediately taken aback with first item which read. 'Five hundred kilos of Semtex explosive – estimated cost $350,000.'

'How are we going to be able to get all that? Before all we could ever get was a couple of kilos.'

'I know a man who knows a man,' JJ replied. 'I just hope Conrad is good for the money and that's only the tip of the iceberg, it adds up to three quarters of million.'

'Show me the rest of the list?' She looked down the paper that JJ had put in front of her then nodded with approval as she read down the list at last saying, 'Good, Uzi machine pistols.'

'Yes, I thought that they would be better than an AK, if we get into trouble it will all be short-range stuff.'

'Let's hope it will not come to that?' Francine added.

'What do you think of the equipment list?'

'It looks fine, but I would love to see Conrad's face when he sees it's going to cost him almost a million dollars.'

'Well, if you are happy I will give it to him in the morning.'

'Yes, but don't forget to tell Abdul in the morning that you've done it. You could also tell him I spent the night here, that we worked late into the night and it was too late for me to go home to Kadikoy.'

'Yes. I like that. I had better say you were in the guest room otherwise he may crash the taksi.'

'I would like to see his face as well. You will be careful? Don't let him think you are making fun of him.'

'OK. I'll be nice. As you are going to be officially staying tonight can we please go to bed? I need you to make love with me, very slowly and for a very long time.'

'Mm, that sounds wonderful,' she said, in that deep sexy voice that seemed to be reserved for comments of that nature.

When JJ was settled into the back seat of Abdul's taksi he said, 'I've got good news, Francine spent the night at the house with me!' Abdul swerved across the road almost colliding with a donkey that was pulling a cart full of vegetables. Before he could say anything, JJ quickly added, 'She was, of course, in the guest room. We worked very late and have completed the equipment list. I'm going to give it to Conrad as soon as we get to school. It all adds up to three quarters of a million dollars.' At that point Abdul swerved over the road again this time just touching the curb which made Abdul swear. JJ asked, 'Would you like to see it first?'

'No, it's OK, best I don't interfere. That's what you are here for.' Abdul made it sound as if he was talking to the hired help, which JJ supposed he was in a way and he knew that it made Abdul feel better. JJ just nodded.

'Hello Ayşe. I need to see Conrad now, is that OK?'

'Good morning, JJ, its real good to see you. Come have some coffee. Ayşe, could you please arrange that?'

'I've completed the equipment list,' blurted out JJ. He had temporarily forgotten his intention of never discussing the job in Conrad's office. Too late now, he thought, better make it sound innocuous. 'Yeah, I've got some really good stuff down and it only adds up to three quarters of a million US.' JJ made it sound like a joke.

Conrad was furious. 'Do you have to laugh at everything?' he stormed.

JJ got up and added, 'Why don't we talk about it over lunch? I must dash, lots to do. Please tell Ayşe sorry about the coffee, another time.'

Conrad was already sitting in Abdul's taksi when JJ went looking for him at lunchtime. They had obviously been talking about JJ – the silence inside the taksi when he got in was ominous. 'Hi, thanks for waiting. Lunch on me today, my boss will let me put it on expenses!'

Conrad spluttered and Abdul smiled, he didn't mind who paid as long as it wasn't himself. Conrad had to fight to keep his temper with JJ but managed it. 'OK,' he said, 'your wish list of goodies. You must think I'm a millionaire. I don't have that sort of money to spend on fire crackers.'

Abdul added, 'I think it's a good price.'

'OK, OK, don't wet yourself, Abdul, but we must try and make savings.'

JJ joined in, 'What do you think we can do without, Conrad?'

'Well do we really need forty Uzi machine pistols?'

'Yes, we do, that's one each for the forty people who will be risking their lives on the night, not swanning off to some American embassy function, and each pistol will have a hundred rounds of ammunition. The remaining thousand rounds will be used during training. I suppose you agree that they should have some training or do you want to send them off with not much chance of coming back?'

Conrad had gone quiet and started to look sick.

JJ said, 'Abdul, you had better stop.'

Conrad was leaning out of the door before Abdul had had chance to park. He leant back against the seat and said very softly, 'I didn't count on any of our people being hurt. I'm sorry.

Yes, of course everyone should be as well-trained as possible; I couldn't do with a memory that I had been too mean to send them off without the proper gear.'

JJ suddenly felt very sorry for Conrad and all the others who had to weigh the value of life against money. 'OK. I'll try and trim the price as much as possible.'

Conrad smiled a sickly 'thank you.'

Abdul had obviously either forgotten Conrad's sickness or was more callous than JJ had thought. 'We will soon be at restaurant. I heard this morning they have fresh fish today.'

JJ said, 'I thought the fish was always fresh?'

'Some days fresher than others, but, always fresh fish is served to customers.'

By the time Abdul had parked, Conrad was looking a better color. Abdul led the way to the door, letting JJ and Conrad enter before him with a mock bow. Conrad made a reference regarding Abdul's parentage as he passed him, the incident in the taksi forgotten.

# Chapter Fourteen

Starting on the meze and the cold bottle of Turkish rosé wine made JJ a little more sociable towards Conrad. However, it was Abdul that first broached the subject of obtaining the explosives.

'Professor JJ, do you know how are you going to get all that explosive stuff?'

'Well,' said JJ, 'I know some guys, from when I was in the army that have set up a small business selling everything we need.' He took another sip of his wine and continued, 'I shall need a ten per cent deposit for the stuff in cash, the balance in gold on delivery.' Conrad looked ill again but carried on eating. JJ added, 'I will need to go to Europe for about two weeks to sort everything out. Do you have any problem with that, Conrad?'

'No, you carry on, that's why you're here after all.'

'Thanks. I promise to get you a good deal. Will you credit my Swiss bank account with, say, a hundred thousand dollars? That will cover my expenses as well.' JJ was delighted that he had maintained his account in Switzerland. It was strange, he thought, the number of times that he had considered closing that account, that he and so many Rhodesians had opened as a way of getting money out of the country during the time of UDI. There had been three possibilities of countries that would allow dealings with the Reserve Bank of Rhodesia. There had been Hong Kong, South Africa and Switzerland. Switzerland had appealed to most as a more stable country for the future and that their hard earned cash would not be impounded by any majority Government that swept into power.

Conrad, being unable to resist a sarcastic comment said, 'Why don't you take the food out of my children's mouths as well?'

JJ ignored Conrad's comment and continued, saying, 'I will leave as soon as possible. I'll drive the Porsche back; get it out of harm's way!' The main course arrived. It was wonderful red mullet cooked on a charcoal grill.

JJ called for another bottle of rosé, and Abdul growled. 'Bring me a man's drink – bring me some raki.' And the three of them devoured the fish in contented silence, each locked in their own personal thoughts.

JJ didn't go back to the school that afternoon, pleading too much wine with lunch. He got Abdul to drop him of at Sirkeci to catch a train home. On his way down the platform he stopped outside the office of the Orient Express company. Pausing to look in the window he noticed the poster of the train in the station with Francine in her belly dance costume offering a tray of Turkish Delight to the passengers alighting from the train. The caption on the poster was proclaiming, "Welcome to Istanbul; Europe's friendliest city". JJ felt a pang of jealousy as he contemplated the picture of Francine showing a magnificent exposed leg through her costume – the skirt was split to the thigh. He entered the office, browsed through the leaflets on display and pocketed a timetable, asked the man behind the counter if he could have a copy of the poster and was disappointed when he was told that they could not be given to the public. He caught the next local train and was home in twenty minutes.

JJ was feeling excited at the prospect of the drive to England but was a little dubious of seeing Elizabeth again, although their telephone calls were most convivial. He decided to phone her immediately and tell her he was coming over. Elizabeth sounded pleased he was planning to visit her and was demanding details of his flight, how long he was stopping. JJ explained that he hadn't made any arrangements but was really asking if he could pay a visit.

Over the next couple of days JJ firmed up his plans. He managed to track down Peter and Kirk, his ex-army comrades, who were now working out of the Czech Republic, which JJ thought was a happy coincidence as Semtex is manufactured there. He planned to drive to Prague, the capital of the Czech

Republic, and meet his old friends on Sunday next. JJ planned his route. He would drive out of Turkey through Bulgaria, Romania, Hungary, Austria and finally into the Czech Republic. He made copious notes in a pad and on the maps he had been studying. The journey distance was just over two thousand kilometers, about twenty hours' driving time. Allowing for the inevitable delays, call it four days. Two days there, allow another two days to get to the UK, which was an easy drive through Germany. He should be with Elizabeth, Thursday, the week after. He phoned Elizabeth. She was delighted, he didn't tell his planes to visit Prague on his way home, she wouldn't understand.

Next hurdle, tell Francine. He knew she would be unhappy about his visit to Elizabeth. Tomorrow was only Wednesday. He needed to see Francine soon, get it over with. Leaving his office he went to see Ayşe. He was, usual, stunned by her elegance. 'Ayşe, I need to get in touch with Francine as soon as possible.'

'That's no problem, I can phone her now.'

'Thanks. Will you ask her to come to Yesilcoy as soon as possible preferably this evening?'

'Is there a problem?'

'Not really, just need to go through some ideas with her.'

'I'll give you a ring when I've spoken to her.'

'Thanks,' said JJ as he left Ayşe's office, 'see you soon.'

Five minutes later his desk phone rang, 'JJ, I've spoken to Francine, she will be at your house about eight tonight. OK?'

'Thanks for your help, Ayşe.' JJ replaced the receiver and wondered how to break the news. He knew there would be a row!

He was correct, the first full-scale fight they had had, tears and shouts of reproach. She launched herself at him; all JJ could do was to try restraining her. She fought back and he landed in an arm chair with Francine on top of him. He did the only thing he could think of – turn her over and gave her bottom a resounding slap. The tears changed to sobbing, the fight was over.

JJ pulled her upright and kissed her very firmly saying, 'Please don't cry like that, I hurt my hand more than your bottom.'

'Good,' she replied through her sobs. 'I hope it's broken.'

'Come on, it's not that bad.'

'Yes it is; no-one has ever slapped me before! I wish it hadn't been you that did it.'

'Come on. Shall I rub it better?'

'You see the trouble your wife causes?'

JJ couldn't think of a reply that would have been acceptable to Francine. He continued to rub her bottom until she pulled away.

'JJ, what are you going to do after we do the job? It might not be safe to stay in Turkey.'

'It probably won't be for either of us,' he replied.

'No, you are right! Let's not talk about that now. When will you come back to Istanbul?'

'I'll be away about ten days.'

'Can I stay here while you are away? I can have some time on my own. I don't like to be around Conrad all time.'

'Yes,' he said with a rueful smile, 'that would be great, and then you will be here when I get back.'

She gave an exaggerated sigh, ruffled his hair, and said, 'Of course I'll be here, I always am when you want me.' She looked sad and then suddenly brightened up and unexpectedly said, 'Take me for a pizza and I'll forgive you for slapping my bottom.'

'We have a whole week before I leave would you like to go away somewhere until then?'

'What do you mean, a holiday?'

'Yes,' he replied.

'Oh! Yes please. Do you mean it? I've never been away on a holiday before. Where will we go?'

'Anywhere you like. It'll have to be in Turkey; don't forget you don't have a passport.'

'Can I think about it for a while? It will make it more exciting. Are you sure you're not doing this just because you're going to visit your wife?'

'Do you still want that pizza?'

'Yes please. It's really my night for treats isn't it?'

They walked to the pizza restaurant arm in arm. Francine kept singing little snatches of a song that JJ recognized the tune of but not the title or where he had heard it before. In between the singing she kept saying, 'You do really mean a proper holiday?'

'Providing you tell me what you are singing?'

'It's my signature tune, it was written for me by my husband, and it is always played when I am dancing or meeting the train. It's even been on the radio.'

'And you complain about my wife!' JJ replied, a little more crossly than he meant. He didn't want to spoil her excitement over the holiday but it was a good opportunity to show that he too had feelings.

'I'm sorry if it makes you unhappy I shall never allow it to be played again.'

'No, don't do that, it's nice that people associate you with a piece of music – even if it's bad music.'

'You're jealous!'

'Only a bit. I don't like to think of other men doing things for you that pleased you. It means that when you remember a happy moment that you had you're remembering him as well.'

'What about your wife? Didn't you have happy moments?'

'I can't explain it, but it's different.'

'OK,' she said, 'no more song tonight. I shall always be able to remember it was you who slapped my bottom and took me on my first holiday.'

'I'm glad; at least I've managed a couple of firsts. Let's drop the subject of your husband please?'

'Can we have the table in the window tonight please? I want

to be seen with you.'

'Is it safe?'

'I'm fed up with safe. I would like the whole world to see me tonight I am so happy!'

She squeezed JJ's arm as they took their seats at the window table

They ordered a large pizza between them. JJ had beer, Francine only wanted water. She explained, 'I don't want anything to dull my senses tonight.'

JJ laughed at her as she was making her little girl face.

'I've decided where I would like to go on holiday,' she announced halfway through her share of the pizza. 'Can we please go to Cyprus? It means we can go by airplane. I've never flown before and my friends say it's very pretty.'

'Of course, we'll go in the morning!' JJ thought before continuing, 'Isn't it your weekend for visiting?'

'Oh blast! I'll phone his mother on Saturday and say I'm sick. I will not let anything get in the way of our holiday. Please hurry we must go and pack. And I need to have a bath and wash my hair.'

JJ laughed at her excitement. 'Come on,' he said, 'let's go, my pizza has got cold with all this chatter.' JJ thought as they walked home hand in hand that it was like having a five-year-old child, for Francine was hopping and skipping down the road pulling him along.

They packed. Well rather, JJ packed – Francine put her meager possessions into a corner of his suitcase. Her possessions consisted of three changes of underwear, five tee shirts and a hair brush, all of which she had left at JJ's house over the past weeks. It really didn't seem to matter to her that she was going on her first holiday with no holiday clothes. JJ resolved to buy her a holiday outfit that she would remember as often as she remembered the holiday. She put her arms around his neck; kissed him and said a very simple, 'Thank you for making me so happy.'

JJ kissed her in return saying, 'It's me that should thank you for making me so happy over the past months.'

Francine was up at six o clock the following morning. She woke JJ with a kiss and a cup of coffee. He put his arms out to her. She backed away saying, 'It's your own fault, you should have let me bath and do my hair last night. I must do it now.'

'I must tell Conrad that I'm leaving Istanbul on my shopping trip and you must tell Ayşe something as to why you are not going back there for a couple of weeks.'

'I'll tell her I'm staying here, house sitting while you are away. Which is true, she doesn't need to know that you don't go for another week!'

'I'll phone Conrad now,' said JJ. 'You phone Ayşe when we get to the airport.'

Francine disappeared to the bathroom. He could hear her singing her song again. JJ resisted complaining, he knew that she was just happy.

Conrad was a little huffy when JJ told him that he was leaving that day. 'You could have given me a bit more warning,' he complained.

'Have you paid the money into my Swiss account yet?' JJ wanted to know.

'Yes, yes, all taken care of, now you keep to your end of the bargain,' barked Conrad.

JJ put the phone down, thinking that he was still unsure about Conrad! Francine was calling from the bathroom.

'I'm finished. Are you showering?' It snapped JJ back to Francine and a holiday.

They drove to the airport and JJ paid the extra to have the Porsche garaged in a guarded compound. Happy that the car would be safe until their return, they put JJ's case onto a trolley, and arm in arm they walked to the terminal building. Stopping at the Turkish Airlines reservation counter, they started the search for a holiday hotel. They had three hours until the next flight to Cyprus. The agent was helpful in suggesting various destinations. They eventually selected a small hotel just outside the old town of Kyrenia. JJ paid for the package deal. Armed with tickets, they set of on what Francine insisted on calling the holiday of a lifetime.

Walking around the terminal building shopping area JJ insisted on buying Francine a bikini swimming costume, a pair of white shorts with a colorful sun top, a pair of sunglasses and a pair of espadrilles – he explained, 'You can't wear your old brown suede boots on the beach.' JJ having to tell her that they were all for his benefit she was delighted, he could tell.

She asked, 'Why do you want to cover me up? Don't you like me naked anymore?' She again adopted her coy expression.

'Francine, I adore you dressed, undressed; particularly in your old jeans, I just adore you.'

She looked up at him and smiled, saying, 'Thank you for my clothes and I love you. I would kiss you but it's not fitting for an innocent Turkish girl to be seen doing that sort of thing.'

JJ, following her banter, said, 'I had better change the hotel reservation for two single rooms in place of the double.'

Francine grabbed at his arm and hissed at him, 'Don't you dare!'

'To hell with protocol!' he declared, and bent down and kissed her.

She gave a long satisfied sigh and said, 'Thank you.'

All through the flight, Francine, nose pressed against the window, gave a commentary on the progress of the plane. The landing was bumpy as they touched the runway. A number of the overhead lockers flew open, scattering badly packed items on to the unfortunates sitting below. Francine clung to JJ's arm, crying out, 'Are we going to crash?' JJ reassured her that in fact they had landed, albeit a bit hard.

The walk to the terminal in the blazing sun was short and hot. They collected their suitcase from the carousel and followed a stream of other holidaymakers to a waiting coach that whisked them off to deposit them at their respective hotels. Francine and JJ were the first off with Francine calling, 'Have a good holiday!' to those remaining on the coach.

JJ hugged her with one arm, suitcase in the other, and whispered in her ear, 'That's no way for a terrorist to behave.'

'This week I'm not a terrorist, I'm on holiday with my lover. I want to do silly things, holiday things; you'll have to show me what.' He whispered to her again and she pushed him away playfully. 'Any more comments like that, we will definitely have single rooms.'

In a happy, relaxed, mood they entered the hotel booking in as Mr. and Mrs. Jamison, which was the name JJ had had to use when he paid for the holiday tickets with his credit card. Francine was delighted pretending to be Mrs. Jamison. Nobody could doubt that they were married; with Francine's mane of blonde hair no-one would ever suspect that she was Turkish. Depositing the suitcase in their room, they changed into shorts and tee shirts and went for a walk, initially in search of food but latterly on a shopping expedition. Francine returned to the hotel with bags, parcels and boxes, excited with the prospect of wearing her new clothes. 'What shall I wear tonight when we go out for dinner?'

'The long one,' he said, indicating a long sapphire blue linen dress, 'and the white shoes.' She looked dubiously at the shoes. 'I've never worn high heels before, I'm not sure I can.' They both showered and JJ lay on the bed and watched as Francine dressed. She looked stunning, her blonde hair down to her shoulders, the sapphire of the dress in contrast and with her olive complexion. It was a breathtaking spectacle. She stood, taking a few tentative steps in the shoes, nearly falling. Turning to JJ she demanded, 'Do women actually wear high-heeled shoes for fun?'

'You'll be fine. Hold onto me, everyone will probably think you're drunk. Remember, we are on holiday.'

'If I break my ankle you will have to carry me everywhere.'

'I promise!'

By the time JJ was dressed, Francine was dancing around the room in her high heels, full of confidence, eager to go and show her new clothes off. JJ was as eager to show her off; she looked stunning.

As the week drew to a close, they walked hand in hand down the gold sandy beach to a little restaurant they had discovered; for lunch on this their last day of the holiday. They were still in the same happy mood that they had been all week. They had sunbathed, walked on the beach, and eaten delicious food with wonderful wine. It was as if Istanbul was on another planet and what they were going to do was a fairy story. They were simply two people in love enjoying a holiday in the sun.

The landing back at Istanbul was softer than that at the start of their holiday. Francine started to cry on the coach between the plane and the terminal building, 'JJ, I'm sorry, it's just that I've had such a wonderful holiday. Thank you. I'm just sad it's over.'

'I am too!' he said gently. 'Thanks for coming.' He whispered in her ear, 'Now we are back in Istanbul you must stop crying remember you are a terrorist again.'

JJ was relieved to find the Porsche was undamaged. They drove back to Yesilcoy in a somber mood. Neither of them voiced their thoughts to the other, JJ wondering about his trip to Prague and to the UK, Francine wishing that JJ wasn't going to see his wife. Both had happy memories of the past week together.

He set off a little later than he had intended. Francine had still been in a holiday mood when they reach home and they dined early on prawns, steak and salad, drunk too much wine, trying to maintain the holiday mood for as long as possible and went to bed early; which had inevitably meant they would get little sleep.

'Bye,' said Francine. 'Please drive careful.'

'I will. See you in less than two weeks.' As he drove away he looked in the rearview mirror. She was standing by the gate waving. He put the window down and waved back. As he rounded a corner, she disappeared from sight.

JJ was setting a steady one hundred and forty kilometers an hour and was halfway to the Turkish border with Bulgaria when the first of the predicted delays occurred. He had a punctured front tire, fortunately not a blow out just a gradual deflating of the tire making the steering difficult. He cruised to a stop at what he considered a safe place to change the wheel. He pulled into a lay-by and parked under some large trees that gave a little shade. He realized how tired he felt. Remembering how little sleep he had had in the previous twenty four hours, he decided to have a few minutes rest before changing the wheel. He put the backrest of his seat down, opened the door to let any breeze cool the inside. He laid back and was instantly asleep.

As he awoke, he realized he had been dreaming again, a nightmare similar to the one to that he had had the first night at the Pera Palace. This time, the belly dancer was Francine in all her splendor. No finger castanets this time, an Uzi machine pistol was held in her hand, pointed at the head of his wife, Elizabeth. Conrad was still the benevolent uncle trying to keep the peace everywhere. A strange figure of a man came into the picture playing Francine's signature tune on a Turkish pipe that looked like a clarinet with a bubble near the end, the type used by snake charmers. To JJ's Western ear it sounded very bad. He had a shaven head and was dressed in a shabby grey one piece suit, the sort that workmen wear. It had a number printed across the back.

# Chapter Fifteen

JJ's journey to Prague continued well, after the puncture. It was very uneventful except a few minutes' panic when he was crossing into Bulgaria from Turkey. His passport was stamped with a visa allowing 24 hours in the country, the visa occupying a complete page of the passport. He drove to the customs check point putting down the window. The customs officer, dressed in a black uniform like a Nazi Gestapo officer with riding breeches and shining knee high black boots, his chest emblazoned with full dress medals, placed both hands on the top of the car and demanded, 'Passport,' which he took, and without looking at it, put it into his jacket pocket. His next remark was even more hostile. With a jerk of his hand he again demanded, 'Out.' As JJ got out of the car, the customs officer got behind the wheel and without another word drove around the car parking area a few times then into what looked like a huge garage. JJ followed not very happily. As he got to the car the customs officer got out and with a deep sigh said, 'Very fine car; I have Porsche as well, but old.' He pointed to the corner where JJ could see an old 924, its pale blue paintwork glistening in the dappled sunlight filtering through the grimy windows. He handed JJ back his passport saying. 'Thank you for letting me drive your beautiful car.' He saluted and said, 'Have a good journey.' JJ was too dumbfounded to reply. He quickly drove away before anything else happened.

His arrival in Prague was heralded by a storm of such intensity that with each clap of thunder the Porsche seemed to tremble. The cobbled road, slick with water, put the car's traction control to the most severe test. As he drove over the Vltava River, the windscreen wipers were hardly clearing the rain, making driving hazardous. JJ, deciding that he was being stupid driving in such appalling weather, stopped at the next bar he saw. He took a small table by the big window to watch the storm. Before he had finished his first beer the storm ended as suddenly as it had started. The sky brightened immediately with a hint of the sun showing through the storm clouds. He drained his glass, returned to the Porsche and as he slid in behind the wheel the sun won the battle with the storm clouds and brought his surroundings to life.

The sun was shining directly onto the car and before JJ had had time to start the engine the roads around him started to steam as the heat of the sun attempted to dry them. He had heard that the view of Prague was best as you cross the bridge into the city so he turned the car around and drove back the way he had come. Once over the river, he turned the Porsche around and started into the city again, hoping for the spectacular view he had been promised. Again he was disappointed as the steam from the drying roads was now obscuring his view; as the rain had on his first crossing.

He arrived at his hotel and parked, without any problem, directly outside. Taking his bag from the back seat he entered the hotel foyer and was greeted by a tall, slim and attractive receptionist. JJ introduced himself. Smiling, she asked for his passport and for how long was he staying. He said that he had business, but didn't think more than a few days. She appeared genuinely sad as she said in impeccable English, 'What a pity you will not have time to see all the sights.'

'I may have some spare time, maybe you could show me around?'

'Perhaps, let's see.'

JJ caught sight of a sign on the reception desk which read very simply:

*If you park your car in the road outside the hotel it probably will be stolen.*

He immediately felt panic at the thought of his beloved Porsche being stolen, asking the receptionist, 'Do you have any secure parking?'

'But of course we do. You should have said when you made your reservation. I think I can arrange a slot for you,' she answered, switching on the radiant smile.

'Thanks,' said JJ with relief.

That smile was magnificent. She was stunning to look at, more beautiful than Francine and more sophisticated. Tall, maybe only a couple of inches shorter than JJ; with short black hair and not the sort that comes from a bottle either. It shone with flecks of red in the sunlight coming in through the window. Her outfit an elegant pink silk skirt and jacket with a cream blouse. She was wearing black stiletto shoes and had a self-assured elegant manner which JJ found a challenge to match. She spoke English with an almost accent-free ease. JJ judged her age as being in her mid-thirties.

She made a phone call and then smiled again. When she smiled it was as if the sun was shining a shaft of light over JJ. 'It's OK; you can have a parking place in our garage. We have an armed guard twenty-four hours a day. He will protect your car. Can you give him some money when you leave your car? His salary is very small!'

'It will be a pleasure. Thank you for all your help. By the way, I'm expecting two business colleagues in about thirty minutes; please call me when they arrive.'

She gave him directions to the underground parking and suggested he move his car without further delay as cars disappeared in daylight as well as at night.

JJ found the garage with no difficulty. Driving down the ramp he was stopped within a few yards by the guard who was armed with a World War Two Sten sub-machine gun, a holstered pistol on his belt and a large knife jammed into the top of his boot. He was a mean looking individual who would probably shoot first and ask questions later. Thankfully this time he asked in pidgin

English, 'You Jamison?'

JJ nodded. The guard jerked his thumb to indicate that JJ should continue down the ramp. Not wishing to upset the guard, he drove slowly down the slope into the cool, electrically illuminated, vastness below the hotel. As JJ got out of the car he remembered the receptionist's request and gave the guard a fifty-dollar note. He looked as if he was going to burst into tears at the sight of so much money. His face lit up with delight. Without any thanks he stuffed the note into a pocket saying, 'Your car safe here, I guard well!'

JJ threw him the keys and said sternly, 'It had better be here when I get back!'

He then walked towards the sign that indicated the hotel was up some stairs.

His room was in fact a magnificent little suite. He entered into the lounge area. The bedroom was up a small flight of wooden stairs. It was furnished in a modern style with loose Persian rugs scattered over the floors. He looked out of the windows and was disappointed as he looked straight towards the next old grey building across a narrow street. As he stood and pondered on his forthcoming time in Prague, the telephone rang.

'Hi. This is Marie on reception; I have your business colleagues. Shall I send them to your room?'

'No,' JJ replied, 'can you put them in the bar and open them a bottle of champagne please? You do have champagne?'

'Yes, of course, this is an international hotel,' she responded, sounding a little offended.

Peter and Kirk were halfway through the bottle of champagne by the time JJ got to the bar and Kirk was more than halfway with chatting up Marie. As JJ entered the bar, Marie was forgotten as Kirk let out an unholy shriek as both he and Peter jumped on JJ sending him to the floor, and then sat on him. Peter demanded, 'Give up, Captain?'

JJ, hardly able to breathe, gasped, 'I give in. You guys have put on weight since we last did this.' They helped him to his feet, everybody embracing everybody. To JJ's disappointment Marie had retreated behind the bar counter out of embracing range. JJ ordered another bottle of champagne as they settled into a corner booth to catch up on what each other had been doing since JJ had left Rhodesia. Peter and Kirk confirmed that when they left Rhodesia shortly after JJ they went in search of adventure and money.

Their first port of call had been Nigeria, then Angola. They had made a lot of money by this time and decided that life as soldiers of fortune, although a great adventure, was something that was better left to the young. In effect, they retired, but still only in their early thirties they did not like the prospect of sitting with their feet up around a swimming pool in Spain or something similar, so they invested their money, around three million pounds sterling, and set up an arms supply business initially operating out of Dublin but soon transferring to Libya, just avoiding an SAS raid on their Irish headquarters. The Libyan government was far more sympathetic to their type of business, although it did mean supplying arms at discount prices to friends of the government. Then, with Eastern Europe opening up, they moved to the Czech Republic. Not only did the government not appear to object, it was good to be in a civilized country where you could get good beer or a long-legged girl without the constraints of the Muslim faith suffocating every move.

JJ had a pang of regret that he had not been part of their exploits but, knowing that his wounded leg would have not let him continue in a combat role, all he could say was, 'You are lucky sods.' He very quickly brought them up to date with his life and the reason he was in Prague.

Kirk said, 'I'll bet a pretty woman back in Istanbul is responsible for your involvement, you never did like working for just wages.' He quickly filled them in about Francine, each time he thought about her he felt guilty about Elizabeth.

It was Peter's turn to be cynical. Turning to Kirk, he said, 'And he called us lucky sods and it sounds as if he's hit the jackpot?' More good-humored banter continued between them then JJ then gave them his shopping list. Peter and Kirk discussed the items between themselves before Peter said, 'OK. Shall we say three quarters of a million dollars and a two hundred thousand back for you?'

JJ was delighted, as he had been expecting only quarter of that. 'That's great, deal done. When can you deliver?'

Kirk answered, 'You're lucky, only about four weeks, as most of the stuff is in stock.'

Peter intervened and asked JJ, 'As I don't suppose you have an "end users certificate" for the stuff? Do you have any thoughts about how we get it into Turkey?' An "end users certificate" is a document issued by the host government to certify that the goods are an acceptable import. This matter had given JJ many sleepless nights. The plan was simple but he had spent a long time wrestling with his conscience. However, common sense prevailed as he was sure Conrad would do the same if the tables were turned.

'Yes,' JJ said, 'we consign the explosives to the school as books, sent by sea. It should be easy. I know Conrad has a contact in the Istanbul Customs, he never has any hassle over imports.' He didn't mention his suspicion that Conrad was working for the government.

'No point getting everyone jumpy,' he thought. They then discussed how the money was to be paid. JJ would keep ten thousand dollars from the deposit and when the rest of the three quarters of a million was paid he would then get his other one hundred and ninety thousand. This was where trust came into the business. Peter and Kirk were happy to take the word of an old friend that the money was available and would be forth-coming. They had agreed that payment would be made in gold Krugerrands. Conrad would make a cash payment to a gold bullion dealer and the coins would be delivered to Peter's and Kirk's bank in Switzerland. They, in turn, would transfer JJ's share into his Swiss bank account in cash. 'OK you guys, are we going to paint the town tonight or what?' JJ asked.

'Marie, my business has been successful; where can you recommend for a good evening out to celebrate and would you like to come with us?' he called across to the receptionist who was still behind the bar.

She walked over to their table with a thoughtful look on her face. She suddenly brightened.

'Yes,' she said, 'I know just the place and yes, I can show you and I will bring two of my friends.' The three of them were delighted at the prospect, but the joy was short-lived as Marie continued, 'Yes, it will be a wonderful evening. We will start by going to the museum, then onto the opera. You can go this afternoon and get the tickets; the cost is very low compared to London or Paris.'

The three men immediately showed signs that they were not completely overjoyed at the prospect, even if they were to be escorted by young ladies. Peter went as far as remembering another appointment.

Marie burst out laughing and said, 'I see you don't like culture. You should have said what you do want. How about taking us to dinner; then onto a club where we can dance and have a few drinks?' Kirk let out another of his unholy shrieks. The three of them grabbed Marie and lifted her to the ceiling in spite of her protests.

'Put me down at once, have you gone mad? Just give me five minutes to phone my friends. Now, do I contact pretty ones or plain ones?' Not waiting for a reply, she ran from the bar to the reception area where she immediately picked up the phone to start recruiting two friends to partake of the evening's festivities with them. The three of them could not believe their luck. Peter remarked, 'JJ, have you ever found out why women find you so impossible to say no to?'

'Yeah, it's my boyish charm and your money. Tonight I assumed is on you. I could never get away with that sort of tab on my expenses with Conrad.'

Peter and Kirk made an immediate lunge towards him. Had they not bumped into each other they would have sat on him again. JJ called to them from the door, 'I'll go see how Marie is getting on with your dates.'

Marie was just putting the phone down; smiling at the prospect of a free evening out with what appeared three fun-loving, good-looking men. She smiled at JJ as he came through the door from the bar saying, 'Mary and Sophie will be here at seven-thirty. I go home in ten minutes then Samuel will be here for the evening and night shift. I'm going home to bathe, please don't drink too much this afternoon or you will not enjoy your evening out in Prague!'

JJ returned to the bar putting his hands over his ears to fend off the abuse that his two friends shouted at him. They finally stopped shouting long enough for JJ to announce that Mary and Sophie would be arriving at seven-thirty. 'OK you guys, I'm going for a bath and to get dressed for an evening of fun. See you back here at seven-fifteen.' They agreed and waved goodbye as JJ left the bar. Marie was not behind her reception desk so he helped himself to his key and went to his room.

The evening started with the arrival of Mary and Sophie who were as beautiful and as tall as Marie. The men were amazed at such a lovely trio. They paired up naturally enough, Mary with Kirk who had let out another of his unholy shrieks at the sight of the girls, Peter with Sophie and Marie with JJ.

They walked to a restaurant close to the hotel. It was a very pleasant evening, the weather warm but not humid. On arrival at the restaurant they were greeted like royalty, the head waiter fawning over them. Marie asked, 'What could you recommend for six very hungry people?'

'I recommend for you a wonderful traditional Czech dinner of pork with dumplings in a thick creamy sauce and a number of the local Czech beer,' he replied.

Looking at the menu, JJ remarked, 'It's cheaper to drink beer here than Coca Cola.'

Much to the amazement of JJ and his friends, the three girls joined in with similar meals to the men. Marie explained, 'We are naturally slim people and we don't eat meals like this every day, so we don't get fat like girls do in the West.' They all commented on the delight of the meal and how stuffed they all were. Marie stood and took hold of JJ's hand and, with a tug; she pulled him to his feet saying, 'Come on, you promised us dancing and a fun time.'

'OK,' he sighed, 'I suppose we had better honor our promise. Come on you guys, let's go. Marie, where are we going?'

'Not far. We can walk off dinner on the way. Come on girls; get these lumps on their feet.'

They all left the restaurant in a very relaxed mood and set off hand in hand down the street. Marie explained, 'We will go to Old Town Square and see what's on there first!'

As they neared the square they could hear the sound of a jazz band mingled with the laughter of people enjoying themselves. The girls tried to speed up the men, looking forward to the entertainment. As they entered the square they could see the band on a small stage set close to a dance floor that was full of swaying bodies. The whole area was bedecked with decorations and illuminated with colored lights. JJ, Peter and Kirk were all for finding a table and having a beer but the girls demanded that they dance before drinking, so the six of them managed to find room on the dance floor. As JJ took Marie in his arms she pulled herself closer to him and laid her head on his shoulder, humming the tune contentedly, as they shuffled around the crowded floor. The end of the tune also signaled a break for the band who announced they would resume in ten minutes. JJ looked round and found the others they had already got a table near the bar and indicated that they had ordered drinks. They all chattered until the drinks arrived then, taking large swallows of the cold beers, they were ready for the band to start again! Start again it did with gusto, an old rock and roll number which JJ declined on the grounds of being too old for a dance as lively as that. Marie appeared happy enough to sit and talk with JJ while the others bounded off. She leant forward and placing a hand on his knee asked,

'Why are you looking so sad?'

'I'm just thinking of why I'm in Prague, of people that are waiting for me to return to Istanbul and to visit them in the UK.'

'Do you want to tell me about it?' she asked in a soft comforting voice.

'Not at the moment, but thank you for caring.' The band started on the next tune, a slower number. JJ said, 'Come on, I can manage this one,' as he led Marie onto the dance floor.

They stayed in the square dancing and drinking until eleven o'clock when the girls announced that they all had work the next morning and should go home. Mary and Sophie shared a flat together; Peter and Kirk seemed to have already made plans for the rest of the night, so they all said good night as the four of them got into a taxi. With waves and shouts of 'See you tomorrow,' JJ putting his arm around Marie's waist asked?

'Do we walk or taxi?'

'We can walk. My house is attached to the hotel. Would you like to come home with me?'

'Yes please; but I'm not going to. I shall hate myself when I get up in the morning for having turned you down; but not as much as I would do if I accept your suggestion.'

'I don't understand, I thought you liked me?'

'I do, very much, that's part of the problem!'

'Tell me?'

So he told her about his wife Elizabeth and about Francine.

That he couldn't involve anyone else in his problems. He wanted to tell her about the job he was going to do when he got back to Istanbul, but didn't. The least number of people that knew about that the better. He hadn't even told Peter and Kirk the exact nature of the job he was planning.

He looked down into her face and he could see that she had sadness in her eyes. She said, 'Thank you for explaining it all to me. I just don't know how to help you.'

'That's easy, please will you have dinner with me tomorrow night; just the two of us? I am leaving the next day.'

'I would be very pleased to have dinner with you on your last night in Prague and I know the perfect place.'

They arrived at Marie's house and she put the key into the lock. She looked up at JJ who took her in his arms and kissed her gently but firmly.

'Goodnight then,' she said, pausing with the door wide open.

'Goodnight,' said JJ. 'I'll see you tomorrow,' and walked away towards the hotel. He heard the door close behind him, with maybe a little more force than was necessary. He didn't know why but for the first time in his life he felt a total heel – the first time he did something right and he felt bad about it!

Having breakfasted in his room, JJ felt more his old self, so by the time he ventured down to reception to await the arrival of Peter and Kirk he was ready for anything the day could throw at him. Marie greeted him with a warm smile and an almost whispered 'Good morning,' which made JJ wish he hadn't been so self-righteous the night before. She was wearing a low-cut, pale yellow cotton dress, which contrasted with her black hair, accentuating her looks, and her lovely figure, and stopping just short of the knee, emphasizing her long legs. She had dressed to show JJ what he had missed last night.

Peter and Kirk arrived on time and in very high spirits. JJ remarked a little frostily, 'I don't need to ask why you are both in such good moods this morning, do I?'

They ignored his comment and, opening their document cases, produced a detailed breakdown of JJ's order. Peter added, 'As you can see most of the items are ex-stock. The Semtex will be brought in from Syria.'

'Syria?' JJ commented.

'Yes, there are more illegal explosives there than in the factory here! And it's military stuff too so it doesn't contain the metallic particles that get picked up on scanners and is odorless so the dogs don't pick it up either.' Peter continued, 'We will have it here in about fourteen days and a week to repack it. The Uzis and ammunition need a bit more thought on how to ship them – too much metal to send as books.'

JJ had a sudden thought and said, 'How about listing them as an air-conditioning system? Everyone knows Conrad is always talking about having one, so nobody will be surprised that he has ordered one from outside Turkey. The local systems are a bit outdated. His friend at the Customs office will just pass it through!'

Kirk added, 'That's a good idea, we will work on that and get this paperwork amended and back to you this afternoon. Now how about some more of that champagne? All this talking has made me thirsty. Do you think they have any left?'

JJ and Peter laughed as together they called to Marie, 'Can Kirk have a bottle of champagne please?'

Peter promised to have the revised paperwork with JJ by mid-afternoon. Their business concluded they said their goodbyes and left JJ alone with his thoughts and to plan the next leg of his journey and probably his life! Marie came and stood behind him and said, 'I've booked the restaurant for tonight. They have music so we can dance if you would like. I booked it through the hotel so it will be on your bill. Is that OK?'

'Yes, that's fine. Thank you for being so understanding.' She cleared away the empty bottle and dirty glasses.

Marie said, as she was about to disappear behind the bar, 'We must leave here by six-thirty as they start at seven-thirty and we need to get a good table!'

'OK, I know; no more drinking this afternoon. See you about six-fifteen.'

'Yes. OK.'

The revised paperwork arrived from Peter and Kirk. JJ spent the next hour going over it. Everything seemed to be in order. He phoned Peter and confirmed the details were acceptable, then spent the rest of the afternoon getting ready for the evening out.

Marie was waiting for him when he entered the bar. She was early which pleased him, obviously excited at the prospect of another evening out as he was. She said, 'We have time for one quick drink if you would like.'

'No, not for me, thank you; unless you would like one. You look very nice this evening.'

'Thank you for the compliment and no thank you to the drink. Shall we get off then?'

JJ escorted her out of the bar out onto the street. They walked together down the road with Marie holding his arm like old friends. JJ was intrigued as to where they were going but she refused to tell him saying, 'It will spoil the evening for you if it's not a surprise, we shall be there in about another ten minutes.' Marie continued, 'You must think me a dreadful woman for inviting you into my home last night but I've not met anyone that excites me as you do, since my husband died. He was a pilot in the Air Force. It was a silly accident, he was being stupid showing off. He was flying too low and hit some trees and was killed in the crash. I mean, you feel to have the same element of danger about you, as he had, so please don't show off and get yourself killed.'

Although JJ made noises of condolence he was pleased with what she had told him. 'How can you afford to live in that house by the hotel? It must be very expensive.'

'The explanation is simple, the hotel and the house belong to my parents.'

It was every bit of a delight to JJ when they turned the corner and found that they were going on a restaurant boat. The boat was moored against a small jetty decorated with colored lights; an accordion was being played on the rear deck. The deck area was set out with tables arranged around the edge of a small dance floor, the tables furnished with white table cloths. The cutlery and glasses sparkled in the light afforded by the colored lights, festooned around the deck area. The accordionist was sitting on a stool by the bar which was under a small canopy adjacent to the main cabin area. The music floated across the water too them, carried on the warm windless night air. JJ stopped and took hold of Marie in an embrace that nearly squeezed the wind out of her. He kissed her on the cheek as he released her and said, 'It is a lovely surprise, thank you for making me wait. It looks wonderful and did you arrange the weather as well? It's perfect for an evening on the river!'

She was pleased that the surprise had made him happy. 'Come on, let's get on board and find a nice table.'

As they boarded, another two couples had also arrived arm in arm. They called a cheerful 'Good evening' to JJ and Marie as they staggered up the gangplank behind them.

The evening was over. It had been absolutely wonderful, the food excellent, the wine a delight, the dancing slow and soft – the perfect evening for lovers. That was worrying, JJ he was determined not to fall in love with Marie, he had enough problems without any more complications. He had not mentioned Elizabeth or Francine again and she hadn't asked any more questions.

They walked back to the hotel holding hands, neither sure what was going to happen when they got to Marie's house. They talked about the evening, the food, the music, neither of them wanting the evening to end. Marie put her key in the lock, opened the door and said, 'The invitation is still there if you want.'

JJ shook his head and pulled her to him kissing her passionately, as they held each other close. He finally pulled away,
saying, 'Much more of that and all my good intentions will
disappear.'

She put her hand against his cheek and whispered, 'You have
many problems; I will wait for you! The invitation will always be
open for you any time you are passing or if you want to talk to
someone. You always seem so sad. You can always reach me via
the hotel switchboard. I am not working in the morning. I don't
want to see you go.'

'Thank you,' he said. 'I am sure we shall meet again.' With
that, she rushed into her house and this time there was no doubt
– she slammed the door. Not wanting him to see her tears, she
leant back against the door, wiping her eyes.

He took a deep breath and walked away.

The following morning when he paid his bill the reception
clerk handed him a small packet with his receipt. 'This packet
was left for you about an hour ago we hope you enjoyed your
stay? We hope you will use our hotel the next time you visit
Prague.' JJ slipped the packet and receipt into his jacket pocket
picked up his bag and headed for the garage. When he arrived at
his car he was amazed, it was gleaming under the artificial
lighting, it had been washed and polished to a high shine a job
that must have taken hours. The guard lumbered over with his
keys, indicating the car he asked, 'You like?'

JJ was speechless for a moment. 'Yes,' he replied, 'it looks like
new, thank you.' He took the proffered keys and replaced them
with a fifty dollar note.

The guard was obviously delighted. He took JJ's hands in his
own somewhat grubby pair and smiled up into his face, 'It was a
pleasure to work on such a magnificent car; I wish you a safe
journey.'

JJ stopped for lunch at a small roadside bar, he ordered a

sandwich and a cold beer. While he was waiting for his lunch to arrive he remembered the small packet that the reception clerk had given him that morning. As he unwrapped the packet he noticed how heavy it was for something so small. As the last of the wrapping came away he had in his hand a magnificent green onyx box, the lid was secured in place with sticky tape. He removed the lid and was sat looking into an empty box! 'What was it for and who had sent it?' He quickly searched the wrapping paper and found a note, it was from Marie and simply read, *You always look so sad, put all your unhappiness into this box and when you come back to Prague we together will throw it into the Vltava; Just give it try, you may be surprised.*

# Chapter Sixteen

JJ phoned Elizabeth from Portsmouth shortly after the ferry docked, to announce that he had arrived back in the UK. She seemed genuinely pleased to hear from him and promised she would have dinner ready by the time he arrived. With mixed feelings he set off towards home, not sure if he wanted to see her or not.

The problems of the past weeks going around in his mind. Did he still love Elizabeth? He had previously decided he didn't, so probably not. Then why was he in England, apart from bringing the Porsche to safety? What were his real feelings towards Francine? Did he love her as much as his body told him he did or was that just pure lust? What about Marie? What was he going to do after Istanbul? He knew he would not be able to stay afterwards. The prospect of going back to work in London at his old job left him with a feeling of frustration. Things had started to become more of a mess than before he had left for the job of his dreams.

He had just joined the M27 motorway when, to his annoyance, he caught sight of a speed camera flash as he passed. Looking down at the instrument panel in front of him he saw he was doing eighty-five miles an hour. The Porsche was perfectly safe and comfortable at that speed; it was capable of twice that. In fact it had done so on the autobahn in Germany only a few hours ago; it was another item of frustration, for JJ. He was not looking forward at all to being back in the UK. As he parked the Porsche, Elizabeth appeared at the front door, the dogs milling around waiting for JJ's call. He resisted greeting the dogs until he had kissed her saying, 'It's good to see you. You look nice.' In fact, if JJ had known how much her outfit had cost he would have been less courteous. The silk Dior suit was in a blue that matched her eyes perfectly. She had obviously spent a lot of time on both her hair and make-up, which was unusual, normally not bothering or not caring, assuming that it was a waste of time to be smart if she was at home or out in the garden, but regrettably letting the same attitude affect her when she went out. The dogs were delighted that he was home; each with a favorite ball in their mouth waiting for him to throw for them. They were dancing around, each demanding their share of attention, their tails wagging so furiously that they were in danger of causing injury to someone or something, running after the balls that JJ was throwing for them.

They were part way through dinner when Elizabeth put down her knife and fork, picked up her wine glass leant back in her chair, and said,

'Well, tell me about your new job, your new career that has taken you away from us all in England.' She said it with frostiness in her voice that indicated her annoyance with the situation that had dared interfere with her life.

JJ didn't reply immediately, trying to decide what to tell her. 'It's different, not the routine and responsibility of designing a chemical plant or a refinery costing hundreds of millions of pounds. I go to work each day not worrying about who has forgotten what or if the budget will be enough to finish the detailed work and if we going to finish on time. I go into my office and am surrounded by young people, all milling around trying to get my attention first – a bit like the dogs were when I came home.' He had decided to end this particular conversation early without getting into a debate on the rights and wrongs of his new job. He continued talking, 'Anyway, it will not be for much longer. I expect to be finished in about three or four months, so really it has just been a long holiday.'

Elizabeth smiled and without saying anything, resumed her dinner. As JJ topped up her wine glass she looked up and smiled at him again this time saying, 'Thank you, I suppose if you finish in a few months you will be coming home then?'

'Well, I can't stay there can I?'

'Well, at least this time you will not be shot full of holes like you were when you came back from one of your adventures when we lived in Rhodesia when you had been off playing soldiers. What will you do, or are you going to retire?'

'I'll probably start to catch the train again, but compared to that, the prospect of retiring sounds good. It makes me shudder just to think about the train, London, and all that it entails. Maybe retiring is not such a bad thought. I would like to still do something though, I don't want to just sit and vegetate!' He didn't say it, but getting shot again was a possibility, this time not just in the leg!

'Maybe you will have some time for me then,' she added.

He didn't say anything, but thought ironically that perhaps the train wouldn't be that bad after all. There had to be something better, but what?

Elizabeth was in an obvious good mood saying to him, 'You go and play with the dogs, and I'll make coffee. Would you like a brandy with it?'

'Please, that would be nice.'

The evening was warm. He sat in the garden throwing an occasional ball for an insistent dog. As he sat, his thoughts drifted back to Francine and how they could possibly get away after the bridges blew up. Francine's lack of passport had always been a concern. Elizabeth's comment about getting shot was also very much on his mind.

Elizabeth's good mood continued for the rest of the evening and was still there the following morning. She was humming to herself as she busied in the kitchen, preparing breakfast for them both. Eventually, with a contented sigh, JJ wiped a piece of crusty bread around his plate, mopping up the remnants of egg and tomato, and then pushed away his plate and drained his coffee cup. Looking across to Elizabeth, he said simply, 'Thank you. I really enjoyed that.'

She smiled happily at him across the table, not speaking.

Later that day when she dropped JJ at the airport, he kissed her briefly goodbye in the car; rather than trying to find a car parking space. He took his small flight bag and waved as the Porsche roared away. What a car, he thought, I shall miss it.

Francine met him at the airport. He resisted embracing her just in case, but thinking of when they got home. To his surprise, Abdul and his taksi were waiting for them outside the terminal building. It reminded JJ of his arrival in Istanbul on that cold damp day in January. Was it only a few months ago? Francine was full of news, hardly waiting until they got into the taksi.

'Mr. Jamison, we have good news. We have another fifty recruits. A cousin of Abdul is the leader of another group of anarchists and has agreed to join us. They are from Ismit, south of Istanbul.' JJ didn't voice his opinion that he would have preferred not to be involved with another of Abdul's relations.

Trying to sound enthusiastic he said, 'That's excellent. I have managed to buy all that we need. Will you get everyone together on Saturday and we will get the training under way. Say, eight in the morning. How about using that old factory building where you first took me to meet your people Abdul; when I agreed to be involved?'

'OK Professor JJ, I fix.'

They arrived at JJ's house. As he got out of the car, he turned to Francine and smiled, saying, 'Francine, I wonder if you will help me with the equipment listings of the stuff I have bought. Will that be OK, Abdul?'

'Sure Professor JJ.' Turning to Francine he said, 'Why don't you stay over? It's late already and I'll collect you both in the morning?' JJ could hardly believe his luck. He had sorted all the paperwork out on the plane from Heathrow so they could have the whole evening and night together with nothing to do but enjoy each other's company. JJ had hardly closed the door when Francine jumped, putting her arms around his neck and kissing him passionately; rubbing her body against his. JJ had almost to push her away in order that he could breathe.

'Oh darling,' she said. 'I have missed you so much. Hold me and tell me you missed me.'

'Wouldn't you prefer me to show you?'

'Yes please,' she gasped.

He picked her up and carried her to the bedroom. Although she was light in his arms she was wriggling so much that by the time he put her onto the bed he was already breathing heavily. She clamped her arms around his neck again, this time he didn't fight to be released.

'JJ, Abdul is here!' Francine called from the kitchen where she had started to prepare breakfast.

'Darn man, why couldn't he have been stuck in traffic for once. I haven't showered yet.'

'Don't worry, I'll give him coffee and show him the paper work we did last night.'

'It's in my briefcase in the lounge.'

JJ could hear her calling to him to park and come inside.

The drive to town was very relaxed. Abdul was very pleased that JJ had got everything that he had promised. JJ said, 'Everything will be here in four weeks, so if the training can go really well we can be ready in, say, eight weeks. We need a night with no moon. Can you find out when the next time that happens – in about two months?'

'OK will do. I suppose lunch in the usual place today so you can update Mr. Conrad?'

'Yes, why don't you come too?' JJ said, turning to Francine.

'Thank you,' she replied, 'we didn't have time for much last night.'

'Good, that's all agreed, Abdul. I'll sort it out with Conrad. Pick us up at about twelve-thirty, phone the restaurant to let them know we are all coming.'

'I'll do that,' said Francine, wanting to be useful.

Opening the taksi door, JJ picked up his briefcase as he got out and shouted over the traffic noise, 'See you both later.'

'Hello, Ayşe, I would like to see Conrad in about ten minutes. Can you arrange that for me please?'

'Sorry, he will not be in until about twelve. I can get a message to him if that will help.'

'Please tell him I'm back and can we lunch at the usual place? I've arranged for Abdul to collect us here at twelve-thirty.'

'OK JJ, that's no problem.'

Ayşe phoned him after about ten minutes confirming that lunch was OK but that Conrad would meet them there as he had other things to attend to.

Lunch was a great success. Francine was in fine form. Abdul and Conrad took it in turns to complain – Abdul about no income after the bridges were blown, Conrad about the amount of money that JJ had committed him to spending. Ishmael had prepared a wonderful lunch. The meze, a wonderful spicy mixture, the fish a delight, the salads crisp and the wine sharp and cold. Conversation was generally subdued but always about the job. There was speculation about the training that was due to start in two days' time.

# Chapter Seventeen

Abdul arrived to pick up JJ at six on Saturday morning. Francine was already in the taksi. They had agreed that as training was starting on Saturday they would not see each other on the Friday night. Abdul set off at his usual frantic speed. Francine shouted over the noise of wind and exhaust, 'We are picking Conrad and Ayşe up next.' JJ was astonished at the news, Conrad had never shown any interest in being at the sharp end so to speak, and as for bringing his wife as well, wonders to behold. They had a slight detour up the Bosporus to the little village of Tarabya. They would cross the Bosporus from there. Apart from adding about thirty minutes to the trip, JJ was happy sitting in the back seat with Francine. He wished he could touch her; but as with most taksi's in Istanbul, the driver has rearview mirrors positioned to see just about everything that happens in the rear of his vehicle.

They arrived at what was to become known as the training camp. Abdul and Francine had done a great job of getting things ready for today, with a proper platform for the leaders from which to address the audience, a vast sandbagged area to carryout weapon training. They had scoured the surrounding area to ensure that nobody was living in a two-mile radius, who may hear, or see, something of the training. All was clear. The original choice of the site had been a good one. JJ told them that he was very well pleased. They beamed in his praise. After the lengthy business of shaking hands and cheek kissing, Abdul called for everyone to be seated and listen to their commander, who was going to lead them to a glorious victory over the capital-istic tyrants. 'Captain Professor JJ.'

They gave him a less than warm round of applause as he rose to begin his opening address to the assembled troops. He had dressed in his Rhodesian army uniform complete with medal ribbons, the three pips on each shoulder indicating his rank of captain. The brown Sam Browne belt shone in the sunlight and it was weighed down on the right by the weight of his nine-millimeter Browning Hi-power automatic pistol. Over his shoulder he was carrying an Uzi machine pistol on a webbing strap. He certainly was dressed to impress and, as he started his opening address, the mood of his audience changed. Not only was he an imposing figure standing there, armed and looking very dangerous, but again he was displaying the same charismatic charm that had won over the Anarchists when he had first agreed to help, only a few months previously.

'Members of our Anarchist movement, over the next eight weeks you will learn to use automatic weapons like this,' he held up the Uzi for them all to see, 'and learn how to maintain them in good condition. I will teach you to kill your enemy without him making a sound, not sticking a knife in his back and hope he dies after he has screamed for ten minutes, and on the subject of killing, you will not fight amongst yourselves. You will not speak of what we are going to do to anyone, no boasting to your girlfriends, wives, or whatever. You will learn to plant the plastic explosives that Mr. Conrad has bought for the fight.' At that, Conrad got a riotous cheer. JJ continued, 'You will become so familiar with it that you will sleep with it under your pillow at night. Remember, it will not go bang until Abdul tells it to. So don't be clever and keep some of it for your own use. Abdul has the privilege of pressing the button in eight weeks' time and we need to provide a spectacular bang. We are going to carry out this mission without hurting any innocent civilians, police or army personal.'

A voice from the audience called out, 'Why teach us to kill if we are not going to?'

JJ put his hand up to try and prevent any more annoying questions and continued. 'You need to know how to kill. If the project is going to be jeopardized by someone catching you on the night, you will then unfortunately have to eliminate that individual. OK?' No-one else said anything. 'Well, if there are no more silly questions, I will continue. The training here will be strict and intense, I would prefer to have you all in a camp away from anyone day and night, but that may draw attention to what we are doing. There would be questions asked if you all disappeared for eight weeks. A lot of you have had army training; therefore I don't propose to waste your time, and mine, with teaching you drill.' This got a unanimous cheer from his audience. 'When you are here you will work hard, you will not have days off, you will not become ill, you will not have hangovers in the mornings. Each one of you will be responsible for another person, your "buddy". You will watch each other and help each other. There will be those among you who will find the training easy and those who will not. It is up to each and every one of us to make the best use of the time we have. I want you all to remember we have only eight weeks.' Again he emphasized the time available. 'If I find any one of you letting down the team, I will personally shoot you. Do you all understand?'

This time they all shouted as one. 'Yes sir.'

JJ added for good measure, 'If anyone doesn't like the rules, please leave now.' Two clean-shaven young men at the back of the audience stood and shuffled away. Abdul whispered to JJ, 'I don't trust them. Shall I...?' He didn't finish his sentence.

JJ nodded, 'Yes, quickly and loudly.'

Abdul spoke into his mobile phone and within less than a minute two bursts of gunfire were heard by the audience. Abdul's phone rang and he grunted to the caller, 'Bring them here.' He spoke to JJ again, 'My men have just searched the bodies – they were army. They are bringing their identity papers over now. We will bury the bodies.'

JJ spoke to the stunned crowd before him. 'Is there anyone else not able to cope with my rules? Remember, you all volunteered for this and you all knew what we were going to do before you came today. Those two were army spies. You can all see for yourselves their identity papers before you leave and remember what you have just witnessed if any of you think about betraying us. One other thing, mobile telephones are not to be used under any circumstance until the day of the explosions, they are too easily traced and calls overheard. Then one of you will steal a phone and it will be used as the trigger to set off the detonators. Now, to save time, you will form yourselves into groups of ten and select a leader who will have the rank of lieutenant. I will visit each group and brief you on your tasks. I may change the members of any group and I will possibly change the leader. Do you all understand?' Again, in one voice possibly louder, this time they replied, 'Yes sir.'

'Now that's all settled, I just want to add that I am in control of your training, particularly the section on explosives. Madam Francine, who you all know, will teach you how to use the Uzi automatic machine pistol. You probably know her by reputation, if not personally. I don't know many of you yet but by the end of your training I will know everything about each and every one of you. When you have sorted yourselves into groups of ten you must then choose the person you will be responsible for and who will be responsible for you. Remember this – you may have to rely on your buddy to save your life or you may have to kill him if he turns out to be a traitor. You have thirty minutes to sort yourselves out. Now move.'

He gave a clenched-fist salute and shouted, 'Up the revolution!'

They all responded with the clenched fist and, as one, chorused, 'Up the revolution!'

'Just like children, just like my African troopers,' JJ said to himself with a sad feeling. 'I wonder how many of you will die before this mess is over?' He resolved, 'None if I can help it!'

Francine came up to him, smiled, and said, 'That was a great speech. You were wonderful. Shame about the army people, but it will serve as a reminder to the others what happens to traitors.'

He looked into her eyes as he replied, 'I was lucky that it happened when it did, it really emphasized my message. Let's hope there will be no more and, more importantly, how did they know about today's meeting and who else knows?' Those must be the most beautiful eyes in the world he thought; the whites so clear and the iris starting blue on the outside turning a light hazel before the black of the pupil. And they sparkled with life. He started to feel a need for her but suppressed it as Abdul joined them.

They had a similar discussion with Abdul about how the spies knew when and where the meeting was to be held and who else knew. They decided to adopt the "wait and see" option, rather than rush headlong into something they couldn't control. JJ was tempted to tell them his theory about Conrad but decided to wait and try to find out more before saying anything.

JJ, Abdul and Francine set off on a tour of their troops. They had formed themselves into ten groups and were assembled in loose formations around the main area that had been used for the briefing. They introduced each other and JJ listened to the tales of disaster that came pouring forth about a brother or father that was imprisoned or had disappeared. JJ was being patient with them, it was their first day and he let them air their problems instead of them being pent up inside. They were all asking the same question, can we really blow up both bridges? JJ tried to assure them that he knew what he was doing and everything would go to plan if they learnt well and followed orders. JJ had no problem with confirming the choice of lieutenant of the first group. Ali was a monster of a man with a great sense of humor and an easy disposition. The second group was a different matter. He was introduced to Ibrahim, an obvious bully who seemed to have a very devious manner. JJ took an instant dislike to him. He continued with the group for another ten minutes, during which time he noticed Ishmael, a quiet man displaying a silent intelligence.

Not an obvious leader but a far better bet than Ibrahim. He continued to watch and make notes.

Francine and Ayşe had miraculously produced sandwiches for them and all the troops as well. During their meal, JJ had the opportunity to discuss his observations with the others. Abdul was of a similar opinion as JJ but his solution to the problem was a little too drastic for JJ. Abdul declared. 'In my country, if you don't like someone, you kill him. It's so simple, no?'

JJ had a better idea. 'No. We can't kill him because we don't like him; we could end up killing them all for one reason or another. Let's transfer him to another group; but we shall need a reason. Can anyone think of something he could be used for apart from target practice for Abdul?'

Conrad and Ayşe, not being part of the strike force, were not being included in the discussion but it was Conrad who came up with the solution. 'I know him, he's a good driver.'

JJ picked up the thought and said, 'Yes, that's perfect. We transfer him to Ali in group one, he should be able to keep his bullying in check. And we make group one responsible for transport and because Ibrahim is such a great driver it would be a face saver for him among the rest.'

Ibrahim did not at first see the opportunity he was being given but when Abdul spelt it out for him he was delighted and when he found out that he was to have a truck at his disposal at night after training he began to imagine all sorts of ways of using it. Ali was very pleased to have the responsibility of transporting the troops and explosives. He could almost see his name in neon lights as the person who single-handedly rid the country of the capitalistic fascist tyrants.

Ishmael, on the other hand, modestly accepted the command of group two with a warm thanks to JJ. 'I'll not let you down Captain, sir.'

To which JJ harshly replied, 'You know the penalty if you do.'

Having resolved the problem of group two's lieutenant, it was now time to review the leadership of the other groups. JJ and Abdul ran through the list they had made during the day. Group three stays with Iskender; group four, Hakim, with a possible change to Fahd. Group five was unanimous Malik. Group six was provisionally given to Mustapha-A. He was not happy to accept the responsibility but Abdul was convinced that he was capable of the job. Group seven, Ahmad, no problem. Group eight, Wahid was the obvious choice; group nine, Jameel, a little weak but he has Hassan as a good number two. Group ten, they could not agree on the choice of Azeem. There was no alternative except to take Hassan from group nine which would leave Jameel without support.

It was starting to become obvious that the men were showing signs of tiredness and JJ was feeling exhausted. He turned and looked at Abdul who had just returned, having taken Conrad and Ayşe home; 'Shall we pack up for the night as well?'

'Good idea, I'm starving.'

Abdul called the troops together for one last word before going. JJ looked down at them from the platform and spoke quietly and slowly.

'It is time for you to go now. Before you do, I would just like to announce the names of the lieutenants that we agree to. They are ...' he read out the list of names. After each name was announced they all cheered as each man came up to be congratulated by JJ, Abdul and Francine. 'Now I suggest that you take your "buddy" out for a beer or dinner and find out something about him that you did not know before. Remember that one day you may save his life or you may have to kill him. Also, don't forget you are no good to me if you have a hangover tomorrow. Goodnight. Have some fun, for tomorrow you may die.'

They all shouted back, 'Goodnight, sir.'

Going over to Francine, who had adopted a small corner for her office, he said, 'We are going home now.'

She looked up at him and asked, 'Who is your "buddy" that

you are going to take to dinner tonight?'

'Don't tell Abdul, but she is a beautiful blonde belly dancer. All we have to do now is convince him to take us both to Yesilcoy and that we are going to work this evening.'

'Don't take a girl for granted – she likes to be asked sometimes.'

'Is this a sometime?'

'No. That would be a waste of energy and I don't want you to be too tired tonight.'

Abdul was sitting in his taksi, engine running shouting, 'Come on, let's go.'

JJ, without waiting for Abdul to move off, said, 'I need to go over some planning tonight with Francine. Does that give you a problem?'

'Not at all, my boy; I now think of you as a son. If a man can't trust his son, who can he trust?' He ignored the fact that JJ was only about five years younger than himself.

Francine whispered to JJ, 'So much for the guardian of my chastity.'

# Chapter Eighteen

Francine and JJ decided on Pizza for dinner that night. It would be a simple meal at the restaurant in the village. It was only a few minutes' walk and as JJ had taken the Porsche back to the UK they had no transport. They needed a walk after the drive home in Abdul's taksi so didn't fancy the idea of another taksi ride. They showered as soon as they got in, neither in the mood and too tired for the usual horseplay. So showered and changed into clean clothes, they set off to walk to dinner. They had only gone about a hundred meters from the house when a police car pulled into the curb in front of them. Two police officers jumped out and stood in front of Francine and JJ, stopping their further progress. One of them, the one with sergeants' chevrons on his shoulders, demanded, 'You come with us.'

They were amazed. How could the police have known so soon? Francine's grip tightened on JJ's arm and he determined to play the innocent Englishman out for a walk with his girlfriend. He demanded in return, and in English. 'Why? What have we done?' The policeman's knowledge of English was obviously limited to, 'You come with us.'

Francine, as usual not looking Turkish, didn't speak. It was a game they often played when they were out shopping. Particularly in the Grand Bazaar, where the shopkeepers could be a little overpowering in a frantic attempt to make a sale. They would pretend not to understand, then with a flourish, she would turn and let forth a stream of Turkish that would make a laborer blush.

JJ was still pretending not to understand what they were saying in Turkish and, being the typical Englishman abroad, he was speaking louder and louder in a vain attempt to make them understand. In fact they were saying little in Turkish except, 'Just get them into the car,' and 'don't hurt them.'

Those few words at least made Francine and JJ feel a little easier. They didn't speak to each other in the car. JJ kept up his demands to know where they were being taken and what had they done wrong. They arrived after a ten-minute drive at the police station in Yenikapi. The area had a large collection of cheap tourist hotels and a few expensive ones preferred by the Americans, the ethnic surroundings of the Grand Bazaar and the Blue Mosque. They were ushered into a waiting room. It was the bleakest most inhospitable room that JJ had ever been in. There were no chairs or other furniture, just rough wooden benches secured to both floor and wall on two sides. The third wall had in it the door that they had entered by, whilst the other wall had the outline of a door opening and what appeared to be a keyhole. No posters adorned the walls; there was nothing to make the visitor feel comfortable. The walls were painted a dark green and were chipped and scarred though years of abuse, the floor was bare wood. They had been in the room for about ten minutes when a policeman roughly pushed a handcuffed youth of about eighteen into the room in front of him and forced him down onto the bench on the opposite wall to Francine and JJ. The young man was in obvious pain. He had a cut over his left eye and his hands had turned blue from the handcuffs being overly tight, reducing the circulation. As he was forced down onto the bench he hissed abuse at the policeman, who just laughed at him and hit him on his already painful hands with his rubber truncheon, telling him to be quiet or he would hit him again. At that point, a well-dressed officer came in and introduced himself to Francine in Turkish. He was, he said, the Station Commander and he knew that she spoke perfect English and Turkish and he needed her help as a translator. She was, he continued, the only one he knew that he could call upon at short notice. He had until then ignored JJ; but turning to him he said that he also knew him as a professor at the English engineering school and he was sorry to have disturbed his evening. He spoke in an apologetic manner, leering at Francine at the same time. He continued. An American tourist had had his wallet stolen and they needed a statement and that they had caught the person responsible, indicating the youth.

Francine looked at JJ, and as she stood, she said in English, 'This shouldn't take long; I will be as quick as I can.' At that, she followed the station commander from the room, leaving JJ in a mild state of shock. What an incredible woman, he thought, so calm and collected. He, the hardened old soldier, was in a state of near panic. It was almost an hour before she returned to the room with the obvious American tourist, the station commander and an elderly Turkish man in a crumpled grey suit and a red check shirt. The station commander said something into the ear of the American, who looked across to the young man, who was still in the room with his guard. He nodded and replied so quietly that JJ could only guess what was being said between them. At that moment the elderly Turk rushed across the room and beat the accused around the head. The police didn't intervene. The Turk stopped the physical abuse but continued with a torrent of verbal utterances. The man was the father of the accused; he said he could not understand how his son could do such a thing and that his mother would most probably die of shame. The man had physically aged in the past ten minutes and when he left the room it was with tears running down his face, his shoulders slumped, and obviously feeling dejected knowing that when he told his wife about their son he would get the full force of her anger.

Francine disappeared again with the group, leaving JJ alone feeling sorry for the old man that had just left the room. He soon found out the purpose of the door-shaped outline on the fourth wall. The policeman guarding the youth produced a key and, dragging his prisoner across to the wall, inserted the key into what had appeared to be a keyhole. Turning the key, he pulled open a door, revealing behind it another door. The guard took the key and inserted it into the lock of the second door; a door of bars. Behind that fourth wall was a row of prison cells into which the guard pushed his prisoner, none too lightly, with the sole of his shoe in the small of the lad's back. He obviously fell onto his hands for he screamed with pain as the guard turned away and relocked the cell door, telling the prisoner menacingly over his shoulder that if he heard any noise from him he would be back! He then performed the ritual of relocking the barred door and the door in the wall as he left the cell area. He looked across at JJ nodded and smiled as he left the room. Five minutes later Francine reappeared, being escorted by the station commander. They were laughing as if sharing some joke. He whispered into Francine's ear at which she turned and thanked him for his gallantry and offered him her hand which he raised to his lips with a click of his heels and bid them both a good evening, escorting them to the main door which, after further goodbyes, was closed behind them. They found themselves on the pavement outside without even a ride home in a police car being offered. They were both trembling at the incident that had just happened to them.

JJ declared, 'Sod the pizza. As we are in town shall we go to the Oriental restaurant in that old hotel? It's only a few hundred meters from here and you can tell me all about it!'

'Let's wait until I've got a large brandy in my hand first then I will tell you all the sordid facts.'

'Good evening, sir, madam, it's nice to see you both again.' They were greeted by the headwaiter. JJ could never remember meeting him before and was too tired to correct him.

'Your usual table in the corner is vacant.' He fawned over them, escorting them to their table and, wishing them a pleasant meal, called a waiter over to take their drinks order, leaving them seated and with a menu in front of each of them.

The waiter arrived very swiftly and JJ ordered two very large "Konyak" the local brandy. He knew from bitter experience that if he had asked for Turkish brandy they would have been given raki. As he picked up his glass he noticed his hand was shaking. Francine laughed as she spoke. 'You should have been with me this evening, then you would be shaking!'

'Tell me what happened?' He turned to the hovering waiter. 'We are going to drink these very slowly then we will order. I will call you when we are ready.'

'He was very polite he offered me coffee and he said that he knew that I spent most nights in Yesilcoy with you, that I was married, my husband being a terrorist was currently in prison and that he knew that I had been in prison. He said we were being watched because you were new in town and they didn't know much about you. They then found out that you are ex-Rhodesian army, an officer. They wondered if they should warn you about my past record and me but that it became obvious you knew about me because you take me to the bus station to go on the prison visits. He then got round to why we were taken to the police station. He was waiting for a victim of a pickpocket to arrive to make a statement and needed it to be in Turkish and that as my English was nearly perfect I could translate. Also that he had wanted to talk to me for a long time. That with my husband in prison and being all alone I should have someone to look after me and all I had to do was call at any time.'

'So it was just an excuse to try and get inside your knickers?' JJ gasped.

'Yes. Can you think of anything lower than that?'

'No, but I admire his taste.'

'Another comment like that and you never will again,' she hissed, and smiled at the same time. 'Instead I will take it as a compliment.'

'Was it definite that young lad did it?'

'Yes, no doubt. He was trying to use an American Express Gold card in a shop. The owner called the police and he kept him in the shop till they arrived. He still had the American's wallet on him. The American positively identified him as well. Open and shut case.'

'What will happen to him now?'

'They will probably keep him here for the next few days until his trial, then they will shave his hair off and send him to prison for about a year.'

'Possibly the one your husband is in?'

'No, he is in an army prison, they will send him to a civil prison. I thought you were buying me dinner?'

They ordered a lavish meal with champagne and French brandy, 'proper cognac' as JJ called it. They were a very satisfied couple that waited for a taksi to take them home. As JJ bent down to tell the taksi driver where they needed to go, the driver that looked up at him was Abdul.

'Hello, Captain Professor JJ, what are you both doing in town?'

'We will tell you on the way home.'

As they drove down the coast road, Francine and JJ, in relays, recounted the events of the evening. Abdul listened in amazement, asking the occasional question until they finished their story. Abdul wanted to report the police station commander for trying to harass a lady. They persuaded him that it may not be a good idea and that JJ would deal with him.

'OK, Professor JJ, you kill him then, for you are now my son, as I told you before, and he insulted my son's wife.'

JJ hadn't thought about doing any such thing, but when Francine confirmed that he was going to, he knew what was being expected of him. He thought what a strange code of conduct the Turks seem to have. There was Francine having an affair with him and was expecting him to kill someone for trying to do the same as he was doing – amazing!

They arrived at JJ's house. As Abdul parked the taksi, he asked, 'Shall I take you home now Francine?'

She responded a little too quickly, JJ thought; 'No. We haven't had chance to discuss tomorrow's plan's yet, pick us up as arranged in the morning.'

JJ looked at his watch, it was almost midnight. He thought, *tomorrow is going to be a long hard day.*

'OK. Goodnight then,' shouted Abdul as he drove away at a little less than his normal roar.

# Chapter Nineteen

The second day of training brought with it a very long and tiring day much as JJ had premised the evening before. After Abdul had dropped them off at JJ's house in Yesilcoy they had both showered again. This time as the consequence of the second cognac, they couldn't resist the horse play and then, of course, the inevitable session of love making. JJ remembered turning out the bedside lamps at three. The alarm was set for five. By the time JJ had showered, Francine had the coffee bubbling on the stove. She had poured him a large mug full of the black sweet nectar. He walked into the kitchen doing up his shirt. She looked at him over the brim of her steaming brew and asked,

'Did we get any sleep at all last night?'

'About two hours, but do you know, I could have managed on much less if you had carried on nibbling at my ear the way you did earlier.'

'It wasn't just nibbling your ear was it?'

He gave her a rueful grin, 'Well, no, you did nibble your way into other parts!'

'Well, you did your share of nibbling as well. Talking of nibbling do you want breakfast?'

'No thanks, we can get something on the way.' At that moment Abdul pulled up outside. 'We can continue nibbling tonight if you can think of an excuse for being here!'

In a somewhat tired and happy mood they left the house and got into Abdul's taksi; they were greeted by a smell of warm bread. He smiled at them and said, 'I didn't think you would have had time for breakfast so I stopped off and bought you bread, and there's some cheese and a knife wrapped up it that bag.' As an afterthought he added, 'You can pay me for the food later.'

Francine and JJ devoured the food before they had crossed the

Bosporus Bridge. As they crossed over the bridge, Abdul sent them into a dark mood as, in a very casual way, he remarked, 'It will be strange when these bridges are no more and all the rubble is at the bottom of the Bosporus!'

Due to the motion of the taksi and the somber mood that Abdul's remark had caused, Francine had dropped off to sleep, her head on JJ's shoulder. It was not long after that JJ joined Francine in a deep sleep. Abdul's cheery voice roused them both. 'Well people, here we are again. I bet you are not the only ones with hangovers this morning.'

JJ growled irritably, 'We'd better be.' Getting out of the taksi, he turned to Abdul and ordered, 'Get them lined up into their groups and ready for the day's work.'

Francine disappeared to her office retreat without waiting to see the condition of the men. She knew that JJ would tell her all about it later. JJ mounted the steps of the platform, not sure how to play things that day. Should he come down like a ton of bricks on any wrongdoers or should he allow them one slip, vowing never to do it himself again. He stood and looked down on them and was relieved to see a sea of smiling, eager faces looking up at him. They had all obviously taken his warning very seriously. 'Men,' he called out, 'last night Francine and I were taken to the police station!' There was a groan from the listening groups. JJ continued, 'They took us from outside my house in Yesilcoy. They would not tell us why they were taking us. Only when we arrived at the police station were we told what they wanted. We were there to help the police take a statement from an American tourist who had had his wallet stolen. After the police had finished with us it was late and we were hungry and still shaken by the events at the police station. We went to eat and have a drink to steady our nerves.' He could see them nodding in agreement that after an ordeal like that a man, and more particularly a woman, would need a drink – maybe even two. 'Men, I must confess to you all I broke one of my own rules this morning – I have a hangover.

What should I do?'

Someone from his audience shouted, 'Go and have a large raki, it will make you feel better.'

'No,' replied JJ, 'not even if I could be sure that I would feel better would I have a drink this morning. I will get through the day and suffer my pain.'

They all cheered him.

'And to show you that I am suffering, we will start today with a session of unarmed combat given by me, so if anyone of you thinks that they can beat me, today is your opportunity.' He was in excellent physical condition. After he had come out of hospital in Rhodesia and had thrown away his crutches, he had been determined to remain fit and not let his wounded leg be a burden. In the wonderful weather of the country he had swum and run and had continued exercising on his return to the UK. The tribute to his exercising was that his old army uniform still fitted as well as the day that it had been made.

They all cheered again.

Two hours later JJ was covered in perspiration, his clothes soiled from the dust on the ground. He had a cut lip and the start of a black eye. He had worked off his hangover and all of the troops respected him for both his honesty and his ability. The eye and the lip were both given to him by the monster Ali, the lieutenant of group one, and in return JJ had broken his nose. After the bout, Ali praised JJ as the only man who had ever beaten him. They hugged each other. The watching men cheered them both. JJ had had no doubt that he could beat any of them and had saved Ali until last, knowing he would be the hardest of them all. JJ went in search of Francine, needing a little tender loving care. She fussed over him and, hearing his recount of the fight immediately going in search of Ali, saying he was in more need of nursing than he. In fact, he was fine. His nose had stopped bleeding and he had straightened it himself using a truck mirror to guide him.

Francine then took over the training. She demonstrated how to strip, clean and reassemble her Uzi automatic machine pistol, the accuracy and effectiveness of it when fitted with a shoulder stock. She explained that they would not need the accuracy, as they would only have to use the weapon at close range.

JJ and Francine were both relieved when Abdul arrived back. He had been to the shops and had brought back more bread, cheese and cakes. JJ declared a two-hour lunch break then more unarmed combat training.

The men groaned, feeling at their already sore bodies.

Most of the men, Francine and JJ, dozed in the shade of the trees surrounding the square. Abdul remained sitting in his taksi, singing gently along with the radio that was turned low. At two o'clock on the dot he sounded the twin tone air horns of the taksi, waking everyone from their slumbers. 'You OK now, Captain Professor JJ? Are you ready to kick Ali's backside again?'

JJ looked at him and said, 'Why don't I start off the afternoon of unarmed combat with you?' Abdul went a deathly white. 'No, OK, you better off teaching those that may need it. You don't need to waste your time on me.'

JJ and Francine laughed. Abdul joined in, still a little shakily, not sure how serious JJ had been. Abdul leant over and reached out his arm to help Francine up. She couldn't resist the temptation to take his hand and bring her leg up, putting her foot into his stomach and pulling him over her in a high throw, landing him on his backside. He landed softly on a pile of straw, breaking his fall. The men who had witnessed the incident all cheered and laughed. Abdul, not feeling like it, had no option but to rub his bruised posterior and join in the laughter. His pride was bruised more than he was. JJ walked over and clapped him on the shoulder saying, 'You're not in shape Abdul, it looks as if Francine has kicked your backside, why don't you come and work out with the rest of us.'

Francine, looking pleased with events, said softly, 'I've

wanted to do that for ages.' JJ looked a little confused, she continued, 'I'll tell you about it later.'

Abdul was still sulking when JJ declared that the day's work was over. He had been sitting, brooding, in his taksi all afternoon. He brightened considerably when JJ said to him, 'It's only five; you can get almost a full day's taksi fares if you drop us off at Yesilcoy, then straight to the airport. You should be in time for the London flight coming in.'

'You OK, Captain Professor JJ. You think about me, not like my son's wife.'

JJ laughed and said, 'Today turned out well.'

Abdul just grunted.

They travelled back to JJ's house in considerable silence. Abdul was still annoyed with Francine for showing him up in front of the men; JJ and Francine were both too tired to care.

'Drop us at the supermarket please, Abdul, we need to get some food in.'

'You are staying again tonight? Good job Captain Professor JJ is my son!'

As he roared away he did not wave as usual.

'That was easy, considering that he's mad with you!'

'Let him be,' she replied, 'have you forgotten he blamed me for my husband being arrested that night?'

JJ had and feeling guilty that he had, said so.

She briefly squeezed his hand as she said, 'That's OK, tell me you love me.'

'Have you looked at yourself in the mirror recently? Yes, I love you, even with a dirty face and scruffy hair.' He grinned at her.

She retorted, 'Was that a grin or a leer?'

He tousled her hair, which he knew would make her mad.

'You can cook your own dinner tonight if you don't stop making me cross.'

'Have you forgotten that a Turkish woman always puts the

needs of her man first?' Reminding her of her comments the first few times she had made him a meal.

She squeezed his hand again. 'What type of a meal would you like to eat tonight?' She phrased her question in such a way that he would not be easily able to turn his reply into a lewd remark.

'Anything light and quick. I think we need an early night. I'm nearly dead on my feet.'

'Not that dead?' she retorted.

'I must be getting old.'

Again she squeezed his hand, saying, 'Let's wait and see how we feel, shall we?'

When they got home, Francine insisted on the first shower, leaving JJ with a cold beer and a stern warning to let her shower in peace.

She cooked him sweet and sour prawns with white fluffy rice while JJ took his turn in the shower. He examined his eye, which was sore and swollen, his lip a little puffy, as he shaved. He emerged from the bathroom feeling wonderful, dressed in a clean shirt and trousers. Francine had a cold bottle of Turkish rosé wine on the table waiting for him to open.

A happy pattern was being set – hard days with early mornings, long relaxing evenings and nights. JJ and Francine were in a continual state of euphoria.

News arrived one day that to some extent spoilt the happy mood that they had slipped into. The first shipment of explosives had arrived in Istanbul and someone had to go to clear the consignment at customs. Conrad insisted that JJ went. JJ argued that Conrad knew the people, so he should go. JJ lost the argument on the grounds that had made the arrangements. Leaving Abdul to supervise the day's activities at the training camp and Francine in bed, having a well-deserved day off, he set off by taksi for the customs shed. At the port he had been told by Conrad to ask for a Mustapha and that he was OK. JJ found to his dismay that Mustapha was on holiday when he presented his paperwork at the main gate.

To his continued horror, the police inspector that he had last seen at Yenikapi police station marched down the path accompanying a customs officer to where JJ had been told to wait.

'Ah! Professor JJ, it is so nice to see you again.' Taking JJ by the elbow and leading him away from the customs officer who was busying himself with a hand full of paperwork, he asked, 'And how is the delightful Francine. She is very naughty, she promised to come and visit but she has not. Seeing the school on the ship's manifest I thought I would pay you a visit on the chance that I may see her.'

JJ thought he should have got rid of him when it was expected of him – instead he had put it off, not really wanting to do it. He replied swiftly, 'She no longer works at the school but I will get a message to her to come and visit you tomorrow. Where will you meet?'

Keeping his voice low, the officer suggested that they meet at his house and added. 'My name is Kemal.' He gave JJ a slip of paper with his address and telephone number written on it in a childish scrawl. JJ slipped the paper into his shirt pocket and promised to deliver the message immediately he had finished with the customs. 'Well, let me see if I can assist you then.' Turning back to the customs officer, he shouted, 'What is the delay?'

'We must examine the cargo before we can release it.'

'There is no need. I can vouch for this man and his cargo. It is only books.'

The customs officer happily took the police inspector's word, producing a pen, rubber stamp and inkpad from his pockets. He started signing and stamping the papers he was holding. With a smile and a salute he handed the paperwork to Kemal, the police inspector, turned and walked swiftly away. Kemal turned to JJ and said, 'Do you wish me to see your books or would you prefer to deliver my note to Francine?' JJ could not be sure if Kemal suspected the consignment was illegal or was just playing games. Deciding on caution, he replied rapidly, 'I will deliver your note at once.'

Kemal smiled. 'Thank you. You do know where she is then?'

He pushed the paperwork at JJ and continued, 'Don't let me detain you anymore.' Escorting JJ to his waiting taksi, he said, 'Abdul is not with you today? You never seem to be without him.'

'He's not feeling very well. He probably drank too much raki last night.'

'Tell him I asked about him, please.' He waved at JJ's departing taksi then climbed into the rear of his waiting car speaking to the person who was sitting waiting on the rear seat in the far corner. 'General, the cargo is definitely illegal but I think we should let this one through and wait for the big one.'

'If you think you can spot the next one, I agree.'

'That will be no trouble with my contacts in their little group.'

# Chapter Twenty

'Hello? Yes, this is Kemal,' sounding annoyed.

'Oh hi, this is Francine. I was trying to confirm my visit to you tomorrow. Shall I be over at say, ten in the morning?' she asked.

As Kemal's voice turned to treacle, Francine felt sick. 'That will be excellent. I am looking forward to your visit.'

'There will be no-one else there will there?'

'No, we shall be all alone, just you and me.'

'That will be wonderful,' she said, looking across at JJ.

'Please don't be late.'

'No, if anything, I'll be bright and early. See you soon.'

'That was great,' said JJ.

'Goodbye Kemal.'

Francine shivered involuntary as JJ spoke.

'Now, how am I going to get into his house?'

'Let's play it by ear in the morning. Take me out tonight so I can try and forget tomorrow.'

'How would you like to eat fish at one of the little restaurants in Kumkapi?' The area was probably the most popular restaurant area of Istanbul with about thirty or forty individual fish restaurants.

'Oh yes please, lots of people and noise.'

'First we must phone Abdul,' declared JJ, 'and tell him we shall not be at training again tomorrow.'

'Good thinking.' She added, 'If we tell him why we shall not be there he will explain to the men we are doing something else more important.'

They showered and dressed. Francine was wearing a new outfit that JJ had bought for her the last time they were in the Grand Bazaar. They set off in search of a taksi. Being unable to find a vacant one, Francine suggested, 'How about going in by train and get a taksi from Sirkeci station? You do realize that it is still only mid-afternoon and early for dinner.'

'Yes,' JJ said, 'it could be a late lunch.' As they were close to the little village station, JJ agreed. They waited on the station platform for the local train, the Orient Express train passed slowly by, heading for the end of its journey, Istanbul. When they also arrived the passengers had already started to pour forth from the comparative giant in its glistening blue and gold livery, all excitedly chattering away at the prospect of the next part of their adventure

JJ caught the sound of the little band playing an unfamiliar tune, but obviously a well-known one to Francine, for she had started humming it when she set foot on the platform and caught the first notes which, to JJ's north European ear, sounded more like a cat being murdered. One of the regular belly dancers was giving out her samples of Turkish Delight. Francine said, 'Let's go and see who she is.' She was obviously missing the attention that she no longer enjoyed from the rich travelling public. It had been too JJ's delight when she had told him that she was giving up dancing professionally. He had not tried to influence her in any way; neither had he tried to persuade her to continue, not liking other men having designs on her body which he now considered his personal property.

'Do you miss it?' JJ asked.

'Yes I think I do, really, but I wouldn't have the time or the energy to carry on both that and the training. Let's talk about it when we have done the job. Would you mind if I started again?'

JJ lied to protect his own jealousy of her dancing for the pleasure of other men. 'No I wouldn't mind, not really.'

With Francine taking his arm, they left the platform and the spectacle that the tourists were enjoying. One American male, so obviously overjoyed at the sight of a scantily clad and very shapely female, was not looking where he was walking, so, as he got off the train, had fallen down the steps onto the platform. His very plump wife was patting him on the cheeks trying to revive him, at the same time saying, 'Well, honey, if this is how you are going to behave now we are in this heathen country; I'm going home to Iowa!'

This time they had no problem securing a taksi.

'Kumkapi, please?' JJ instructed the driver. 'Take us to a good restaurant with music and dancing.' As JJ settled in the seat next to Francine for the short journey he risked holding her hand – something he dare not do in Abdul's taksi. When they arrived in Kumkapi they were immediately surrounded by noise. The atmosphere was vibrant. The traffic was heavy, making their progress slow. It gave them an opportunity to soak up the local character. They had been before but not as often as either would have liked, for JJ objected to paying the exorbitant prices for something that was caught and then landed on the quayside opposite. They eventually arrived at the restaurant of the driver's choice, the virtues of which establishment he had been praising for the last ten minutes. He probably received a kickback from the owner for taking him customers which was why he had insisted that he would deliver them to the door when JJ had suggested that it would be quicker if they walked the last few hundred meters.

The food was wonderful, the music raucous. JJ had only one opportunity to dance with Francine when the little band picked up on a slow waltz tune; he was not a lover of dancing. He, as always, enjoyed holding her close. She glided with him around the floor making him forget the almost imperceptible limp, which normally made him feel clumsy. 'You are such a wonderful dancer,' JJ remarked, 'you would make Fred Astaire look like a three-legged camel.'

'You do OK,' she retorted, 'but I think you are better at other things.'

'Is there anything in particular that I'm very good at?'

She reached up and kissed his cheek as they danced and replied, 'We are her to eat fish, not for you to fish for compliments.'

By the time they resumed their table, the restaurant had filled up with tourists. With the influx of bodies the room was beginning to get warm, in spite of the air conditioning, and with extra bodies there is the inevitable rise in noise. The band picked up tempo, the lights dimmed and the diners became silenced. The little dance floor that they had just vacated had become an arena for not one, not two, but three belly dancers who drifted onto it as if on a cushion of air. They were dressed in various styles and colors of the traditional dance costume and as they wove around the floor the audience had become mesmerized, as much by the hypnotic music as the spellbinding movements. Francine whispered, 'I know them all. The one in red was at school with me, the one in yellow was at my ballet school, and the one in blue is married to Ali, the man who gave you that black eye. He will be here somewhere – like you he doesn't like other men looking at her.' It was the first time she had ever made any reference to JJ's possessiveness. He had thought she had never noticed.

The four girls acknowledged each other as the dance progressed. Ali's wife beckoned Francine to join them in the dance. She waved back and shook her head.

JJ said, 'Why don't you? It will look like you're a tourist who knows how to dance and I'm sure you would like too.'

Francine caught the attention of Ali's wife, and nodded her acceptance. She rose, kicking of her shoes, as she joined the other three dancers. For a few seconds JJ was worried she was going to do a striptease as she shed her jacket, then her blouse, then her skirt, which was a wraparound affair revealing her underclothes, which looked remarkably like her short-skirted dance costume. JJ realized immediately it wasn't, as it was without the little coins that jingled as she moved. The band switched their music and started playing Francine's signature tune they must have recognized her. The four of them glided around the room. Francine now had on a pair of finger castanets, beating out the tune in their tinny, ringing, notes. JJ couldn't help his pangs of jealousy as some of the newly arrived tourists shouted out lewd comments to the girls. Francine and her friends ignored the comments. JJ was considering going to stop the shouts but before he could rise, a couple of waiters were there, getting them all sat down and quiet. The girls moved backwards and forwards and from side to side as they shimmered and shook, the band reaching a deafening final crescendo, then, silence. The dance over, the crowd roared their appreciation. The dancers disappeared behind the bandstand. Almost at once, Francine with Ali and his wife were standing at their table. Ali introduced his wife, Karli. He explained the name meant "covered with snow".

'Hello, Professor JJ. So at last I meet the man who broke my husband's beautiful nose.'

Ali was very quick to respond with, 'You see what I did to his eye?' The remains of the bruise going yellow.'

They all laughed. JJ invited them to join them but Karli declined for both of them, saying that she still had another hour yet before she had finished dancing for the day, and with a wave, they said their goodbyes. JJ asked, 'Why do I always like the people you know?'

'You mean the pretty female ones? If you can tear yourself away from my friends we could go home, it's almost nine and I may turn into a pumpkin! I have had a wonderful evening. Thank you darling.'

As they took a taksi back to Yesilcoy, Francine said, 'Thank you again, darling, it was wonderful dancing again. The problem is I still can't help thinking about tomorrow. I hope you will be OK, Kemal has a terrible reputation.'

'So have I. Remember I broke Ali's nose.'

They both laughed at the memory of their brief encounter earlier that evening with the giant Ali and his diminutive wife, Karli.

Having both enjoyed the evening out, they were reluctant for it to end, but with the thoughts of tomorrow's meeting with Kemal on both their minds, Francine declared, 'It's no good going to bed yet. I'm not in the mood for sex and I shall not sleep. It's only ten-thirty. I did promise to be early. How about going now and trying to catch him hopefully off guard, or still asleep?'

'How long will it take to get there?'

Francine consulted her watch before replying, 'We could be there in an hour.'

'No, that's much too early he probably will not even be in bed yet; how about watching a movie for a couple of hours?'

'If you like, but I feel very restless.'

JJ selected a video and they settled on the settee together with JJ only drinking a beer and Francine on water; both conscious that they must be alert later and would need their reflexes at their keenest. Although they watched the film, neither was paying it much attention. They had both seen it before so were able to doze and still follow the story. JJ turned the TV off two hours later, grumbled about it having been a waste of time. Francine squeezed his hand and kissed him on the corner of his black eye. He winced at the contact and said, 'OK. Let's get changed.'

Francine put on her most glamorous dress and JJ slipped into dark trousers and shirt with soft-soled shoes. Looking at her as she dressed, he couldn't resist remarking, 'Are you sure you don't fancy sex?'

She threw a shoe at him, that caught him near to his injured eye, although it had turned yellow, it was still partially closed. He yelped at the sharp pain and made a grab for her. She evaded his hands reminding him, 'I said – I don't fancy sex tonight.'

They both laughed, the tension of what was to happen later was eased from their thoughts for a short while!

JJ was stripping and cleaning his nine millimeter Browning Hi-Power pistol, reloading the magazine, easing each brass and nickel cartridge gently into place; a task he had performed so many times previously, before going into action when he had been in the army. He thought back to the day he had bought it. It was on their first monthly R & R weekend from Rhodesia to Johannesburg; paid for as part of the salary package that all the mine contract workers received from a grateful employer. JJ had bought two weapons – the Browning for himself, and for Elizabeth, a Walther PPK that would fit easily into her handbag when she went shopping.

The seemingly strangest part of the incident was that he had bought them at Johannesburg railway station. A South African that he worked with recommended the gun shop, being convenient to Commissioner Street Police Station where they would need to go to get firearm permits before being allowed to actually take the weapons from the shop. JJ was never sure why he had thought it strange that a shop selling firearms would be located on a railway station platform.

They had always found shopping a funny experience after the purchase of Elizabeth's weapon. Due to various terrorist activities, shops and department stores employed security guards, they were mainly black, to check everyone, black and white, entering their establishments for weapons or bombs. They would stop Elizabeth at the door and politely ask, 'May I see in your bag, madam?' Then, seeing her pistol, they would produce a huge-toothed, shining grin and continue with, 'Thank you, madam. You may enter.' They seemed to be happy that yet another white person was armed and in their store. It all seemed very strange thinking back. In fact, the whole period of their stay in Rhodesia during the bush war had had a very unreal feel.

JJ's feeling at the moment was not of some real incident about to happen, but a life-threatening event was about to unfold. What would happen when Kemal realized that JJ had accompanied Francine? He didn't doubt that he would be able to handle the situation; his only concern was what the Americans call "collateral damage", with, maybe Francine being hurt, in the event of a gun fight. Francine, impatient to get going, chided him to hurry.

'Wait a minute,' JJ shouted. 'How are we going to get there at this time of night? We'll never find a taksi and if we did don't you think he would be straight onto the police when it's announced that a murder has been committed near to where he took two foreigners? He would sing like a skylark.'

'Damn! Why did you have to take the Porsche back to the UK?'

'That would have been just as bad. How many cars like that do you see in Istanbul at three in the morning particularly with foreign license plates?'

'Yes, you are right, we shall have to give it another three hours before we can start and even then we shall have a lot of walking to do! Would you like me to make you something to eat?'

'Please, a nice greasy bacon sandwich and a cup of coffee.'

'Trust you.' She didn't voice her revulsion at the thought of cooking bacon. Her Muslim upbringing still showed through at times, particularly where pork was concerned. She dutifully prepared JJ his breakfast, which he devoured with obvious relish. It was, in Francine's opinion, time that they should be on their way. JJ was still hesitant about the lack of people likely to be around. It was still only three-thirty. He gave way to her superior knowledge of the city and when it started to come to life. 'Come on then, it's time I worked off that sandwich, it's sitting like a lead balloon in my stomach.'

Francine had slipped on over her head a large black shawl that not only hid her mane of blond hair but also covered her shoulders and the top part of her dress. 'No point looking like a tart until I have to.'

'OK.'

Taking his hand and squeezing it, she smiled up at him, 'It'll be fine, and please don't worry.'

To JJ's surprise the trains were running and fairly busy. Their journey was swift and uneventful. Crossing the road from Sirkeci railway station to Eminonu ferry terminal presented all the hazards normally encountered in the rush hour. JJ remarked how right she had been about Istanbul coming to life early in the day as he was narrowly missed by a taksi as it went rushing to deliver its passenger to a pre-requested destination. They took a less busy ferryboat to Kadikoy. It was now five forty-five.

'OK,' Francine said, 'now we walk.' From the bag she was carrying she produced a pair of walking shoes, quickly changing them for the high heels that JJ had bought for her when they had been on holiday in Cyprus. 'I am not walking three kilometers in those,' she said, as she placed them carefully in the bag, 'Besides, I don't want to spoil them – they were a present from someone very special.' They smiled at each other, remembering the week they had had together walking, talking, swimming, sunbathing, and how close they had been to each other.

Fifteen minutes later they arrived outside Kemal's house. It was in a prosperous area; the house neat and well-looked after, a highly polished car standing in the driveway. The roads around still quiet, JJ whispered to Francine, 'I bet he didn't get this place on a police salary?'

She quickly changed back into her high-heeled shoes, wrapping her shawl around her shoe bag with her walking shoes in, then stuffing both under a hedge, hopefully to remember to collect them if; no, when they left. The street was narrow and still with no sign of life. They slipped quickly around to the back of the house hoping that he didn't have a dog or an alarm system. As JJ was holding a fence for Francine to step over they heard a door open behind them.

'Good morning. I was expecting you earlier, probably before daylight. No, don't turn around yet. Please bend forward and place your gun on the ground.' JJ did as he had been instructed.

'Good, now turn slowly this way.' Kemal was standing before them with his service revolver pointing directly at JJ, leaving him in no doubt that he would pull the trigger if he made any attempt to do anything that Kemal didn't like.

'You probably would like to know how I knew to expect you.'

'It would be nice to know who betrayed us and who I shall kill next – after I finish with you.'

'Don't be so sure of yourself. I have heard all about your army days. I'm not some native savage for you to trick. I will shoot you, and the beautiful Francine, if you both don't do exactly as I say. Do you understand?'

They both nodded that they understood.

'Good, it's so much easier when I deal with intelligent people. Now, will you turn around and continue to walk to the rear of the house.'

JJ walked past his discarded pistol, not looking down as he almost trod on it.

'Excellent, you have learnt very quickly. Now when you get to the large doorway in front of you, you will enter. There are two chairs in the middle of the room; you will each sit on one of them. They are secured to the floor so it will be pointless for you to try anything and make me shoot you both so soon. I'm not concerned about the noise as this room is soundproofed and anyway I am a senior police officer, so nobody would take any notice.'

They sat as instructed. JJ clasped his hands together on his lap, Francine let hers hang beside her, in a very dejected manner.

'Aren't you going to say anything? No? In that case let me tell you a story. My very good friend Abdul phoned me last night and told me that you had ideas of coming to kill me. He told me that you had guessed that I knew the cargo was illegal and you didn't want me to expose you so you offered me this lovely lady as a bribe, knowing that I wouldn't notify the customs department until I had had the delights that she can provide.'

Francine, flashed JJ, a look that could kill, and then burst into tears. 'I thought you loved me!' she shouted.

As she fumbled into the pocket of her dress for a handkerchief, she slid her hand straight through the bottomless pocket onto her thigh clasped the butt of her small Smith and Wesson 38 magnum that was in a soft suede holster, strapped conveniently to the top of her leg, and fired. The hollow point bullet hit Kemal directly between the eyes, slightly above the bridge of the nose and, flattening on impact, exited larger at the back of his head, taking with it a lot of blood and grey brain matter. He stood for a moment with a surprised expression on his face before dropping his revolver and falling onto his back, knocking over a small table that was behind him. The table broke but nobody heard it splinter, it happened so quickly after Francine's shot that the two sounds merged as one. Francine and JJ both jumped up and turned to each other. JJ noticed that she was not crying – she had only pretended to – but was in obvious pain. They walked towards each other, Francine limping on her right leg. JJ held her. She quickly lifted the hem of her dress and removed the holster and the little gun that had caused so much damage to Kemal's head and handed them to JJ asking him, 'Put these under your jacket please.'

He rammed the gun and holster into the inside pocket of his jacket. 'You were wonderful. Why didn't you tell me that you were going to be armed?'

'I'll tell you later. Let's get out of here before the police wake up.'

'Hold my arm.'

'Don't be so stupid, it's nothing.'

They walked slowly around to the front of the house, JJ stooping to pick up his discarded pistol on the way. The road was still deserted. Francine retrieved her shawl and walking shoes. She put her shawl on again and changed back into her walking shoes, relieved to be out of the high heels that were aggravating her leg.

'Now we walk back to the ferry. Please hold my arm in case I stumble over. I don't want people to think I'm drunk. Now please, no talking until we get on the ferryboat.'

JJ did as she bid and took her right arm. He also insisted on carrying the bag containing her high-heeled shoes. She was able, with his aid, to set a good pace. As the ferry terminal came into view she let out a load audible sigh. He bent and kissed her check saying, 'Only another couple of hundred meters hang on.'

As they bought the tickets for the crossing to Eminonu, she managed to force a smile for the ticket clerk. He smiled back and wished them a good crossing.

'She will be OK after breakfast, it was a great party,' JJ said, indicating a somewhat woozy Francine.

They found seats on the near-deserted upper deck. The air was still fresh; the heat of the day had not yet started to build.

'Now tell me what happened to your leg. I can hardly lift your skirt to look for myself.'

'The little holster was something that I dreamt up. The gun I have had for a long time. I have ruined a perfectly good dress by cutting the pocket out. I have also hurt my leg by not being able to pull the gun out of its holster when I fired. I must have burnt my thigh. It's OK, don't look so panic-stricken, it's my outer thigh that's hurt.' She smiled weakly at him and passed out. JJ left her propped into the corner so she wouldn't fall and went in search of a bottle of water. He located the refreshment seller and also bought the syrupy cake known locally as baklava. Taking both, he hurried back to Francine who was just coming to as he sat next to her again.

'Try and sip this water when you're up to it. I've also got you a baklava, it's full of honey, it will help you to feel better.'

'Thank you.' She mouthed the words, being too weak to summon the energy to speak the words aloud.

By the time they docked at Eminonu, Francine was feeling, and looking, much better. She had eaten the cake and got syrup all over her dress and shawl. JJ washed her hands and mouth with water from the bottle.

'Come on, let's be positive and go find a taksi.' As he helped her up, she stifled a cry of pain as she put her weight onto her injured leg. With JJ's help she limped off the boat, mingling with the crowds of people all eager to get to their destinations, hoping that no-one would notice them.

Taksi's at that time of day were plentiful. When they pulled up outside JJ's house he noticed the time, it was still only eight-thirty.

# Chapter Twenty One

When JJ got Francine into the house, he set about dressing her leg. It wasn't as bad as he had expected. She had probably fainted on the ferry as much out of the shock of shooting Kemal as the pain from her injury. She must have moved the barrel of the gun upwards when she had pulled the trigger, thus avoiding the main blast onto her leg. It had been a remarkable shot considering the speed at which she had fired and from such an angle.

'Now that doesn't look too bad. How do you feel and why didn't you tell me you had a gun? Bad news, I'm afraid you shot a hole in your dress as well.'

'It feels much more comfortable, thank you. It throbs a little but I hope that it will wear off. I didn't tell you I was carrying a gun because I didn't want you to think that you could rely on me. I have never killed anybody before in cold blood and didn't know if I could!'

'Well, you did a much better job than I did, given that Kemal had the drop on us. What are we going to do about Abdul?'

'You know what we have to do.'

'Yes, but he is your father-in-law.'

'That is not important, we must think about what we are fighting for, but firstly we must find out why he is doing it.'

'What will you tell your husband?'

'Let me worry about that.'

They discussed what to do for the next hour, finally deciding that they would tackle him the following day.

'Do you want to sleep with a cripple tonight or shall I go in the spare room?' she asked.

'It's only ten in the morning, are you suggesting that we go to bed now or are you getting presumptuous?'

'Well, we didn't get any sleep last night. We are not working today. If the police are onto us it doesn't matter where we are, they will come for us so let's try and make the most of our day off.'

JJ had given Francine some tablets for the pain in her leg and had had a very large whisky himself so by the time they climbed into bed they were both so sleepy that apart from a brief kiss goodnight, they made no further contact with each other.

The ringing of the telephone woke them both at five that afternoon. It was Abdul – could he come over for a chat? He had just heard the news about Kemal! JJ agreed.

'Why did you say yes to him?' Francine was in a rage. 'He is a police spy – why do you think he will want to come over? Not just for a sympathetic chat. It will be to try and get evidence that we did it.'

'It's better to know what is happening, don't you think? Now calm down he will be here at six-thirty.'

'Well, I shall be wearing my gun again. I am as good a shot with my left hand as I am with my right and now I know I can kill someone you can rely on me to get there before you. I will hesitate because he is my husband's father. I will not hesitate because of what he made me do to Kemal.'

'Just be careful please,' was all he could say.

Abdul arrived on the dot at six-thirty. As he entered the house he had a curious look on his face as if unsure of himself. It was unusual, as he was normally so confident, in everything he did and said. 'Well, I have heard that Kemal has been found. Shot in the head they say, straight between the eyes and the bullet blew the back of head off. Was he still alive when you left?'

'No,' said JJ, 'he was very dead.'

As he spoke, he pulled his gun and pointed it straight at Abdul. 'He said that you had phoned him.'

Abdul started to stammer, 'Now, Captain Professor JJ, please do not do something that we shall both be sorry about. Let me explain.'

'You've got two minutes; make the most of them, they could

be your last.'

'Yes, I told him you were coming and that you would probably try to kill him. I had no choice. He had been to see me and told me that if I knew anything about what you were doing and I didn't tell him, he would have my son hanged. What could I do?' By this time he had broken down, sobbing like a baby.

'Keep going, you've got less than a minute,' JJ said sternly.

'What could I do?' sobbed Abdul. 'I couldn't let them do that, the poor boy has suffered enough already.'

'It would be better than serving another seven years in that place. Just shoot him now, before he uses any more excuses.' Francine was now in tears.

'If you don't, I will,' she said, producing her gun out of her pocket.

'JJ my boy, can't you stop her?' Abdul was holding hands in front of his face as he pleaded. 'I knew that you were more than a match for him.'

'Abdul,' JJ demanded, 'why didn't you tell me about Kemal? We could have worked something out instead of you letting us walk into his trap.'

'He said he would know if I contacted you and that would be my son's death warrant. I didn't dare do anything.'

'How did you know that he had been shot and that the back of his head had been blown away, if you are not working with the police?'

'Mr. Conrad told me and told me to get over here and find all I could and report back to him.'

JJ was thinking aloud. 'Conrad again, I wonder?'

'Abdul, are you sure that what you have told us is the whole truth?'

'Well, I still think we should kill him.' Francine was almost jumping up and down in her rage. 'I'll do it, like I did to Kemal; I'll shoot you between the eyes and blow the back of your head off. No, I've got a better idea; I could skin him, like you would a rabbit.'

'Francine,' JJ said, 'who'll clean up the mess?' It was the best thing he could have done for she dropped the barrel of her gun towards the floor and laughed.

'Well, he'll make more mess than Kemal; he's got a bigger head.'

The tension in the room eased a little. JJ had not moved the aim of his Browning, it was still unwaveringly pointing at Abdul's heart. Abdul removed his hands from his face and wiped his eyes on his knuckles. Turning to face Francine, he asked, 'Why did you think I could do anything that would harm my son's wife? Have I not always tried to protect you, even when I thought that Captain Professor JJ was having an affair with you, did I not try and protect you?'

'OK, father-in-law, you win for the moment, but if I find that you have lied I shall be more liable to take a knife and skin you rather than waste a bullet.'

Abdul visibly shuddered at the prospect, and babbled on that they need not worry for he was telling them the truth.

JJ replaced the pistol in the waistband at the back of his trousers. 'OK, Abdul, for the moment you live, but you have still to prove what you are saying is true. Let's go find Conrad.'

Conrad was still at his desk at school when the three of them walked in. He stood in surprise at seeing them. Unable to compose himself before he spoke he blurted out, 'Abdul, I told you to report back to me, not bring them too me.'

'We insisted,' JJ said. 'Now sit down and keep your fingertips pressing hard on the top of the desk.' Conrad sat hurriedly as JJ's Browning appeared. 'I said, press hard, if your knuckles are not white in five seconds and stay white; I will kill you.'

Francine couldn't resist joining in, out came her Smith and Wesson. 'If JJ doesn't do it, I will. I may just anyway, the times I've had to fight you off in the office and at your home when Ayşe was out. You make me sick with your clammy hands and foul breath. How my sister could ever let you touch her is beyond me.'

'Unlike you, my dear, she likes money and what money buys. She likes to look nice and have nice things, not like you. You are just a slut, from terrorist parents, married to a terrorist, been in prison and now playing house with him.' Conrad sneered as he indicated JJ.

JJ thought she was going to pull the trigger. He called to her, which made her pause. 'Let's try and get some information first. If he doesn't co-operate fully then you can.'

Conrad could see the rage in her eyes and obviously knowing who her parents probably had been, had no doubt that she would kill him without thought.

'I'll tell you anything you want to know, just keep her under control.' He was gradually getting his act together and was now more composed. JJ noticed that he was also releasing the pressure that his fingertips had been applying to the desk-top.

'I shall not tell you again. Fingers, pressure, apply, desk, got it?'

Conrad's knuckles went white again.

'Well,' said JJ, 'do you know what your sister-in-law promised to do to Abdul if she found he had lied? Tell him, Abdul.'

Abdul's fear returned, due not so much to what she had said but her voice when she had spoken left no doubts that she would take pleasure in doing it.

'Mr. Conrad, she said that she would take a knife and cut off all my skin.'

'You were always an old woman, Abdul. You don't think she could do anything like that. Maybe shoot you, but to skin someone would take a person so callous and depraved, that I could not imagine.'

JJ didn't know where she had got it from. He was as amazed as the other two men when she was standing there with a stainless steel skinning knife, the type that hunters use to skin an animal that they had killed to take home as a trophy. The men could see that she wouldn't bother to kill first but would skin any of them alive, given the right provocation.

'OK, Francine, let's not frighten them to death before they tell us what's going on.'

Conrad started to talk. 'It was really your sister's fault. She always wanted more and more things – clothes, jewelry, bigger house, bigger car, why would anyone in their right mind want a big car in Istanbul, for God's sake? The school wasn't making enough money to keep her satisfied. Kemal knew of Francine's past and approached me on the pretext of checking on her, we became friendly, he was pleasant male company. He knew lots of people and the school, through his friendship, had started to do well. Sons, relations and friends were all clambering for places. Ayşe was happy; so I was happy. Then Kemal took me to dinner one evening and suggested that he knew of an anarchist cell operating in Istanbul and that we were all involved and that Abdul was probably its leader and that Ayşe and I had been involved since before our marriage. Francine was still as active as ever in it. If I would like to make even more money, he would pay me a million dollars if I would arrange for Abdul to plan, and to recruit an overseas specialist to buy arms and explosives and train your people and blow up a Bosporus bridge.'

By this point in his explanation his voice had started to become hysterical and he slumped forward across his vast desk, completely forgetting to keep his fingertips pressed on the top of the desk. Francine brought him back to his senses as she stuck the tip of her knife, none to gently, into the back of his right hand, causing his blood to fountain all over the desk as well as her own hand. Conrad got the message and if he had pressed any harder he would have either broken his own fingers or made holes in the top of the desk.

JJ broke the silence. 'Abdul, we have to get him out of town. Let's take him to the training camp and get the rest of it out of him.'

Francine interrupted him. 'If we wait about half an hour until it is dark, there will be less likelihood that anyone will see us get him into the car.'

So they waited, in almost total silence, broken only by the traffic passing outside and the occasional wail of anguish from Conrad. Francine was keeping him under close watch, her knife an ever constant reminder to him of her intentions if he moved or made a noise. That, in itself, was sufficient to cause an involuntary wail to pass his lips.

The shadows had been getting longer, cast by the trees on the opposite side of the road, and then suddenly they were gone, merged into one dark mass.

JJ indicated it was time to go. Conrad was in such a complete flunk that he had wet his trousers. Abdul was complaining about having him in his taksi, should his bowels also involuntarily let go.

'Come on, let's get moving, we have wasted enough time already.' They bundled an uncooperative Conrad out of the school and into Abdul's waiting taksi. They squashed him in the rear seat between Francine and JJ. She was keeping her knife very much in evidence. Conrad was as if mesmerized by the sight of it. JJ said, 'Watch the bumps, Abdul, or Francine will cause Conrad to ruin your upholstery.'

'You bet, Captain Professor JJ, don't want that.'

The journey took over an hour, due to the volume of traffic all trying to be the first home and every one that pulled out to change lanes because they thought it was moving faster than the one they were in, caused that lane to have to slow, which added to the chaos. Conrad had become a whimpering, whining, pathetic, little man. Sitting there, wet trousers, tears running down his face; occasionally looking at JJ and pleading, 'Don't let her touch me with that knife. I'll tell you everything. I'll give you money. What do you want? Please don't let her loose with that knife.' At these moments JJ would either glare at him or Francine, digging him in the side with her knife was sufficient to silence him for a few minutes.

They finally arrived, much to the relief of JJ and Francine, as they were able to stretch their aching joints and ease Francine's burnt thigh, also pleasing for Abdul without Conrad ruining the taksi's upholstery. They hauled Conrad out and made him kneel on the ground before them.

'Now talk, shout, cry, whatever you want to do, you know that nobody will hear you out here. Tell us what you had told him and who he told.'

'I only told him that you had been recruited and he accepted that you were a good choice. I told him about your suggestion to blow both the bridges which appeared to delight him. That you had bought explosives and guns and that training had started. I told him where this training camp is.'

'Why do you think he was pleased because I had suggested that we take both bridges out?'

'I don't know it was as if he was pleased how well things were going. Originally, all the expenses for the explosives and guns were supposed to be paid for out of my million dollars to make sure you weren't being wasteful with the money. He said he was so pleased how well things were going he would pay the half a million I gave you to buy the stuff with. Those two men you killed the first day worked directly under him. I don't know how because they were army and he was police.'

'Who did he report to? Who authorized him to spend so much money to set up a terrorist attack?'

'I don't know any more,' he whined, 'please let me go.'

'Just tell us, one more time, from the beginning.'

He told his story four more times, until eventually they were satisfied that they had been told the truth, as Conrad's story never varied. It was either the truth or he had learnt his lines well. They left him lying in the dust, an utter, weeping, hysterical lump while they retreated to Abdul's taksi to discuss their next move.

Francine wanted to kill him. Abdul thought he had told the truth and that probably no-one else knew about the plans and that Kemal, for some reason, wanted their plan to succeed. JJ tended to agree with Abdul that Kemal wanted their plans to succeed but he wasn't sure about nobody else knowing.

'What are we going to do with him? We can't just let him go.'

'I'll skin him alive, the treacherous snake,' was Francine's vote.

Abdul was for letting him go. 'He's seen what will happen to him if he betrays us again. I think we should give him a chance.'

The casting vote was JJ's, 'We can't take the chance that he will betray us but I don't like the idea of killing him.'

'I'll do it,' Francine volunteered, too enthusiastically for JJ's comfort.

'If anyone does it, I will. It's my duty to protect us all,' JJ stated, and Francine looked disappointed.

JJ got out of the taksi and walked over to the crumpled pile that had been Conrad. He drew his pistol and pointed it at Conrad's head, closed his own eyes and pulled the trigger.

# Chapter Twenty Two

The Browning kicked in JJ's hand and the report drowned out the thud as the bullet shattered Conrad's head. An immense sadness descended upon him. He had killed men before, even women, but always in the heat of battle. He didn't know how many he had killed. When you fire an FN rifle on automatic spraying the dense bush from where you are being shot at, it's not possible to see, or even hear the bodies. You know if you've succeeded when you stop being shot at. After his first contact with the terrorists he had felt remorse at killing, the senselessness and futility of it. But after seeing the carnage inflicted on a mission hospital, the mutilation of the nuns who were trying to care for villagers that had been attacked for little, or no reason other than being there; the wanton destruction of the building with all of the patients still in their beds, too sick to run. He had become hardened to the act of killing. Killing Conrad had been his first execution. He felt sick. He wanted to get away, get on a plane and fly away to escape to anywhere; even to England, away from the place that had turned him into a terrorist no better than the ones he had killed all those years before. He felt Francine's presence, he hadn't heard her. She reached out and took his hand, the one that was holding the pistol, and lifted it to her lips and kissed the back which was white from the pressure he was exerting on the butt, and then rubbed it against her cheek. He started to relax as she spoke.

'It was essential to stop him from passing any more information. With Conrad and Kemal both gone, that hopefully, will be the end of the killings and we can revert, to our aim of a bloodless victory.'

Still holding him by the hand, she led him to the taksi and helped him into the front passenger seat. He let her take his pistol, which she laid on the floor before him.

'Abdul can arrange to have things cleared up here after he takes us home. Would you like to stop for something to eat and have a drink before we get to Yesilcoy?'

'No thanks, just home please.'

'OK, Captain Professor JJ. Let's hope there are not too many of them damn dangerous taksi drivers on the road tonight!'

JJ smiled. He was glad that he hadn't had to kill Abdul. He always seemed to say the right thing at the right time, even if most of it was stupid. He leaned back in his seat, and before Abdul had started the engine, he was asleep. By the time they arrived home he was feeling much better. He had slept for almost an hour and it had revitalized him to some extent.

'The Captain Professor JJ is now awake, Francine, and we are in Yesilcoy. Why don't I drop you at the pizza restaurant? You both need some food and a stiff drink.'

JJ nodded.

'I will join you for one drink, I need one too, and then I must go make some money. One good fare from the airport to the Hilton may just cover my expenses today. I also need to use the restaurant telephone to start the cleanup operations.'

They sat at the table in the window again. Francine looked out of the window and declared, 'No-one around watching us tonight, thank goodness.'

'Well, at least we appear to have had some success if we are not being watched,' JJ remarked.

Abdul rejoined them at the table with a huge smile, 'Drinks are on the way and my phone call was OK. Everything is being dealt with.' He downed his raki and said goodnight, adding, 'I will not collect you in the morning, I think you both deserve a day off.'

They wished him goodnight and waved to him from the window as he drove away.

'Food, now what would you like to eat?' JJ asked.

'One of those really spicy ones that will give me indigestion and keep me awake all night please.' She was trying to keep his mind off of what had happened.

JJ ordered two, extra spicy, and a bottle of their favorite wine. They sipped their cognacs until the pizzas arrived. The waiter opened the wine, poured two glasses, and wished them a pleasant meal, then departed, leaving them to eat. They ate hardly anything as the pizza was too spicy. JJ called for a second bottle of wine.

Francine declined further alcohol. 'No thank you, I'm not in the mood.'

JJ drank another glass without any real enthusiasm and then signaled for the bill.

They walked home with Francine's hand linked around JJ's arm. They hadn't spoken about Conrad or Kemal since the killings.

'We need to talk,' she declared, 'it will do neither of us any good until we have.'

'We will, when we get home!'

They settled themselves onto the settee with a bottle of cognac and two glasses close by. They didn't touch each other – it was almost as if they had only just met. Normally, one or the other would reach out to the other and touch a hand, an arm, to feel comfort and give support in times of stress or just when passing each other in the room.

'You start please darling,' she said.

'I'm not sure where or how; I just feel so bad inside so disgusted with myself. I never gave him a chance to defend himself. I am as bad as those communist trained terrorists that I hunted in the bush for killing those nuns during the war. I have no right to just put a gun to someone's head and blow it apart. This is not my country, not my war. I am your hired killer, a murderer.'

She slapped him a resounding blow to his face, hitting him just below his black eye. 'Just stop feeling so self-pitying. I thought you were a brave man, a soldier of fortune. How much did you personally make out of that deal you did in Prague? Just snap out of this stupid mood, you have killed many people. This morning I killed my first and I enjoyed doing it.' She screamed at him. Calming down a little, she continued, 'Yes, I enjoyed shooting Kemal – he needed to be destroyed before he could destroy us. If I hadn't, he would have shot you, raped me, then sent me back to prison and probably had my husband executed as well. I always knew that I was an excellent shot with a handgun and now I have not only proved it but I have also proved to myself that I can stand the pressure of combat just like you my darling. I know that anyone can depend on me, the same as we know that we can depend on you. In a way the killing of both Conrad and Kemal were the same.'

JJ stopped her. 'No, they were not the same at all. You acted in self-defense. I just murdered Conrad.'

'That's what I'm trying to tell you. You acted in self-defense too. If you hadn't shot Conrad he would have carried on passing information about us to the police or the army – to anyone that would pay him.' She trailed off into a tearful, sobbing, shaking jelly. She jumped up and rushed to the bathroom. JJ could hear her being violently sick. He didn't go to her; giving her the privacy that he thought she needed. She returned after about ten minutes, her face white, her hair wet around the edges, holding a towel to her mouth. As she reached JJ she threw her arms around him and sobbed onto his chest.

'I'm sorry I hit your eye, did it hurt?'

'Yes, it did, very much.'

She kissed the corner of his eye. He didn't wince at the contact as he had the day before they went to Kemal.

'I'm sorry that I got hysterical and I've been sick, but I think the realization of what I did to Kemal and what I would and could have done to Abdul and Conrad, has just hit me! I was happy to kill them cold-bloodedly and without any feeling of right or wrong, without remorse. I now know that what you and I did was necessary and justified. That we acted in pure self-defense. It was either them or us. The thing that was wrong was that I had taken pleasure in shooting Kemal and stabbing Conrad in the back of his hand. One should never take pleasure from an act of violence. One can be pleased they have the ability, the technique. I had become a little crazed with my ability, now I hope it is under control and you can rely on me in the future never to let you down. I will also tell you when I'm carrying a weapon so you never have to worry about protecting me. By your sentiment over the shooting of Conrad, it showed me that someone can carry out what you did calmly and justly and not to take pleasure in it. Now please pour me a drink to wash away my sickly taste.'

He poured two glasses of cognac, as he handed her one, he toasted her with his glass.

'You are quite a lady. I am glad you're on my side.'

'Well, just let me have a quiet five minutes, and then I'll show you just how much of a lady I am!'

They sat together in silence, sipping their drinks, their fingertips just touching, each locked in their own private thoughts. The phone rang. JJ groaned, 'Now what?'

'Professor Captain JJ, all mess cleared up. I got an absolute idiot fare. "Hilton," this American shouted, "Hilton Hotel quick." So we got there pretty quick. You know how good I drive. He goes into Hilton, shouts to a porter, "bags" and rushes up to the reception and bangs on the desk. You know how snooty those reception guys are. "Sir?" he said. "I'm Hoover," this guy shouts, "I got a room reserved in this 'otel." Banged down a piece of paper. The clerk looked at it, moved it with the tip of his pen in order to read it and said calmly, "Not here, sir, that's the Sheraton. Goodbye!" This American picked up the paper, looked at it, swore, turned to the porter that had brought in his luggage, shouted "Bags, taksi" and looked at me and shouted some more.

"You brought me to the wrong hotel," he shouts. "Sheraton, and be quick." Well, that doubled his fare. He even gave me twenty-dollar tip.'

'That's great, Abdul, thanks for the call.' JJ quickly put the phone down before Abdul could start on the story again. He knew that it would be his topic of conversation for a week. 'I'm going for a shower before I go to bed, I feel still feel dirty about shooting Conrad.'

He was standing, just letting the hot water wash over his body, thinking about Conrad's brains splashing on the ground. The shower door opened. Francine was standing there, wearing nothing more than a big smile.

'Is there any room for me?' she purred.

The burn on her leg looked very red still and she whimpered slightly as he soaped her all over. With Francine he never knew if it was pain or passion that made her whimper so. He hosed her down with the shower spray.

'Thank you, now it's your turn.'

It was just getting light outside when JJ woke. He got quietly out of bed and made his way to the kitchen, making her a chocolate and coffee for himself, in large mugs. As he gently put her drink on the bedside table, she roused, her eyes flashing open, her face grim. Seeing him standing beside the bed, the expression on her face changed to a huge self-satisfied smile.

'Thank you, darling. I love you.'

'I love you too,' he said, bending over to kiss her. 'What shall we do today?'

'We could always do what we did last night.'

'Don't you ever have enough?' he asked.

'Not of you.'

'Shall I hire a car and we can drive up to the Black Sea and have lunch?'

'It will make it an expensive lunch.'

'That's OK, remember, I made a lot of money on the arms deal in Prague.'

'You are a soldier of fortune?'

'Only a poor one. I'll tell you about it while we drive.'

He rented an open-topped VW beetle and they set off for a day by the sea. The road from Istanbul is a twisty narrow track as it meanders through the forest to the coast. The weather was perfect for a drive in an open topped car. They had been before but last time it had been a windy day; the waves had pounded the beach making it too dangerous to venture near to the sea. This day was the middle of summer. With no wind, the beach was crowded with tourists, the edge of the sea full of bathers. They walked hand in hand along the beach feeling a little disappointed that they had to share the day with other people. They found a small beach bar that was about to serve lunch. Having stopped to look at the menu, they were encouraged in by a waiter who, while about to start work, couldn't without customers. Standing on the restaurant steps, he confirmed that they did have fresh lobster. 'Please, you wait, I show you – very alive and fresh.' He reappeared in a couple of minutes with a large wriggly lobster in each hand, their claws clamped firmly shut with stout rubber bands.

'OK,' said JJ. 'We'll have those two with a salad and a bottle of cold champagne.'

The waiter could not believe his luck at such an expensive order, he knew that the owner, the patron, would give him a big bonus.

'We don't need both do we?' she asked.

The waiter looked crestfallen until JJ said, 'Yes we do, today is a celebration.' The waiter departed with the wriggling creatures before JJ could be persuaded to order just one. JJ hadn't told Francine about his trip to Prague before – she had never asked and he didn't want to tell her about Marie. He had promised to tell her about his windfall but wasn't sure what her reaction would be.

'You think I made a lot of money out of my trip to Prague don't you? Well, I made some, but not a fortune. I got paid ten thousand dollars.' He lied, hoping she wouldn't see that it was not the whole truth – the other one hundred and ninety thousand he hadn't actually got yet.

'That's a lot of money to a Turk!'

'But don't forget, I'm only being paid as a school teacher by Conrad, not a military consultant, so I took the opportunity to get a bonus. Do you think that's very wrong?'

'No, not in your world, but it is in mine. I have a good mind not to eat your expensive sea creature and drink your wine, it's decadent.' At that moment, lunch was served. It looked and smelled wonderful. 'Well, maybe just a little.' She couldn't say any more as she was attacking a claw with her neat white teeth. They cleared their plates and had a second bottle of champagne. The waiter was beside himself at the prospect of the huge bonus he was sure the patron would pay him.

'For a capitalist, you certainly know how to please a lady, thank you.'

'For a terrorist, you certainly know how to please a man.'

'You are the only one I have ever pleased like that.' She smiled at him. It was a smile that JJ could never tire of. It contained warmth, love, tenderness and her outstanding beauty. 'And it's only because I love you,' she finished simply.

He reached across the table and took her hand. They held hands across the table, without speaking, for some minutes. Then, without saying anything, she turned his hand palm down and kissed the back of it and rubbed it against her cheek as she had only the day before, after he had shot Conrad. It was as if she was reaffirming her love for him.

He felt guilty about lying to her about the money he had made, but he knew she would not be able to comprehend someone getting that amount of money.

'Come on,' she said, 'I feel like a sleep in the sun after all that wine and food.' She pulled him to his feet. JJ left the waiter a huge tip which almost brought tears to his eyes. Francine scolded him for being extravagant and making such a shameless display of his capitalistic wealth.

They managed to find two unoccupied sun beds under a thatched sunshade. Within minutes they were both sleeping. A group of children playing some game known only to other children, which involves making the maximum amount of noise and chasing each other round and round, had woken them both. They must have been asleep for over two hours. They had one last walk down the beach and returned to the car for the slog back into Istanbul. They discussed the day in the car and agreed it had been a good day. Tomorrow it was back to work.

# Chapter Twenty Three

Abdul arrived punctually at six the following morning. As they got into the taksi, he commented that they both looked better than the last time he had seen them.

JJ said, 'We went to the Black Sea yesterday, had lunch and slept in the sun.'

'You're lucky, I had ten hours at the training camp and I still ache.'

Francine couldn't resist asking, 'Unarmed combat or aching backside from sitting all day?'

They all laughed. Abdul set of at his usual breakneck speed and asked, 'Did I tell you about my American fare from the airport to the Hilton?'

'Yes,' said JJ. Abdul took no notice of his reply, launching into the story again. He told them the story three more times on the journey, each time suitably embellished from the previous version.

When they arrived, JJ was impressed with the display that was before them. All of the men were standing to attention in lines, behind their respective lieutenant, all smartly turned out. As Francine and JJ got out of the taksi they all shouted as one, 'Good morning, sir.' He called out, 'Good morning,' in return.

Someone called out, 'Three cheers for the captain.'

They all cheered. JJ waved an acknowledgement, turned to Abdul and asked, 'So this took you ten hours to perfect?'

'Sure did, Captain Professor JJ, think it was worth it?'

'What did you tell them?'

'That I watched you put your gun at Conrad's head and blow his brains out and that Francine had shot Kemal, the dangerous police man. Many of our men have known him and have been tortured by him. That her superb shooting, without drawing her little revolver, had shot him between the eyes and that if they didn't smarten themselves up and show you the respect you deserve one of you would probably shoot one of them as an example.'

'Abdul that was a wicked thing to say, we would never do anything like that.'

'You know it, and so do I, but they don't.'

'Well, I must say it appears to have worked. Now I will talk to them. Get them sat down.'

'Men, we thank you for your welcome. Do you see the wonderful job that Ali did to my eye? Today I have no hangover.' Laughingly he carried on, 'I am going to give you all a chance to black the other one.' They all laughed with him, but doubted that anyone from their ranks, not even Ali, would try if the captain was without a hangover, for had they all not seen what he was like with a heavy head and Abdul had told them that he was capable of making a man kneel and put a pistol to his head and kill him. He was pleased that Abdul had not told them all that before pulling the trigger he had closed his eyes so he didn't have to watch what he was doing.

'After lunch, we shall again benefit from Francine's experience with the Uzi machine pistol. Then I will show you how to make an explosion to demolish a Bosporus bridge. Our explosives have arrived. Then we can all go home and look forward to doing it all again tomorrow and the next day, and by the time we get to THE day, all of you will be able to shoot like Francine and fight like Ali and I can expect a few more black eyes.' He made a mental note to agree an actual date, as he couldn't keep referring to THE day.

As the morning passed by with only a few of the men showing any spirit or determination to beat JJ, he called a break, left Abdul to get them sat and quiet them down. JJ mounted the platform and set into them, verbally calling them every foul name that his Turkish vocabulary allowed. 'What is wrong with you all? Are you all of cowards? You are certainly acting like a load of woman!'

'Captain, please may I say something?' Ali stood smartly to attention, waiting for JJ's permission to continue.

JJ nodded at him, 'Go ahead.'

'Well, sir, the men and I respect and like you, we do not want to fight with you.'

JJ fingered his black eye.

'I'm sorry, sir, I really just meant to hit you gently.'

'So did I, when I broke your nose.'

They both laughed. The men cheered.

'OK,' he said, 'I thank you, but I do need you to show some spirit. If I do not take part, but watch and give instruction? Would you prefer that?'

They all cheered again.

'Well, get on with it then,' he barked.

Leaving the platform, he was met by Abdul and Francine.

'The thing that Ali didn't tell you is that they all afraid of you, even Ali,' Francine said smugly. 'And it's all Abdul's fault for telling them those terrible things about you.'

'Don't be too harsh on Abdul, he meant well,' JJ defended. 'He also told them about how well you can shoot. I hope you don't have a similar problem with them this afternoon!'

'I'll be fine; we are not going to be dueling.'

The day wore on. Francine had been correct. If anything, the men had shown greater attention and were eager to learn how to shoot so well as to hit a man between the eyes. JJ took over in the late afternoon and announced, 'Good news! We have received our explosives. Now I can show you what it does.' He had in his hand a piece of Semtex, which he rolled into a ball about the size of a golf ball. He threw it to Ali, who caught it and as he did the watching men groaned and, as one, dived to the ground with their hands over their heads. Ali had broken into a sweat, the perspiration running down his face like tears. He was holding the plastic ball very gingerly with his fingertips.

'As you can see,' he continued, 'it doesn't go "bang" until it's told to.' He took a small piece from the ball and shaped it. Going to an old door that had been erected on the platform behind him, he squeezed the plastic explosive onto the door knob and inserted a small electronic detonator into it. He had in his hand a small black box which he waved in the air, and called to his audience. 'Who would like to be the first to test the Semtex and the detonators?' No-one moved. 'OK then, I'll choose a volunteer.' He looked slowly at them all in turn, seeing the fear on the faces of some. 'Ibrahim, come on, you can have the honor.'

Lieutenant Ali's number two in charge of transport lumbered onto the platform with a look of cockiness on his face. JJ handed him the transmitter that would activate the detonator. 'Stand about one meter from the door, slightly to the side, and press the button when I give the order.'

'Why to the side?' asked Ibrahim.

'When the door knob comes off it will come very fast and I'm sure you don't want to lose your manhood.'

He quickly moved away from the direct line of the impending flying door knob.

JJ shouted, 'Detonate now.'

Ibrahim didn't move a finger.

'What's wrong? I said, detonate.'

'We are too close.' The cockiness gone, replaced by fear.

'You are just in the correct place; now do as I tell you. Detonate now.'

This time, Ibrahim pressed the button. As predicted by JJ, the door knob flew across the platform, landing amongst the men who had crowded together. When it landed it was still warm but had lost its momentum over the ten meters it had travelled before running out of energy. As the smoke cleared from the door, JJ walked towards Ibrahim, who was still standing riveted to the spot with fear and trepidation. He had to prize the transmitter out of Ibrahim's fingers; and, going to the door, he called out to the assembled men, 'Come and see, not a mark on the door.'

They crowded around the door. Some patted Ibrahim on the back, commenting on how brave he had been to be so close and all exclaimed how wonderful it was to make such an explosion and only send the door knob across the platform without any damage to the door. Ibrahim was still standing motionless but his face had adopted a huge grin.

Abdul arrived at seven to take Francine and JJ home. Ibrahim was still in a state of mild shock. After he was able to move from the platform, he had started to shake and then had been violently sick. He was still trembling at the memory of the door knob flying past him and the violence of the explosion. JJ felt pleased he had chosen Ibrahim. It had demonstrated to everyone that he was probably not good enough for any form of actual combat. Being a truck driver was his forte, now he and the men knew it. He brightened visibly when JJ declared time to go home and almost ran to his big red truck.

Francine came out of the bathroom having had her shower. She was wearing the thick toweling bathrobe that JJ had bought for her.

'Thank you darling, it's wonderful, all fluffy and snuggly, like having a big towel around me.' JJ looked at her for a moment; unable to speak an idea was forming in his mind.

At last he spoke, 'Yes, it could work. If you would have your hair cut and dyed, and with the right make up you could pass for Elizabeth.'

Francine immediately responded, 'I don't want to look like your damn wife. I thought you loved me because I am so different, at least that's what you've told me before,' she shouted, as she stormed out of the room. JJ felt immediately guilty. They had agreed months ago not to say things which compared them with the other's husband/wife after Francine had thoughtlessly said something silly which had compared JJ in a bad light with her husband. JJ was still upset at the remark.

He went after her immediately. 'Darling, don't be mad. I have just had a wonderful idea to get over you not having a passport. We can make you look like my wife. Don't you see? If I could get her passport, I could get you out of the country with me? The authorities may still be onto us, we don't know who else was involved. We must keep it just between ourselves. We have seen how people that we thought we could trust turned out to be traitors.'

'It would never work!'

'If we don't try, we shall never know.'

Francine was very reluctant, but she agreed that next time JJ went back to England he would bring Elizabeth's passport back with him and they could then check if she could be made up to look like the photo in it.

JJ showered and they had an early night, both tired after the day and still somewhat troubled from the killings of the previous days they fell quickly into a troubled sleep. Francine woke JJ in the middle of the night.

'I've got an idea,' she declared. 'If I'm to look like you're damned wife, we still need a plan to get away. Why don't we try and make them think that we are going to get away on the Orient Express? If we set up a routine about a week or so before THE day; meeting at the station so if we disappear one day they will assume that we have gone to the station as usual! We could be in Greece in Conrad's Mercedes before they found out that we weren't on the train. We shall have to make a reservation and buy tickets though. Will you mind wasting all that money?'

'I think I may just be able to afford it.'

'It's OK, I forgive you for saying I look like your wife if you are going to waste all that money to help me.' They didn't get back to sleep again that night. They were still lying in each other's arms when the alarm clock announced that it was five o'clock and time to get ready for work.

Abdul was his usual cheery self as they drove out of Yesilcoy and onto the main highway. Turning to talk to them over his shoulder as he drove, he asked, 'What are you two going to do after we blow the bridges? It may be better to get out of Istanbul like me.'

JJ replied for both of them. 'It's a coincidence, but we were discussing it last evening, over dinner. We thought the same as you, get away from Istanbul, maybe somewhere around Bodrum, a lot of English are living there.'

'We couldn't agree if we should stay together or go separately,' Francine added.

Abdul, always eager for people to take his advice, was unable to stop himself from saying, 'I think much further south. Have you ever thought of Cyprus?'

They replied together. 'No.'

'Is that a good place?' JJ asked.

'It's a great place,' stated Abdul. 'Ideal for a holiday by the sea... I'm surprised you've not been.'

'I've never had time. What about you?' JJ replied, turning to Francine.

'No, never could afford to go there,' she answered.

'Think about it,' was Abdul's advice.

'We will,' they assured him.

JJ was wondering if Abdul knew about their little holiday on the Island and asked, 'Where are you going?'

'Sorry, JJ my boy, but those things are best kept to yourself, you never know who may find out.' He appeared to be concentrating on his driving; something he never normally bothered about. The discussion had taken nearly all of the journey time, for within ten minutes they pulled off the tar road onto the dirt one to take them the rest of the distance.

The routine was the same as previous days. Unarmed combat, with JJ almost being a spectator, firearms training, explosive training. When Francine took over for the work with the Uzi, she said, 'It will be better when the new Uzis and the ammunition arrive. I can do only so much with one gun and almost no ammunition.'

'They should be here hopefully within the next week,' JJ replied.

On their way home, JJ got Abdul to take them via Conrad's house for they needed to tell Ayşe that he was dead.

# Chapter Twenty Four

'Ayşe, we have some very bad news.'

'Is it about Conrad?'

'Let me tell her, Francine,' JJ Interrupted.

'Yes, it's about Conrad. I'm afraid he's dead.'

'That's not bad news. If he was coming home tonight, now, that would be bad news.'

'I don't understand,' Francine said.

'He's a pig, a brute. When he touched me, he felt like a clammy dead fish. I'm not sorry he's dead. When he went out I used to pray that he wouldn't come back. He often stayed out all night and when he didn't come home from work last night I assumed that it was another all night drinking party with one of his cronies. Do you know what happened to him?'

'Yes, I shot him. He had been selling information about us to the police. You were there on that first day when I warned everyone what would happen if anyone betrayed us. I am not sorry for doing it but, if it makes it any easier, I didn't enjoy it.'

'I'm OK, as I said, I'm not sorry he's dead but it will take some time to adjust to the thought that I'm never going to have him touch me again. He really was an animal and very violent. I was never allowed to say anything or complain about his behavior, if I did, he would just lash out with anything that came to hand. If you look at my back you can still see the bruises from the last time.'

'I'm your sister, why didn't you tell me?'

'Remember what our mother used to tell us? You are married for life.'

'I never told you about Conrad either. If he managed to find me alone at the school, or here, he used to try grabbing at me and touching me. He said if I ever told you he would throw me out and I would have nowhere to live and no job. He never actually managed to do anything to me but it was horrible!' Francine and Ayşe hugged, crying on each other's shoulders.

'I'm beginning to think that being shot was too good for him. I now wish I'd let you at him with that knife.'

'This is what it really means to be a Turkish woman. I'm glad you stopped me from using my knife. I would have hated myself afterwards, not because it would have been Conrad, but because of actually doing something like that. You know what I was like after I shot Kemal!'

'When did you do that?' Ayşe asked. Francine brought her quickly up to date on the events of the past two days, particularly the bits about Abdul and Conrad.

'Didn't you know that Kemal was a friend of Conrad's? They used to go out drinking together a lot. I didn't like him either; he was always staring at me. There was another man, someone in the army, I don't know his name, Conrad always referred to him as "The General".'

'Maybe there is still someone out there after all. We had hoped the killing would stop now. Let's wait and see if anything happens next, we've come too far to stop now,' JJ said, very subdued at the prospect of more killings.

Francine persuaded Ayşe to let her stay with her overnight. She did not want to leave her alone after the news she had just received, even if she was declaring she was pleased to hear that her husband was dead. Before he left them together, he took Francine to one side and quietly asked her to find out what Ayşe's plans were for the school, as the arms were due soon. JJ was pleased that he had had confirmation from the bank and the guys in Prague that Conrad had paid the outstanding money for the explosives and arms.

'Don't worry, darling, I will be with you tomorrow night. It's only one night and we can always make up for one lost night,' she said as she kissed him goodbye before she rejoined Ayşe.

'If you have any trouble, over anything at all, phone me

straight away. Have you still got your revolver? Goodnight.'

'Don't fuss so much. Yes, I have it. Goodnight, I will see you tomorrow.'

Abdul drove JJ to Yesilcoy and on the way he questioned Abdul about other people Conrad met and where he used to take him. Abdul was not able to come up with any new names or places that JJ had not been to. It appeared that JJ knew all of Conrad's friends, people he met on a regular basis but as neither he or Abdul had ever heard of Kemal before, as a friend of Conrad's, he could not rule out there were others in the army or police that neither of them knew. JJ didn't mention anything about Ayşe's reference to "The General". He didn't know why, but decided it wiser not to discuss him with Abdul yet.

JJ dined alone that evening on pizza and beer. He and the waiters had started to become friendly. They joked with him about the lack of female company. Had he sold her for many camels? He joined in with the banter, being relieved to have someone to talk to. He went immediately on the defensive when one of the waiters made reference to Francine's friend, Ishmael, who owned a restaurant on the Asian side of the Bosporus. He had asked if JJ also knew him and did he see him very often? An innocent enough remark, made so soon after the shootings of Kemal and Conrad, it had made JJ immediately suspicious of the man, someone else to be careful of, he thought. As he drained his glass, it was immediately refilled by the waiter with the all the questions. He had been hovering. As he sipped his fresh cold drink, he pondered on if that waiter had hovered when he had been in the restaurant with Francine. Had he overheard their conversations? Was he just interested in his customers? Was he spying for the police? Now he had two more people to worry about – The General and the waiter!

He didn't have long to wait. The restaurant had emptied, leaving JJ sitting alone in the window table. The waiter came over to his table with another bottle of beer, which he offered to JJ,

'Professor JJ, would you like more beer?'

'No more, thank you.' He shook his head as he replied.

'My name is Ali. Can I talk with you?'

'Carry on.'

'No not here. Can I come to your house later?'

'What's it about?' asked JJ, getting alarmed.

'I can't talk here. Can I come to your house later please?'

'OK, I will give you five minutes.' He paid his bill and walked home, deep in thought about his impending meeting with Ali.

Ali's knock came on his back door after about ten minutes. JJ opened the door and let Ali into the house. He appeared very calm and relaxed.

'Thank you for letting me come to your house. I needed to talk in private.'

'Tell me what you want then.'

'I know that Ishmael and some of his friends are involved in some movement to overthrow the government and I would like to join them.'

'Why ask me?' JJ queried.

'Your friend Madam Francine and her husband are good friends of Ishmael so I hoped that you would know what they are doing and let me be involved.'

'How dare you come here and accuse me and a good friend of being involved in some plot to overthrow the government? I know nothing about it. Now, get out before I hit you. I should call the police and report you. If I find out that you have said anything about this to anyone, I will report you to the police.'

'You won't call the police. I know you and that blonde are playing house. It's very wrong of you, with her husband in prison.' JJ cut off any further comment from Ali by punching him in the mouth then, grabbing him by the scruff of the neck, pushed him to the front door, opened it with his free hand and with a resounding kick, sent Ali head first towards the road, shouting after him,

'Don't forget, if I hear one word of this from anyone I will report you to the police.'

Ali couldn't speak; he was too busy pulling broken teeth from his lips.

JJ slammed the door as he re-entered his house. His knuckles were bleeding from the contact with Ali's teeth. Going to the bathroom, he ran cold water over his hand as he reached for the first-aid box. He applied a liberal dose of iodine straight from the bottle, to the cuts which made them sting. He stood shaking his hand and swearing to himself, trying to relieve the effects of the iodine, mopped off the excess blood and applied a large sticking plaster. Still felling very annoyed with himself for hitting Ali without getting any real information from him first, he poured himself a very large whisky, which he took to the terrace overlooking the rear garden. He sat sipping the amber liquid, thinking about what would happen next. The clamorous ringing of the telephone woke him from his deliberations.

'Hello, JJ, it's me. We have just been for a walk in the park and we were followed by two men,' Francine reported breathlessly. 'They are hanging about outside in the road.'

'Listen, Francine, I have just had a visit from one of the waiters from the pizza restaurant and he said he knew all about us and wanted to join the team. When I said I didn't know what he was talking about, he started on about you and I playing house etc. So I punched him. I think you should phone the police and make a complaint about those men following you and let's see what happens next. Apart from that, how's it going?'

'OK. Ayşe is fine. I'll phone them now and report back later. Love you.'

'Love you too. Bye.'

JJ showered, his hand still sore from Ali's teeth. He was still walking around the house wearing a towel around his waist when the phone rang again.

'JJ, I phoned the police as you said. They have just been and taken the two men away in a van. There was a bit of a fight before the police got them into the van. It looked genuine.'

'OK. Phone them again in the morning and ask what is happening to the two men. Have you had chance to talk to Ayşe about the school and the arms?'

'No, I haven't, not yet. I will later.'

'Thank you. Goodnight, I'm going to bed now.'

'Goodnight.'

JJ slept badly with his thoughts, killing Conrad, punching the waiter and missing the closeness of Francine. He woke before daylight and, being unable to sleep again for the thoughts that were milling around in his mind; he got out of bed and headed for the bathroom. Stepping into the shower turned onto cold, he soon started to think with a clearer head.

'Good morning, JJ darling. I've good news all round. Ayşe is going to carry on running the school so we get our arms without any more complications. I've spoken to the police. They want Ayşe and me to go and make an official complaint about those two men this morning. As soon as we have been to the police station they have promised to have them in court.' She sounded a little flustered, as she mumbled into the phone. 'We are going now.'

'Don't let them trick you into saying anything you don't intend. Take care and phone me again as soon as you get back. Bye.'

'Bye, JJ. I wish you were here.'

The phone clicked loudly in his ear as she hung up. It sounded like a door slamming. He was worried about her; she had never displayed nervousness before, always being very optimistic, calm and practical. He pondered on her attitude during their brief conversation, as he replaced the receiver. What was happening? Walking to the kitchen, he poured himself a large whisky which, he took back into the lounge. The phone rang as he sat down. It startled him to such an extent that he spilled his drink.

'Hello, JJ.'

'Elizabeth! This is a surprise.'

'A nice one I hope?' She sounded a little terse, as she continued, 'I thought that you must have forgotten me. You didn't phone last week.'

She sounded close to tears, Elizabeth's answer to all things where he was concerned, just turn on the tears and make JJ feel guilty. He tried to avert the impending session of incriminations by quickly saying, 'I'm so sorry but I was not feeling very well. I am better now. I was going to phone you tonight.'

'What was wrong?'

He thought he caught a trace of concern in her voice. 'Flu, I think. My head was really painful. All my body ached.'

'That's OK so long as you are OK now. You're too old to be running around like you do. You should take more rest. I don't suppose it stopped you having a drink did it?' The mother hen syndrome had replaced the tears, at least for a while. For the next few minutes she continued to lecture him about looking after himself; to rest more and drink less. Finally coming to what JJ surmised the real reason for her call, 'Have you got a date yet for when you will have finished playing around out there?'

'Not yet, but it will definitely be less than eight weeks.'

'Please let me know as soon as possible,' she retorted frostily. 'I thought you said when you were home that you were finishing soon.'

He couldn't be bothered to argue with her, his mind still very much concerned with Francine and the problems facing the safety of the whole venture as well as the physical danger to both Francine and himself. Trying to get her off the phone without being rude was going to be difficult.

'Elizabeth, I will come home for a couple days in a few weeks' time, then we can have a chat about our future, maybe book a holiday for when I finish. I'm hoping for a bonus.'

'OK, but do not make it too long.'

'No, it won't be. Bye.'

'Bye. Love you.' She sounded close to tears again.

'Love you. Please don't worry.'

For the second time in less than an hour, the phone being hung up sounded very loud. He was halfway to the kitchen to replenish his spilled drink when he stopped with a feeling of guilt. Elizabeth was right, he did drink too much. In place of another whisky he poured himself a large glass of milk.

The phone rang again before he had returned to the lounge. Assuming that Elizabeth had forgotten something, he lifted the receiver and asked, 'Hello, what did you forget?'

Francine sounded perplexed. 'No nothing. I don't think I have anyway.'

'You didn't tell me you missed me last night,' JJ replied quickly. 'I thought you had phoned back to tell me.'

'You told me to phone when we got back home after the police station, didn't you? We have to go back at two this afternoon. Those two men are going to be in court and we have to give evidence against them. It will be awful standing there, saying these men have been following us and loitering outside Ayşe's house.'

'That is very quick. Are the courts not very busy?'

'They treat matters like this very seriously in Turkey. We are married women. I just hope they don't look us up on the police computer. If they find out about me they won't bother prosecuting the men and I shall get into trouble for wasting their time. Once you've been in prison you don't have many rights left. I need a hug!'

'Will you be able to come over to Yesilcoy after court this afternoon?'

'I'll try. I will phone you this afternoon, when I know the verdict.'

'OK darling. Don't worry, good luck.'

'Bye, JJ. I do love you.'

'Bye. Love you too.'

Forgetting his lecture from Elizabeth, he poured himself a very large whisky. The sun had broken through the summer storm clouds, flooding the patio outside in brilliant sunshine. He took his drink into the garden and sat drinking and thinking and worrying. After his phone call with Elizabeth, he was concerned about his future. Not his safety, but his future with Francine. How could he achieve a life with her?

The phone woke him from his thoughts yet again. This time it was Abdul. He had heard that Francine and Ayşe were pressing charges against two men. JJ told him the story of how they had both been followed. Abdul sounded sympathetic, then, to JJ's surprise asked, 'Can you get Francine to drop the charges? I know those men. They work taksi's with me. They are good men.'

'They sound bad men to me. Are you sure they are not spies?'

'I'm sure, Captain Professor JJ, they both good men. Please will you speak to Francine?'

'I will speak to her, but I make no promises. Bye for now.' He put the phone down before Abdul could say anything else.

He returned to the garden, taking with him the near empty whisky bottle. He sat again and poured the contents of the bottle into his glass. Drinking and thinking was all he seemed to be doing today. Now he had another mystery to solve. How had Abdul heard about those men and what was his real connection with them? He would have to talk to Francine but he resolved not to ask her to drop the charges. Abdul's phone call and explanation seemed too pat.

# Chapter Twenty Five

It was almost six when Francine called again.

'They got twelve months each. The judge was a friend of our mother. The defense attorney wanted to introduce evidence about Ayşe and me. He said that he had proof that we did not deserve to be protected from men, that his clients needed protection from women like us. The judge was furious and would not let him speak about us. He was really very sweet. He knows about me and my husband and I don't think he liked the defense attorney.'

'That's fantastic news. How soon can you be in Yesilcoy?'

'I'll be there before eight.'

'OK. I'll get some food in. We need to talk in private.'

'Get some prawns and crab please, and salad stuff. I'll make dinner when I get there. Love you. Bye for now.'

'Love you too, bye.'

JJ wasted no time. He walked briskly to the shops where he bought the fish requested by Francine, and salad, a loaf of bread, still hot from the oven from the bakers. Stopping at the supermarket, he selected a bottle of whisky and two bottles of champagne. Tonight they had something to celebrate and they had some serious decisions to make. He was whistling softly as he poured the dressing over the salad, tossed it lightly and decorated it with crab claws and prawns. Covering his culinary effort with plastic film, he placed it into the refrigerator to keep fresh, poured himself another large glass of whisky and walked happily into the garden looking forward to a pleasant evening and, he hoped, an early night to bed with Francine.

She disturbed his thoughts as she let herself into the garden by the side gate. Letting it slam shut behind her made JJ jump back to the present from his thoughts of the future.

'Hi,' he shouted to her, for it was obvious she hadn't noticed him sitting in the garden, 'you got here before time.'

'Would you like me to go again?' she asked, smiling at him. For she knew that his answer would be a resounding, no!

'Shall we sit out here and have a drink? I've made dinner. It's in the fridge with the wine.'

She seemed as if she was about to cry. 'JJ, why did you make dinner; don't you like the way I prepare your food?'

'Of course I do, I wanted to do something nice for you for once.'

'You always do nice things for me.'

'Well you weren't here last night. I'm getting old; my memory is not as good as it used to be.'

'OK, I forgive you just this once, but you must never do it again. Do you understand me?'

JJ could see that she was serious and he nodded his agreement.

'Now please would you get your girl a drink before she dies of thirst?'

JJ retreated to the house and reappeared in a few minutes with two glasses of bubbling champagne. He handed her one and said, 'I now propose a toast. To the sweet old judge, may God bless him for his wisdom and for him being a friend of your mothers.'

They sipped their wine in appreciative silence.

Francine was the first to speak. 'Tell me what's so secret that we had to eat at the house?'

He looked at her and smiled. 'Well, firstly you will not let me kiss you in public or touch you, both of which I'm going to do a lot of tonight. Secondly, we have to talk about your father-in-law.' He told her of the phone call from Abdul.

'OK. A kiss first,' she said.

Having to use most of her strength, she pushed JJ away and, breathing heavily, she gasped, 'I said a kiss, this bench is too hard to make love on, please wait till later.'

JJ reluctantly agreed, for it was obvious that Francine had

made her mind up and it was no use hoping she would change it, he knew her too well. 'Let's go in and eat then,' he declared. Taking her hand he pulled her to her feet. 'You're getting heavy.'

'It's all the lunches and dinners we have.'

As she dabbed her mouth with a napkin, she sighed with pleasure. 'If I wasn't such a good little Turkish girl I would let you make all my food. That was lovely.'

'If you were a good little Turkish girl I probably wouldn't want too. Now we must talk about Abdul.'

She agreed reluctantly. 'He always spoils things.'

'Did you learn anything about those men in court today?'

She shook her head so vigorously that her mane of blonde hair flew over her face, covering it like a veil. Pulling the hair from her eyes and mouth she said a simple, 'No.'

'They must have more of a connection than just being on the taksi's with Abdul. Have you ever seen them before?'

'I don't think so.'

'Do you think there is any way we could get a photo of them?'

'Yes, that's easy, we buy a newspaper in the morning, there was a cameraman at court he will have taken pictures of them.'

'That was lucky, if we show them around someone may know who they are. We need to know what the connection is with Abdul.'

They were luckier than they expected. The newspaperman had done an excellent job, the paper contained not only color pictures of the two men but an article giving their name and brief life history. The most significant thing was that they had only recently left the army and that they were still unemployed. There was no reference to the identity of the girls that had brought the charges. As they pored over the paper, drinking coffee and eating croissants, Abdul drew up outside.

Usually he would wait for them to come out. Today was different. He banged hard on the door. As JJ opened it, he pushed his way in. It was obvious that he was in a foul mood, for without even the usual pleasantries he shouted at JJ, 'I thought you said you would get this stupid girl to drop the charges against my friends?'

'I said I would try. We didn't speak after you phoned until the trial was over and I only said I would try.'

'You are both a big disappointment to me.' He turned to Francine, 'Why did you have to phone the police? Those poor men, they are ruined now.'

'What about me and my sister shouldn't we be protected from men that follow us? We didn't know if they were going to attack us, so we had to do something. Anyway why are you so upset about them? I would have thought that you would have been more concerned for the safety of your son's wife.'

Abdul was calming down, he had obviously decided he wasn't going to get anywhere by complaining, his friends were already in prison. 'Well, let's go, shall we? Otherwise it will be lunchtime before we get there.'

It was one of the quietest drives to the training camp they had had. Abdul was still in a sullen mood, JJ and Francine both sitting thinking about Abdul and what his real connection was with the two ex-soldiers.

The day was predictably arduous, long and hot. By the time they packed in the evening, Abdul had cheered up considerably, even joking with Ali about his broken nose that was still displaying signs of bruising. He even managed a comment to JJ on how well he thought the day had gone, considering. At least it was an improvement on that morning's open hostility.

Driving back into Istanbul, they encountered a police road block. Not an unusual thing, but on this occasion Abdul was particularly agitated. When it was their turn to have their documents inspected, he didn't have his usual interchange with the duty officers. He was very subservient and made none of his usual wise cracks. Not only did they check all of their identity documents but also Abdul's taksi documents. The police, appearing satisfied, waved them through the check point. Abdul, evidently relieved, was starting to make his jokes about police time wasting – when they should be out catching criminals instead of delaying innocent motorists.

Abdul's strange behavior was another thing for JJ to add to his growing list of things to worry about.

That evening Francine and JJ went to the pizza restaurant for dinner. The waiter that JJ had punched in the mouth was not there. Much to their relief, their usual waiter was on duty and told them, with some relish, that the other waiter had been fired for apparently fighting. JJ said nothing. They had taken with them the morning newspaper. JJ showed it to the waiter and asked him if he had seen the men in the photograph? He shook his head and called Mustapha, the restaurant manager, over. This time the jackpot, he had seen them, they were friends of the waiter he had just fired. He had recommended them to Mustapha, knowing that he was desperately looking for staff. The manager hadn't liked either of them and had refused to hire them.

So a link was starting to emerge. Two friends of Abdul and of JJ's waiter, following Ayşe and Francine and asking questions about Ishmael and his restaurant, who is a friend of Francine and her husband and supposedly also of Abdul's. The waiter would have had no problems joining the anarchist group, having two friends who were friends of Abdul. It was just possible that the waiter didn't know Abdul, but JJ considered it unlikely.

What was Abdul up to?

Later, when Francine and JJ discussed the evening's revelation, Francine laughingly said, 'I've still got my knife. You should have let me skin him when I wanted to.'

'Now, don't start that again, you know you couldn't before, that was different,' JJ retorted a little angrily. He didn't like to think of her as someone capable of such an act.

'I was only joking. You know I couldn't do it now. I think I could have that day, I was a bit unhinged at the time.'

'It's not nice to even joke about it, darling.'

Francine went silent; the events of the day when she had shot Kemal flashed though her mind. She shuddered at the memory.

'I'm sorry JJ; but what are we going to do?'

'I don't know; we must make a plan to trap him.'

'How are we going to do that?'

'Let's sleep on it shall we?'

'OK darling, I love it when you make such masterly decisions.'

The following morning brought with it a midsummer rain storm of such intensity that only the brave or stupid ventured out onto the roads. One of those was Abdul, who arrived only five minutes later than usual to collect them

# Chapter Twenty Six

Abdul was back to his old self – very cheerful and complaining as usual about the traffic congestion and how all the taksi's added to the problem. He was overly polite to Francine. JJ was once again referred to as "my son". He made no fuss when Francine asked if they could stop off for bread and cheese as they had had no breakfast. To be honest, they had both overslept. The combination of an early night and two bottles of champagne were to blame.

None of them made any reference to the previous day's argument over Abdul's friends. In spite of getting little sleep they hadn't spoken further about how to try and trap Abdul. Their night had been filled with lovemaking and any discussion that had taken place was only that which takes place between lovers. They ate the bread and cheese as if they hadn't eaten for a week. Abdul joined them in their breakfast feast; he, however couldn't resist complaining about the lack of coffee. A contented Francine linked her arm through JJ's and was soon fast asleep, her head on his shoulder. JJ was also feeling very content. He and Francine had just spent a wonderful night together and he had just had a satisfying breakfast and now she was snuggled up against him. He sighed, a very self-satisfied sigh.

Abdul's complaints about the traffic on the bridge roused him and brought him back to the present. He didn't move; although his left leg was stiff; for fear of disturbing Francine. She was in a deep sleep and making those little mewing noises of someone in a perfectly happy sleep.

'Don't worry, Abdul, the bridges won't be here much longer.'

Another moan from Abdul about lost income woke Francine. She reached up and pulled JJ's head down towards her face and kissed him. She let him go and mumbled, 'I love you,' as she went back to sleep. Abdul made no comment.

JJ had to shake her to wake her, for when they arrived at the training camp she was still in a deep sleep. They spent the day instructing the men on the deployment of the explosives, a very time-consuming exercise with them all. JJ had decided that they all should have a rudimentary knowledge of the most critical part of the plan – the actual planting of the explosives. He would select maybe ten men to actually carry out the job with him. There were already a few who showed a natural attribute for it. He was pleased that the giant Lieutenant Ali was one of those. With his help, JJ was sure that he would have no problems getting the job done. He would let Ali lead the men on the raid to plant the explosives on one of the bridges while he would lead the assault on the other bridge.

Over the next few days, those with the natural talent for explosives became more confident handling and placing it in position; molding it into shape as they placed it in the small scale mock-up of the bridge that JJ had built for them to practice on.

How to trap Abdul was the main thought on the minds of both JJ and Francine. When they had a spare moment away from the others they would discuss the problem. Abdul, on the other hand, was proving to be a very useful member of the team, always ready with a 'Well done,' and other words of praise or a practical comment like, 'I know where I can get backpacks to carry the explosives in.' It was the small items that JJ's planning had overlooked, not due to carelessness but having to try and think of everything with no-one to discuss the finer points with. He couldn't talk to Francine about it; she assumed he was in complete control of his thoughts as well as his body and actions. She was the devoted wife, good for the ego but bad for the practical side of a terrorist raid. Was this why her husband had been captured because she couldn't see the errors she was making in her planning, assuming he was godlike in his abilities and couldn't be harmed? Abdul now couldn't be trusted. Conrad was no longer with them. He decided to try talking to Lieutenant

Ali, but needed not to show a weakness to one of his troops; to them all he must show a complete picture of self-reliance and control. He discussed how to arrange a meeting between him and Ali with Francine. She immediately suggested that she would invite Ali and his wife, Karli, for dinner one evening as soon as possible, declaring that it was ages since she had had chance to gossip with a dancing friend.

Ali agreed readily that he and Karli would love to come to dinner – this was without consulting her. As the following day was Saturday, they agreed that dinner would be in Yesilcoy at eight. JJ managed to suppress a groan – dinner in the middle of the night did not agree with his body but as the other three naturally dined much later, he didn't complain. Francine was in a buoyant mood, looking forward to entertaining in JJ's house. She looked at him and said, 'It's really just like being married, having friends for dinner. We shall have to prepare a very special meal and as the party is tomorrow you may help but I'm in charge of the menu and the preparation, do you understand?' JJ nodded his agreement. Francine hurried away to start preparing the menu. *Now,* she mused, *what shall we start with? A meze, of course!*

The choice of items that the meze would consist of was the next problem. Should it be an all fish or meat and fish? She decided on fish with various vegetable dishes. It took her two hours to complete her menu. Taking it with her, she rushed over to the area that JJ was using for his explosives training, eager to seek his approval. As she entered the sandbagged area, a violent explosion took place, the blast of which sent her spinning to the ground, knocking her head on a rock as she fell. She screamed out, but no-one could hear her, they were all rubbing their ears trying to shut out the ringing that the blast had left them with. Ali was the first to spot Francine lying on the ground and, pulling at JJ's arm, pointed to her. They both rushed across the fifty meters to where she lay. JJ reached her first and flung himself onto the ground beside her. He lifted her gently by the shoulders, allowing her head to lie on his lap. Ali was standing looking down at them and produced a water bottle, which he offered to JJ. 'See if you can get her to sip this.'

As he lifted the bottle to her lips he realized that the front of his trousers was stained bright red and the patch of blood was spreading as he looked down. He managed to get a little water in her mouth, which caused her to cough and lift her head. JJ called out for the medical kit and, as Ali passed it to him; already opened it in readiness for JJ's searching hand as he tried to find cotton wool. Grabbing a large wad of it, he soaked it in water and gently bathed the back of Francine's head. Francine was now fully conscious and cried out a little as his ministrations increased the pain in her head. Looking up, she smiled at him and said, 'Thank you.'

'Thank goodness you're all right. I'm sorry, that was a demonstration of what to expect if you use more Semtex than necessary. You don't blow the knob off the door, you blow up the door compete with knob. Nothing was left.' He wanted to kiss her but knew that she would be very upset if he did in front of half their little army. Instead, he helped her to a sitting position in order to examine her cut head. He declared, 'You have a gash about the size of a walnut and it's swelling up. How do you feel?'

'Bit of a headache, but I think I'll survive. Any painkillers in that bag?'

JJ gave her two, and held the water bottle for her she swallowed her tablets and drank most of the water that was left in the bottle. She smiled up at him again saying, 'Let me stay like this for a couple of minutes. I'll be fine.' She closed her eyes and promptly went to sleep. She cried out as she woke some fifteen minutes later and put her hand to her head and tentatively prodded her wound, which had stopped bleeding.

'I don't know about the size of a walnut, more like a tennis ball. Help me up please.'

JJ, and Ali, who was standing by his side looking very concerned, helped her to her feet. She shook her hands free from JJ's protective grasp and promptly fell backwards into Ali's arms.

'Sorry,' she said looking up, 'just a bit dizzy.'

Ali picked her up in his arms and carried her to Abdul's taksi. Abdul was nowhere to be seen. Together, Ali and JJ got her onto the back seat where they made her as comfortable as they could.

'Shouldn't you take her to hospital?' Ali asked concern in his voice.

'Let's see how she is in half an hour. I know that she would hate to be at the hospital.'

At that moment Abdul reappeared. 'I was about a kilometer away and heard the explosion. I thought I would go and see if I could shoot some rabbits. There was nothing for me to do here.'

'What, without a gun?' JJ asked, looking at him.

'I must have dropped it hurrying back to see what the noise was,' Abdul hastily replied.

All JJ could think was, another nail in your coffin, Abdul!

'JJ,' Francine called out.

To his relief, when he got to her she was sitting up with a hand on the lump on her head.

'Thank you for looking after me. I am feeling much better now.'

# Chapter Twenty Seven

Francine took the following day off. She was still complaining about a headache. JJ had tried insisting that she went to hospital for a check-up, but she would not listen to his pleading.

'You go with Abdul and I'll get dinner organized for tonight.' she said, dismissing it lightly. 'I'll phone Karli and get her to come over this afternoon. You get away early this evening and don't forget to bring Ali home with you. Now go, before I change my mind and go back to bed.'

JJ couldn't resist saying, 'In that case I had better stay at home and look after you.' She pointed at the door and ordered him out. He kissed her briefly on his way out.

Abdul was very talkative on their journey to the training camp as they discussed possible dates for the explosions and agreed the tenth of next month, as it would be a moonless night. JJ realized that it was only twenty-two days away and he needed to visit England to borrow his wife's passport and set up their escape plans. He would have to go within the next week or he would not have time to fit everything in. Another row with his wife Elizabeth and probably with Francine as well – he wished they both understood him a little better. He was so preoccupied with his thoughts that he almost missed Abdul's next comment about his relationship with Francine.

'I was very angry with you both when I first realized that you were having an affair. Then I began to understand that you both needed the affection and support of the other to carry out what we planned. The killing of Kemal and Conrad made me see this clearly and if we are going to succeed with the main plan of blowing up the bridges, hopefully without the loss of life; well, civilians anyway, you will need each other. I only hope that you don't hurt each other when this is all over and you leave the country for good. Francine will be very lonely. You have your wife to go back to. You will be OK.'

'Abdul, I don't know what to say. You and I have become friends and she is married to your son. I didn't mean it to happen,' he continued lamely. 'It just did. Neither of us expected it.'

'Don't worry JJ, my boy, what's done is done, just don't expect it to continue. You do know she doesn't have a passport, so can't leave the country and you will not be safe in Istanbul in twenty-two days' time.'

JJ didn't answer at once, he was once again thinking of the future, of life with Francine in England, where would they live. How was Elizabeth going to take it? She was bound to make a big drama out of it. He was also wondering if they were correct in their assumptions that Abdul was a traitor or just doing and saying all the wrong things. He genuinely liked him and hoped he wasn't going to have to kill him.

'Don't worry, Abdul, I will not be around after the bridges go up. I'll be long gone.'

That appeared to make Abdul even happier and he started to sing Francine's signature tune. 'My son wrote this tune for his wife as a wedding present. Did you know that?'

'No.' JJ wondered why Francine had not told him the whole truth about the tune. Oh hell, life is just getting too complicated, he thought, and closed his eyes. Abdul had to wake him when they got to the training camp.

The day was hard. JJ was not in the mood for unarmed combat, he was too preoccupied with his thoughts from the morning's taksi ride. He let one of his troops get the better of him in one bout, knocking him to the floor, and took it out on the poor chap that was next, breaking his arm unnecessarily. He felt very bad about it and insisted that Abdul take the man to hospital at once.

Abdul reappeared after about two hours. He reported to JJ, 'Not a very bad break, they just put it in a plaster cast.'

'Thank goodness for that. Let's call it a day. I've had enough for today. Call all the men together; I want to talk to them.'

When they were all standing before him, he mounted the stage to their applause and raised his hands for quiet. 'Men,' he shouted, 'we have a date for our operation – it is to be the tenth of next month and, as a token of my respect for you all, I am declaring that tomorrow will be a holiday. You have all done very well and I shall expect to see you all on Monday morning without hangovers. Have a good rest and goodnight.'

They cheered him as he left the stage. He felt a little happier as he and Ali got into Abdul's taksi for the journey home.

By the time they arrived at Yesilcoy he was feeling more relaxed. He had insisted that Abdul take them via the house of the man whose arm he had broken. The man and his wife treated them like royalty, insisting that he should take tea with them, only to have that changed when Abdul came in carrying a case of raki that JJ had had him stop and buy for the man as a peace offering. JJ forced down two glasses of the white cloudy liquid, trying not to show his dislike of it. Shouting farewells to each other as they left the injured man and his wife, JJ, Ali and Abdul resumed their journey. Abdul commented that the man's arm would now be less painful because of JJ's visit.

JJ had decided to tell Francine about Abdul's conversation with him in the taksi that morning but not to mention her signature tune being a wedding present, he thought that she deserved one little secret.

When he opened the door to let Ali and himself in, he could hear laughter coming from the kitchen. Obviously Karli had arrived and she and Francine were catching up on old times. Francine rushed to greet them, demurely shaking hands with Ali then threw her arms around JJ and kissed him. He was shaken by her open display of passion in front of others, 'I hope you don't mind,' she blurted, 'but I've told Karli about us.'

Karli was standing in the kitchen doorway with a glass of

champagne in her hand, smiling. She lifted her glass in a salute, 'To you, Captain JJ. Thank you for making my friend so happy.'

Ali, unable to remain quiet, grabbed JJ's hand and stated, 'I don't know the full story, but if Karli approves, so do I.'

JJ, pulling himself together from the shock, turned to Francine and demanded, 'Why haven't you got champagne for Ali and me?'

'It's waiting in the kitchen.'

'Well, cheers to you all.' They all raised their glasses to the toast.

'By the way, Francine, Abdul also knows about us. We spoke about it this morning in the taksi,' JJ announced. 'He seemed OK about it – he still called me his son.'

'Well, let's sit down and enjoy this champagne. Dinner will be twenty minutes yet.' Francine was obviously a little shaken by JJ's news.

The meal was a great success, Francine the perfect hostess, enjoying her role of JJ's wife. She, with the help of Karli, cleared the dining table leaving only Ali and JJ's glasses, together with the remnants of a bottle of wine. Karli called from the kitchen, 'Coffee will be ready in 15 minutes.'

They carried both the coffee and French cognac into the lounge and set them down on a small table. JJ smiled at the picture as the two women poured out the drinks for their respective husbands, the way they appeared to glide around the room. First the coffee, then the brandy, stopping only to enquire if they needed another cushion behind their backs, and then kneeling on the floor beside to hold the offered cup and glass, not touching their own coffee until her husband was leaning back with a full glass of brandy. JJ sighed, smiled and looking across at Francine, said, 'Thank you very much you make me a very happy and contented man. Unfortunately we need to talk about Abdul and what, if anything, we are going to do about him.'

Francine said, 'Tell us everything you know about him. Karli wants to be part of it as well. I told her this afternoon what little I know.'

'There is not much to tell, it's more of a feeling but I'll tell you what I know. Firstly, how did the two army men find out about the first meeting and how convenient was it that they had their identity papers with them? Secondly, he told Kemal that Francine and I were going over to Kadikoy, that day. He admitted that, blaming everything on Conrad.'

'But Conrad admitted it,' interrupted Francine.

JJ frowned at the interruption and continued, 'The waiter who tried to get me to help him join our group, who had the two friends that he had tried to get jobs for at the Pizza restaurant were the same two men who followed Francine and Ayşe and were friends of Abdul. The other day at the training camp when Francine hurt her head because of the explosion, Abdul claimed to have been out of camp shooting rabbits but didn't have a gun. Ayşe said that Conrad referred to someone as The General – someone who has an army connection otherwise why were the first two spies army and not police! That's all the facts that I know but as regards the feeling he always seems to be there at the right moment; always say's things as if he knows them to be fact; when he was talking about holidaying in Cyprus the other day I would swear he knew we had been there. How could he know I can't think? Well, anyone anything to add?'

'Well,' Francine said, 'he was the first to suggest that we should recruit a mercenary. Sorry JJ, that wasn't meant as a dig at you.'

JJ interrupted her at that point saying,

'Conrad admitted that Kemal had paid him to arrange that.'

Oh yes sorry but if we go back to when my husband was arrested, he blames me for it but knows that he agreed to the plan. The only thing that was different was that my husband went, not me. Does anyone want more coffee or brandy?'

The discussion about Abdul ceased while cups and glasses were replenished.

Once more able to lean back with full cups and glasses, they became quiet and thoughtful, almost morose. No-one wanted to be the first to say, 'Do we have to kill him?'

JJ once more took charge of the conversation. 'Well, I personally like him but I don't trust him. I vote a bullet.'

Francine spoke next, 'I have never liked him. He is my husband's father and I agree with JJ, I don't trust him either. My vote is a bullet as well!'

Ali stood and walked to the window, looking into the darkness across over the road and railway to the sea beyond, little points of light sparkled and bobbed as the crew of the small boats searched for fish. 'Captain JJ, I have never disagreed with you before but now I feel that I must. There is no conclusive evidence that Abdul is a traitor. I agree with both you and Francine, I also do not trust him. I would like to suggest that we give him one last chance. Maybe we talk to him and tell him of our concerns and say that if he doesn't start to show that he is totally committed he can expect a bullet in the back of his head.'

Karli walked over to her husband at the window and, taking his huge left hand in her two small delicate ones, turned to JJ and said in a somewhat shaky voice, 'Well, I'm not sure if I am allowed a vote, but if I am, I will vote with my husband, I do not like the idea of killing anyone, particularly Abdul. I always found him sweet and courteous. I'm sorry, but if I do have a vote, I vote no to killing him.' By the time she had finished speaking, tears were running down her face.

Francine rushed across the room to her friend and, putting her arms around her in a comforting manner, said, 'It's OK, Karli, I'm sure we can work something out.'

JJ was still sitting sipping his drink. Francine looked across at him. 'We can, can't we?'

'Well, I suppose we can teach him a lesson and if he is guilty it will serve as a timely reminder of what he can expect. Come on and all sit down again and let's see if we can devise a little surprise for Abdul. Francine, would you make more coffee please? And pass the bottle on your way to the kitchen.'

'Yes, sir,' she laughed, as she sprung lightly to her feet. 'You're almost like a Turkish husband when you speak like that. Will you give me a hand Karli, and we'll leave these two masterminds to their planning?' As she passed him the almost empty bottle she added, 'Darling, shall I pass you your worry beads and backgammon board so that you can practice to be more like a Turkish husband?' The two girls could be heard laughing in the kitchen as they started to prepare another pot of the thick black coffee.

'Well, what do you propose, Captain?' Ali was once again the humble lieutenant.

'Not sure yet, but we need to give him an almighty fright. I think if we tried a mock execution it would be too hard on him if he isn't guilty, but it needs to be something that will shock him. Have you any ideas, Ali?'

Ali took the question with a solemn, 'Thank you, sir. Yes, maybe. Perhaps we could get one of the men to confess to being a traitor and tell Abdul that he has implicated him and that we were going to have a trial and that he could put his side of the case to us all, the whole group, about a hundred men and women. That should shake him.'

'I like it. It's simple and should be sufficiently frightening for him without being unduly callous. Well done, Ali.'

The girls arrived at that moment with a fresh pot of coffee and a new bottle of Cognac. JJ was delighted, he couldn't wait for the coffee to be poured before he was explaining Ali's plan. Karli beamed with delight at the praise that JJ was bestowing on her husband.

She asked, 'When are planning this little surprise?'

While JJ and Ali were discussing the fine-tuning of Ali's plan, the girls concentrated on making sure that glasses and cups were again filled.

'Well,' Ali said, 'if you will permit me, Captain, I think that we should wait until Monday and confront him after the lunch break. He will be more relaxed then.'

'Well done, Ali.' JJ was once again praising him to the continued delight of Karli.

'OK you guys, get the furniture moved, we are going to dance for you,' Francine ordered. 'Come on, Karli, let's get dressed.'

'Dressed?' said JJ and Ali as one.

'Changed then, is that better?' demanded Karli.

# Chapter Twenty Eight

Francine was awake first on Sunday morning. It was eight o'clock when she woke JJ with a good morning kiss and a cup of hot strong coffee. She handed him two painkiller tablets and knelt there beside the bed with a glass of water.

'Now take them with a sip of this water and stay there while I make you breakfast. I assume a greasy bacon sandwich will be acceptable?'

JJ nodded and started to speak. Francine stopped him by placing her hand over his mouth and saying gently, 'Tablets first, then coffee, then relax, then breakfast and if you feel up to it I will come back to bed, but I think you have a big hangover – yes?'

JJ swallowed the tablets with the proffered water. Francine placed the coffee cup on the bedside table and gracefully glided from the room. As she was closing the bedroom door she heard a quiet, 'Thank you darling.'

She was smiling happily as she returned to the kitchen, thinking about last evening; entertaining friends and the delights of being open with them about her relationship with JJ. She had never had a home with her husband. They had stayed with her sister Ayşe and Conrad or with his father Abdul. It was, in fact, the first time she had been the hostess in her own home – although of course it wasn't, it was JJ's, who always insisted that she think and treat it like her own. Today she felt different, somehow more content, more fulfilled. She knew she was being silly but she was in love with a wonderful man, had a nice house and she was going to make breakfast for this man who had a bad hangover. Even that was a new experience for her. Her husband never drank alcohol and it was the first time JJ had drunk so much. Well, there was that time when he had had a little hangover and broken Ali's nose. She knew that today he would feel far worse. He had drunk champagne, had red wine with dinner, then he and Ali had consumed the best part of two bottles of cognac. She briefly wondered how Karli was getting on with Ali. She decided to leave JJ for another ten minutes and took her hot chocolate into the garden and sat in the morning sun just daydreaming, imagining what it would be like with their children playing in the garden, the boys with a football and the girls pushing little prams around with their dolls, all dressed for a day in the park.

Suddenly, without warning, she remembered shooting Kemal. The thought made her shudder and, standing purposefully, returned to the house to prepare JJ's breakfast. As the bacon was crisping in the frying pan she forced all memories of Kemal from her mind and concentrated her thoughts on JJ. It would be nice, she thought, having a baby boy for JJ – or would he prefer a girl?

The bacon was cooked. As she placed the rashers onto the sliced bread she felt a little sick, the thought of eating pig. Although she wasn't a Muslim, her schooling had instilled in her the basics of the religion and one of those was the fear of pork of any kind. *If I didn't enjoy eating steak and juicy spring lamb*, she thought, *I could be a vegetarian.*

JJ had drunk his coffee and was lying with his eyes closed as she re-entered the bedroom. He must have heard her open the door for as she knelt again at the bedside he reached out to hold her hand. Instead of her hand she neatly placed the plate containing his breakfast into his groping hand.

'Remember what I said – breakfast, then, if you feel up to it...'

She didn't finish the sentence as at that moment he grabbed at her with his other hand, smiled up at her and said, 'I always feel up to it.'

'You didn't last night. Something to do with drinking too much I think,' she retorted playfully. 'Now eat your sandwich and stop talking! I'll make you another coffee.'

'Don't be long.'

She was back in less than five minutes as JJ was wiping his greasy mouth on the bed sheet. 'Please don't do that, use a serviette.'

'Yes, darling, sorry.'

She removed her dressing gown before slipping back into bed beside him and as he reached for her she could smell the bacon on his breath, which made her pull away. She put her hand up and said, 'Not until you have cleaned your teeth. You smell of burnt pig – and a shave would be a good idea as well.'

She could hear JJ complaining all the way to the bathroom and smiled when she heard the sound of the shower. 'He's not taking any chances!' she thought.

Monday morning arrived too quickly for the two lovers. They were, however, ready and waiting as Abdul drew up outside the house and they were soon into the thick of the morning traffic. Conversation was subdued as they headed towards the Bosporus Bridge to take them to them to the training camp. It was the start of a new week after JJ had unexpectedly given everyone the weekend off. JJ was deep in thought at the prospect of the impending showdown with Abdul, his visit later in the week to the UK and seeing Elizabeth again.

JJ had dressed in full uniform rather than his usual fatigues. His Sam Browne and holster shone his brass buttons glistened in the morning sunlight. Ali had seen them arriving and had quickly organized the men into their respective troops. As he alighted from the taksi, JJ heard him shout, 'Company, attention!' He turned and saluted JJ. 'Good morning, Captain, your troops are ready for inspection.'

JJ returned the salute and, with a nod of thanks, started his inspection – the first for many weeks. He thought to himself, *they are starting to look like a fighting force*, then grunted in disapproval as he caught sight of Ibrahim, the man that was Ali's second in command. His shirt was torn, his lip swelling, and both his eyes turning a deep blue. He had obviously been fighting.

'Why have you been fighting? Don't you remember my strict orders about fighting among yourselves?' Ibrahim just stood there not saying anything. JJ was furious. Turning to Ali, he said, 'I will see this man after parade. Make sure he is there.'

Ali jumped to attention and saluted, shouting, 'Sir.'

JJ ended his inspection with a speech from the platform. 'Men, you are, with the exception of one, rapidly becoming a force to be reckoned with, one with which I am proud be associated and call my men. I am saddened to find that one of you has chosen to ignore my orders. You are all here as volunteers so I do not understand why this man disobeyed me! I intend to find out and will deal with him accordingly.'

Abdul and Francine were standing next to the stage. JJ glanced down and caught sight of Abdul's worried face.

'Thank you for all your hard work. Lieutenant Ali, I will see you now, please?'

Ali dismissed the assembled troop. JJ watched them move into untidy groups. It was obvious what the topic of conversation was about – Ibrahim.

When Ali found JJ he was smiling, 'Yes, Captain, sir, you wanted me?'

'Yes. What the hell happened?'

'Well, if you recall our dinner on Saturday? This was a starter for Abdul's surprise!'

'Yes, but what's Abdul got to do with Ibrahim? Thank goodness Abdul wasn't here,' said JJ with relief.

'I hit him, with his permission. He is going to be the one that confesses that he and Abdul are traitors. He has changed a lot since you transferred him to me. He thinks you are a hero. Remember you gave him a truck? He's made a lot of money with the use of it when he is off duty.'

JJ couldn't help laughing. He slapped Ali on the shoulder and said, 'Thank you, I'm glad you are on my side. I hope you hit him while everyone was watching?'

'Yes, sir. Any chance of a case of raki for him tonight?'

'I think one for each of you.'

Ali, not able to resist a joke with JJ asked, 'Any chance I could have a case of that French cognac that made me stay in bed most of Sunday?'

'I had the same problem on Sunday. We must do it again before it's too late! You had better fetch Ibrahim before people start talking to him. Bring him here and be a little rough again.'

JJ could hear Ibrahim's shouts as Ali dragged him around the corner. Despite his shouts, when he saw JJ he smiled. JJ smiled in return and held out his hand. 'Thank you for agreeing to help. I hope Ali didn't hit you very hard?'

'No, sir, just enough to get the right effect,' he said, fingering his lip. Both his bruised eyes were running!

'OK, let's go through the rest of the plan I'm not fully acquainted with all the changes since our original planning.'

'It's better if Ali tells you Captain, sir,' Ibrahim said.

# Chapter Twenty Nine

They all sat on boxes that had once contained the 9mm
ammunition for the Uzi machine pistols – chairs had never been
used in the training camp. JJ was of the opinion that his men had
enough to do and learn and that they could best do that standing
up. It wasn't that he was being a heartless leader but a hard, fair,
one for he applied all of his rules to himself as well as to Francine
and his men. Ali started to explain how things had got to where
they had.

'Well. Ibrahim wanted to repay you for helping him the way
you did at the beginning and to apologies to you for his manner
towards you. He says he felt a resentment towards you, coming
to our country, telling us you knew how to do everything better
than we did.' Ibrahim was looking embarrassed, JJ thought, but
it was difficult to judge anything from his face with the bruises
and cuts. Ali continued, 'I knew how he felt towards you and, as
we had decided on the plan on Saturday evening, I approached
him this morning with the plan and he agreed happily, so I beat
him a little to show everyone that I had caught him at something
but didn't tell anyone what.' He patted Ibrahim on the back
saying, 'He took it like a hero. You would have been proud of
him had you been there.'

'Yes, I would like to have seen that.' JJ was still not able to
dispel his dislike of the man.

'Now,' Ali continued, 'we need to get Abdul and tell him that
we have caught Ibrahim spying and that we are going to put him
on trial before all the men.'

'OK,' said JJ, 'you stay here with Ibrahim, I'll go and find
Abdul.' JJ's search was swift – he found Abdul sleeping in his
taksi. JJ nudged him with his foot, 'Come on, Abdul, we need
you, we have another problem.'

Abdul asked when he saw Ibrahim, 'What's going on, Captain

Professor JJ? Who did this to Ibrahim?'

'I did,' replied Ali.

'Yes,' JJ added, 'Ali has caught him spying and we have decided that a full trial is in order rather than just to execute him. He may have more information and possibly an accomplice.' Ibrahim was protesting his innocence very loudly. Ali hit him again which brought tears of remorse and pleas for his life and he pointed to Abdul and wailed, 'He made me do it.'

'Abdul, you stay there and don't move. Ali, I'll get Francine to come and watch him. Don't let them talk to each other.' When JJ returned with Francine some minutes later she had brought with her, her skinning knife, which she waved at Abdul, saying, 'You should have let me do it the other time when we first suspected him after I shot Kemal.'

'Just don't let him move but try not to kill him, yet,' JJ added.

He marched off calling over his shoulder as he went, 'I'll get everyone assembled then I will call you. When you hear my call bring them both out with their hands tied behind their backs. OK?'

'Yes, sir,' said Ali and Francine together.

JJ mounted the platform and, seeing his men dispersed all around; he drew his Browning and fired one shot into the air to gain their attention. 'Men,' he called out, 'we have another case of spying and I would like you all to listen to the evidence and be both judge and jury, for the men we have are your comrades as well as mine.'

'Bring them out!' he shouted. Francine appeared first dragging Abdul along behind her. Then Ali turned the corner, pushing Ibrahim in front of him.

The assembled men were at first silent then, one by one, they started to shout 'Traitor!' as Abdul and Ibrahim were bundled onto the platform. The shouting had reached deafening levels as JJ once more drew his pistol and fired another shot into the air for silence.

'Men,' he called out, 'these are the accused. You will all listen to what they both have to say; then you may also ask questions of them. Then you will give your verdict and the punishment.'

'OK, Ibrahim, you go first.' He rose to his feet swaying slightly. JJ thought, *What a great actor*, or had Ali hit him a bit too hard? He started to plead for his life.

'Friends, I was made to do it, to spy on you all, by Abdul, to find out things about you and your families. I have not told him anything that I have found out about anything or anyone! I was weak, he offered me money and then he threatened that he would tell the police that I was involved, would tell the army that I was a traitor and a terrorist.' He paused to hold his head, which was obviously causing him pain. Ali prodded him in the back with the Uzi he was holding. Ibrahim took the hint and continued with his story. 'Abdul offered me much money and you all know how weak I am when money is involved. I just couldn't say no to him.' At that point he collapsed into a heap on the platform.

JJ turned to Abdul and said, 'Now it's your turn.'

'JJ, my son, I have done nothing. What this man has told you are all lies. I admit that when I was under the control of Kemal I did as he instructed, he was threatening to have my son executed. I did that for you as well as him.' He turned to Francine, his eyes pleading.

She retorted, 'You never do anything for anyone except yourself, I would sooner they hang him now than have him spend another seven years in that place.' There was no sign of remorse on her face as she said those words, just the detached expression of someone who was not involved and not interested. She continued, 'Tell us all, Abdul. How did they know that he was going to plant explosives that night? Why do you blame me for his capture?' Suddenly her expression changed. 'Of course, it was you that told the police what was going to happen. You didn't know that I was sick and that my husband went in my place. That's why you blame me, not for having made bad planning but because I was too sick to go and you were responsible for his capture, not me!'

Abdul was totally distraught, his shoulders sank. He was swaying as if about to fall over. 'Yes,' he sobbed. 'It was me. I am to blame. Kemal knew all about us even then. I didn't care about you being arrested.' He glanced at Francine. 'I thought you were not worth bothering with – a child born in prison to notorious parents. Kemal paid for my first taksi and always gave me money. Then, after my son was captured I began to know you better and saw how upset and concerned you were about what had happened, and I knew I had misjudged you and your relationship with my son, that you were both a good woman and wife. Then it was too late and he was in prison.' Francine prodded him with the skinning knife that had reappeared in her hand.

'Don't stop now, Abdul.' She spat venomously at him.

'I have never passed on information about anyone except my own son. I am not worthy of any trust but I swear that I have not been in contact with anyone since that tyrant Kemal was shot by my son's wife.'

'Where were you on Friday when Francine hurt her head and you claimed to have been hunting rabbits but had no gun?' JJ asked.

'I swear to you that I dropped it when I heard the explosion. I was in such a hurry to get back to find out what had gone wrong.'

One of the men in the audience jumped up waving a double-barreled shotgun in the air and shouted, 'Sir, I found this on my way home on Friday. I was going to hand it in then all the fuss between Ibrahim and Ali made me forget.' Abdul looked relieved, a little color had returned to his ashen face.

JJ held up his hands for silence. 'Men, I have a confession to make to you all, an apology to make to Abdul and a thank you to Ibrahim and Ali. Let me explain. Kemal had admitted that Abdul was in his employ when we visited him that morning before

Francine shot him. Conrad confirmed that both he and Abdul were working for Kemal. Abdul was out of camp on Friday with no excuse other he had been hunting rabbits, but was not carrying a gun, he claimed to have dropped it when he heard the explosion. One of you had found that gun and unfortunately delayed reporting it.

'In an attempt to find out if Abdul was a traitor we devised this plan – that Ibrahim would confess that he was a traitor working for Abdul in an attempt to get him to betray himself. You have all heard the results. Abdul has admitted that he had betrayed his own son but no-one else. His gun has been found. I propose that we find Abdul not guilty but caution him to show we all can trust him.' Abdul was now smiling. 'Ibrahim, thank you very much for all your efforts and allowing your face to be hit by Ali. I remember how mine hurt the day he gave me only one black eye. Thank you also Ali, for your part in the proceedings. What say you men?'

The audience, which had been standing in stunned silence since Abdul's confession, erupted into applause and shouts. Francine was now standing at the front of the stage with her knife in her hand and rage on her face.

She rounded on JJ. 'How can you just pass it off so easily? Didn't you hear him confess to having betrayed me? My husband was caught, not by Abdul betraying him, but by me being too ill to go.' Abdul was now looking frightened and had started to shake. 'I don't think we should let him off. I say we execute him as the traitor he has confessed to being.'

The audience, sensing blood, had now starting to jeer Abdul.

JJ was visibly distraught at her outburst and reached a hand out to her shoulder, which, for the first time ever, she pulled away, not allowing contact. He held up his arms to silence the assembled troops. 'I can understand that Francine is upset. If I had just heard that my father-in-law had betrayed me to the police I would probably feel the same way. This, however, is not a personal family fight, this is about the broader picture of why we are all here. The fight is with your government. You all expressed your views to me when I agreed to help you in your fight. It would ruin all the hard work that we have all put in if we kill one man who has admitted his crimes and none of us except his own son was involved. Abdul will have to live with the memory of what he has done to his family, which will probably be a greater punishment than a bullet in the head!'

Francine was now just standing with her head hung down, the knife still in her hand but her arms at her side. Her anger subsided. JJ called to the audience, 'Well, do we kill Abdul or let him suffer with his conscience?'

Francine raised her head as if to speak but just dropped her knife to the floor and walked slowly, as if in a trance, off the stage.

The troops hadn't replied to JJ's question. They were talking amongst themselves. Ali, sensing that things were not going well, called out, 'I'm with the captain. Who's with us and the revolution?'

One by one the men held up their arms in the clenched fist salute. JJ took the cue and joined them in the salute, 'Up the revolution!' he shouted. His men all shouted back,

'Up the revolution!'

JJ nodded his thanks to Ali for taking the initiative, which appeared to have saved the day. JJ continued speaking to his men, 'You have made a wise choice. You are putting the cause before your personal feelings. We must put behind us our mistrust and dislike of the man – he is still one of us. I assure you all that if I find any evidence of any more betrayal on his part I will personally shoot him on the spot. He will not be allowed any more chances. The man who found Abdul's shotgun is to be thanked, as without it, Abdul would now be dead. In the months and years to come he may wish that he was but now the fight must continue.' Raising his clenched fist one more time he shouted, 'Up the revolution!'

The troops responded in a mass roar. A number of gunshots were fired into the air from the excited crowed. JJ sensed, rather than heard, Francine's presence just behind him. She was standing there, waving her fist in the air, shouting at the top of her voice, with tears streaming down her face. JJ turned and looked at her. She smiled weakly. He returned her smile and immediately felt relief that she was once more the stable Francine he had known and would need to finish the task ahead.

# Chapter Thirty

JJ found Francine sitting on an ammunition box where they had had their meeting before the showdown with Abdul, her knife lay across her knees she had stopped crying but was obviously still distraught. He walked across dragging another empty box towards her and when it was positioned in front of her he sat down with a sigh. 'What a mess,' was all he could say? They sat quietly, each deep in thought.

Francine broke the silence, 'I'm sorry I shouldn't have shown my anger in front of our people like that, I showed that I didn't believe in you anymore, which is not true. I think you are doing a fantastic job with the training. All the men think of you as a great leader and I gave them a reason not to trust you as they should. I believe in you and love you as well, if that helps any?'

'Thank you I know it will be hard but you've got to face Abdul without your knife in your hand and hate in your heart. Abdul will get his punishment from his family, what do you think his wife and sons are going to say when he gets home tonight? I wouldn't want to be in his shoes. I also love you, I think coming back on stage the way you did helped and as for Ali? It would all have been lost now if it hadn't been for his quick thinking.'

She smiled across at him, 'I'm OK now,' and handed him her knife which he took with a simple, 'Thank you.'

He handed it back to her saying, 'You keep it, it will serve as a reminder to you of today's events.' She jumped up and through her arms around his neck and kissed him.

They were still holding each other as Ali and Abdul came around the corner. Francine rounded on Abdul and screamed in his face, 'I hate you for what you did and for what you are. I hope you never forget what you did to your son, my husband. I am sure that your wife will never let you forget it either so you will get your punishment every day as long as you live.' She continued more calmly, 'Knowing that, I feel that I can continue to work with you for our cause, but, once the job is done I never want to see you again.'

Abdul started to raise his hands towards her, but seeing the hate on her face dropped them with a sigh of despair!

JJ ignoring Abdul spoke quietly to Ali, 'Thank you for your help out there without it I think we could have had a riot!'

'I'm proud to have been of help it was for all of our benefit.'

Now JJ turned his attention to Abdul, 'We are going to continue as if today hadn't happened; we all need the help of each other so let's try and get through the next three weeks without any more trouble.'

'Whatever you say, Captain Professor JJ, you can rely on me.'

'I had better be able to,' growled JJ.

'Now home I think.'

Francine and JJ settled in the back of Abdul's taksi. This time JJ held Francine by the hand not bothering what Abdul thought. He knew that she needed the comfort that the closeness would bring.

'When we get to Yesilcoy drop us at the supermarket we need to buy food.'

'OK, sir.'

After Abdul disappeared around the corner out of sight JJ said, 'I wouldn't want to go through what he is going through and will get when he gets home, by then your mother-in-law will have heard the news about him.'

'It serves him right, the rat! What shall we have for lunch?'

'The usual, I think please, prawns and white wine followed by steak and red wine followed by cognac and coffee and then...' He didn't continue as he saw a strange faraway look on her face.

They walked the few hundred meters to the house carrying their shopping, the bottles clinking together in the bag that JJ was carrying. Once inside she took his bag and said to him, 'You get showered and I'll start lunch; then you can set the table in the garden and sort the wine when I shower.' She had started to sound more like her old self.

JJ had done as she had requested and was sitting in the garden with a glass of cold white wine, thinking to himself how great it was to be in Turkey, *You go to the supermarket to buy wine and it's already chilled, how civilized.* Francine came out fresh from the shower hair still damp and dressed in the shorts and top he had bought her at the airport on the way to their holiday in Cyprus. She had refused to wear the espadrilles except when walking on the road. He handed her a glass of the cold wine, so cold that it was causing the glass to form condensation on the outside which was running down and dripping onto Francine's bare legs which made her jump and squeal. Not the Francine of shooting Kemal or wanting to skin Abdul but the Francine on holiday where everything had excited her, it was nice to see the innocent child like outbursts about the drips of water being cold. He reached across and touched her bare leg rubbing her thigh were the gun shot that killed Kemal had burnt her leg. She sighed contentedly and declared lunch was ready.

They sat at the table for almost four hours, the food had been wonderful, the wine nectar. Francine broke the tranquility of the afternoon, reaching across she took JJ's hand and announced, 'It's only twenty days until we do the job we should start to put your escape plan into operation. When are you planning to go to England for your wife's passport?'

'I suppose soon but I hadn't really given it much thought with everything that has been going on. I'll get another bottle of wine and a pen and some paper and we can make a plan.' He returned from the house with what he had gone for and with an anxious look on his face.

'What's wrong?' Francine asked.

'I think the police are watching the house!'

'Are you sure? I'm going to look.' She returned within a couple of minutes also wearing a worried expression. 'You're right there are two on the road pretending to be talking and two more in a car down the road near the corner. One of those in the road I recognize from that night when we were in Yenikapi police station.'

'That's what made me suspicious I thought I had recognized him as well.'

'What do we do?' Francine asked.

'Nothing for the moment let's carry on making our plan.'

He noted the items on a piece of paper as he spoke, 'Item one – I need to move back to the Pera Palace hotel. Item two – you must move in with Ayşe.'

She screwed her face up at that and retorted, 'Well at least Conrad will not be there.'

'Item three – we make it look like we have had a fight and have fallen out.'

'Does that mean you hit me again?' she asked with a smile on her face.

'No we go to the pizza restaurant in a few minutes time and start an argument then you can slap my face and storm out get a taksi to Ayşe's and then we meet at Sirkeci station in two days' time, when the Orient Express arrives. At three-thirty be at that little bar where we first met. I'll go back to the Pera tomorrow. We meet at the station for six days. OK.

'Item four – the day after that I'll go back to England for three days.'

Tears had started to run down Francine's cheeks, she reached out a hand to JJ and sobbed, 'Can't we do that tomorrow so at least we can have one more night together?'

JJ was torn between keeping to his plan and another night with Francine, he easily persuaded himself. 'OK, you win, pizza for dinner tomorrow.'

She threw her arms around his neck, 'Thank you, I just hate the thought of you in England with your wife.'

'Item five – when I get back from England we continue to

meet at the station at the same time.'

'Item six –' Francine announced, 'You take me back to your hotel with you and show me how much you missed me, like the last time you went to your wife.'

'Good idea, item six – make love.'

'Item seven—' He never finished. Francine had stood up and removed her sun top and shorts, hooked them on a finger and threw them over her shoulder and with a flick of her head sent her hair over her other shoulder and danced away to the house. JJ emptied his glass and went off after her, all thoughts of the watching policemen forgotten.

JJ woke at two in the morning with thoughts of the watching policemen on his mind. He went into the kitchen trying not to disturb the sleeping Francine, her thick mane of blonde hair spread across the pillow. She had the trace of a smile on her face as if remembering something wonderful. He hoped it was a memory about him. He looked out of the window and there were two men in the same place as that afternoon and he could make out in the faint glow of the remnants of a dying moon a car parked at the corner of the road. *Damn police*, he thought. *I wonder what started them off again.*

At that moment Francine called out to him, 'JJ, are you OK?'

'Yes fine. Would you like me to make you a hot drink?'

'Yes please, chocolate and a biscuit.'

JJ carried a tray with two steaming mugs of chocolate and a plate with biscuits on into the bedroom to find Francine sitting up in bed waiting for him. She was displaying none of the signs of her prudish upbringing which would have in the past sent her scurrying into hiding under the bed clothes. As he passed her drink he mentioned as casually as possible, 'The police are still outside.'

'Oh!' she answered. 'We had better try and get some more sleep. I wish you hadn't looked.'

'I wish I knew why they have started again? Please pass the

biscuits.'

'Don't get crumbs in bed,' she said, passing him the plate.

# Chapter Thirty One

Abdul never arrived the following day. JJ was annoyed, Francine pleased that he was showing his reliability was once again suspect. Using the excuse of having a free day off from the training camp, she declared to JJ, 'I'm going to see Ayşe, have lunch with her and a natter. We haven't seen each other since we told her about Conrad.'

'Will you be home late?'

'No, I'll be home in time to prepare dinner.'

She had dressed in her old jeans, suede boots and tee shirt, putting her old blue jacket over the top, in spite of JJ's protests about it being too hot and why not wear a dress? She kissed him briefly as she left the house. He watched her walk down towards the train station. As always he felt a pang of regret almost as if he would never see her again – she had always reappeared at the promised time.

This day was different. JJ felt it, but didn't know why, it was as if something in his head was trying to tell him not to expect to see her again. As the day passed and as the level in JJ's whisky bottle was becoming lower with each passing hour, he became more and more restless. He contemplated phoning Ayşe on a number of occasions. He knew Francine would be upset with him if he did, so had resisted the temptation. When she had not arrived home at six in the evening he couldn't resist phoning and when Ayşe answered he wished he hadn't.

'Why hello, JJ,' she purred,

'This is a surprise. How's Francine? I haven't heard from her for ages!'

'She left here at ten this morning to visit you,' JJ replied, feeling total despair. 'Where can she have gone?'

'I don't know, you know more about her and her moods than anyone now!'

JJ put the phone down and reached for his whisky glass. Finding it empty he picked up the bottle and to his annoyance discovered that it too was also empty. He finally snapped and threw the bottle across the room. It smashed into fragments as it hit the opposite wall. He picked up his keys and money as he stumbled towards the door. The telephone ringing halted him.

He rushed to answer and he couldn't believe the sensation of relief as the voice at the other end of the line said calmly, 'Hello JJ, it's me, Francine. I've done something very silly and need you to come and fetch me. Will you please bring me some clothes? A cool dress and some shoes would be great.'

JJ started to ask what had happened but all she would say was that she was OK and just needed some clothes and that she would explain everything when he got to her. She gave him an address in Kadikoy and asked him to hurry. He threw the requested items plus underclothes in case into a bag. He remembered to phone Ayşe and tell her that Francine had phoned and she was OK but for some reason didn't tell her about the request for clothes.

He flagged down a passing taksi and requested to be driven at all speed to Eminonu and promised a large tip for a fast journey.

As he took a seat on the deck of the ferry boat, he looked at his watch. It had been twenty minutes since Francine's call. He sat and cursed the slowness of the boat as it bounced across the wake of warships and tankers heading for the open waters of the Black Sea or the Sea of Marmara. He remembered the first time that he had made this trip back in early spring. He had then thought he was embarking on a romantic journey, not the life-threatening voyage that had resulted from his flirtatious nature. He still could not really believe all that had happened to him. He still had nightmares about the calm way that Francine had shot Kemal, and how he shot Conrad.

The ferry docked with only a slight bump and the passengers

streamed to the disembarkation points. He hurried and joined the end of the waiting queue, hoping that a taksi would be available to whisk him to the waiting Francine. He could hardly believe his luck – a passing taksi was empty and looking for business. It pulled into the side as JJ frantically waved his arms. He threw his bag containing Francine's clothes into the vehicle before he climbed rapidly in behind it. He gave the driver the address that Francine had given him earlier and promised another large tip for speedy passage. As they drew up at the address JJ was dumfounded when he realized that he was outside the house of Kemal. He paid the driver and doubled the tip as the driver hesitantly asked, 'Are you sure you are at the right address? Not a very good place to go by mistake.'

JJ reassured him that it was all OK and he would be fine. He decided not to try the door of the main house because as Kemal was dead no-one was likely to be at home. He passed around to the rear, walking the route that he had walked before, not sure what to expect. He was pleased he had had the foresight to pick up his Browning as he left the house and the weight of it felt comforting in the waist band at the back of his trousers. JJ resisted drawing his weapon as he reached the door of Kemal's torture room. He turned the handle slowly and eased open the heavy door.

Francine was there with her skinning knife in her hand standing over Abdul who was naked and covered in blood. He had had pieces of his skin on his chest and arms sliced away. She looked up as he entered the room smiled and said, 'It's not as easy as it sounds, to skin someone, but at least I've killed him. It's more than he deserves. His torture is over, which is more than his son's is, he still has another seven years to put up with – all because of him.' She prodded the lifeless form of Abdul with the toe of her suede boot which, like her, was covered in blood. 'I'm sorry to get you involved but I didn't expect so much blood and I needed clean clothes.'

She appeared perfectly rational, which surprised him, as, after shooting Kemal she had shown signs deep of distress.

'Are you OK?' he asked, in as sympathetic a voice as he could muster. He was feeling only revulsion towards her, for her cold-blooded act of murder and mutilation. JJ noticed the other body on the floor and asked, 'Who's that?'

She was still staring at the body of Abdul, but glanced across at the other mound on the floor. 'Kemal, they must have never found his body.'

'We need to get you cleaned up, is the house open?'

'Yes, that's where I met Abdul. I needed to get him to the house in order to do what I had to do. I phoned him from in there. I phoned you from over there.'

She pointed towards the far corner where he could just make out the outline of a table.

'You go into the house, shower and get into some clean clothes.' JJ handed her the bag of clothes that he was still holding. 'I'll try and sort out this mess. We need a big fire to try and get rid of the bodies.' Francine smiled her thanks to him.

JJ searched the room for something to make a big fire with but could find nothing. Determined to find something, he continued his search in the house using the rear door to try and avoid being seen from the road. Outside in the yard was a small brick building which, after forcing the door open, discovered it housed heating system which ran off of bottled gas. His luck was still holding as he felt the gas bottles. There were three full ones. He dragged them one by one into Kemal's torture chamber – but then, what to use for a fuse? He remembered Abdul's taksi was parked in front of the house and the ball of Semtex that was in the glove box, along with an electronic fuse which he had given to Abdul to assure him that it was safe until primed with the fuse and detonated. He went swiftly to the taksi and retrieved his explosives. Stuffing them into the pocket of the light jacket he was still wearing he returned to the building where the carnage was everywhere. He pulled the body of Kemal onto the top of Abdul, removed the Semtex and a fuse from his jacket pocket and assembled them. He stuffed the explosives under the bodies as at least he was sure neither would survive in sufficiently sized pieces as to be identifiable. He removed the caps from the gas bottles and cracked opened each valve to test that they were, in fact, containing gas. Satisfied with his rough bomb he left and went in search of Francine. He found her still in the bathroom, grumbling about the lack of a brush to calm her hair, and pulling her fingers through it in an attempt to make it look presentable.

'Come on,' JJ urged, 'let's go before our luck runs out.'

'Ready,' she announced. 'What shall I do with my old clothes?'

'Bring them with you to the chamber. I'll explain what I've done.'

As they entered the room, Francine took a step back in horror as she saw the mess she had made. JJ took her bag of clothes and pushed them between the bodies of Kemal and Abdul. He explained that the blast from the Semtex would totally destroy her old clothing and the ensuing fire would destroy anything else that was left. He fully opened the valves on the three gas cylinders, grabbed Francine roughly by the arm and shouted, 'Come on, no time to waste.'

He started Abdul's taksi and with Francine sitting on the back seat they roared away. JJ pulled up when they were about five hundred meters away and grabbed his detonator. Pressing the button, he prayed it would work at the range. The whole car shook as the explosions erupted. He looked behind him to see a plume of flames and smoke rising into the sky. They had trouble with both their hearing and coordination for some minutes after the first explosion. JJ turned the taksi around and drove past Kemal's house. What was left of the house? The whole area had been devastated. Smoke was rising from the piles of rubble, the garden was flattened with a hole that would accommodate a car where Kemal's torture chamber had once stood. The houses on

both sides had scorch marks on their walls to testify to the
ferocity of the explosions. JJ said idly to Francine, 'There were
four explosions – the Semtex in the gas-filled room and then
three more, as each of the gas tanks went up. Let's get out of here
before the neighbors come to investigate.' He accelerated away
out of the area and, he hoped, out of danger.

# Chapter Thirty Two

They abandoned the taksi in a town center car park. Before finally leaving the vehicle they rubbed down the interior in an attempt to remove fingerprints. Not that they needed to remove their own prints, as they were known to the police to be regular users of Abdul's taksi, but in an attempt to make the police think that whoever had used it to get away from the remains of Kemal's house had tried to conceal their identity.

As they walked away from the taksi JJ was wondering what was going to happen when the police worked out the cause of the explosion at Kemal's house. He was fairly confident that the severity of the blast was sufficient to have removed any trace of the two bodies. Would they work out that Semtex had been used to trigger the gas tank explosions? *No.* He convinced himself that the use of Semtex would not be detected.

Francine was holding up well. She was behaving as if they were on a day out shopping, rather than having recently sadistically murdered her husband's father, showing no sign any of the stress that she had displayed after she had shot Kemal. That was something else for JJ to worry about. Was it a display of bravado or had she become incredibly callous?

It took them three hours to get to Yesilcoy. They stopped and looked in shops, had a beer at a pavement café and backtracked over their route, trying all the time to detect if they were being followed. JJ, finally happy that they were not being followed, declared it was time to head for home. They caught a little train from Sirkeci. Alighting at Yesilcoy they carried their parcels home, evidence of a day out shopping and that JJ had been summoned to assist the overburdened Francine with her goodies. JJ noticed that two policemen were standing in the same place as when he had first noticed them and a police car was still parked on the corner. They entered the house and, with a huge sigh of relief, dropped their parcels and flopped into armchairs. They were both shaking. JJ was about to fetch glasses and a bottle of cognac when the bell on the front door rang. JJ opened the door to find the two watching policemen, he also noticed that the car had moved from its position on the corner to outside the house. Without waiting to be invited in, they just pushed past JJ into the lounge. Over their shoulders JJ noticed the look of horror on Francine's face.

'JJ what do these men want?' she asked, almost too quickly, as she attempted to cover her first reaction.

'All we would like you to tell us is where you have been today, who you saw and who you spoke to.' One of the policemen took JJ by the arm and led him into the kitchen.

'You can have your say when the lady finishes, in the meantime just sit and be quiet. In fact, pour us both a drink.'

JJ did as he was bid and passed over a large tumbler of cognac, raising his own as he did and said, 'Cheers.'

After about fifteen minutes and two glasses of cognac the policeman who had been questioning Francine called, 'You can bring him in now.'

Emptying their glasses, they both stood. JJ allowed himself to be escorted back into the lounge to the waiting Francine, switching off the light as he left the room. The policeman that had questioned Francine and obviously the senior of the two officers, said to JJ in a curt manner, 'OK, now it's your turn to tell me what you have been doing today.'

JJ started from the beginning, 'Francine left here about ten to visit her sister. I hadn't heard from her all day so around four this afternoon I phoned her sister to find out what time she would be home. Her sister, Ayşe, hadn't seen or heard from her all day. Shortly after that I got a phone call from Francine asking me to go over to Kadikoy and help her with her shopping. She had bought many items and the packages were large. Also, she still wanted to continue shopping in Istanbul on the way home. I then caught a train to town, then a ferryboat to Kadikoy and met her there. Then we came home via many shops. Oh, and we stopped at a bar and had a beer, the only one all afternoon.'

The police officer consulted his notebook and nodded a few times then asked, 'You didn't say where in Kadikoy you met today.'

JJ thought for a moment, where would Francine have said? Then without pausing he continued, 'Why, at the ferry port of course. She had a taksi waiting with all her shopping.'

He closed his notebook, snapping the elastic that secured it, and said in a low voice, 'A very competent and full set of answers. We will leave you now but expect us to return later.'

JJ couldn't resist asking, 'What are all the questions about? I think you have been outside watching this house and as a visitor to your country I think I am entitled to an answer.'

He looked at JJ for a long moment before replying. He nodded and said, 'Yes, you are entitled to know what my investigations are about. Late this afternoon an explosion took place at the home of my commanding officer and there is no trace of his where-abouts. Do you know anything about the explosion?'

'No, even in my army days I could never understand the principles of how explosives work. I know that you need a detonator or a fuse but that's all.'

That appeared to satisfy him and the police left the house with thanks for the help that JJ and Francine had been to their investigations.

JJ closed the door behind them as Francine came rushing up to him, 'That was wonderful...' Before she could say anything further JJ grabbed her and put his hand over her mouth and put his finger to his mouth as a sign that she should say nothing at the moment. She nodded her understanding and took his hand away.

JJ walked through into the kitchen and looked out of the window of the darkened room. He saw the two men talking at the gate with the men in the waiting car. They all got into the car and drove away. He watched the car disappear around the corner. As it disappeared from view, he shouted to Francine, 'It's all clear, they've gone.'

She rushed into the kitchen and shouted, 'You were wonderful. You knew that I had told them that we met at Kadikoy ferry station?'

'Well, we did the first time. I was sure you would use the truth as much as possible. Now the next thing is our fight in the pizza restaurant. I'm afraid it must be tonight.'

She looked sad, as if about to cry. She roughly rubbed her eyes with her fists to send away the tears before they arrived. She looked crestfallen. If JJ hadn't seen her earlier that day his resolve may have weakened but having seen what she had done to Abdul, he honestly didn't want to be with her.

'Well, let's go and do it, I'm also very hungry,' she said, seeing that JJ was determined not to change his mind, as he had the day before.

They walked to the restaurant in silence, thankfully noting on the way that the watching policemen had left their position on the roadside but that their car was still in attendance. One of the occupants got out as they rounded the corner. As they took their usual table in the window, he took up position on the opposite side of the road – leaning against a wall, pretending to be reading a newspaper. It was more perfect than JJ had dared dream. All they had to do was enact their fight as planned. They ordered their pizzas with a bottle of rosé wine. Francine asked for water, at which JJ made a rude comment. The waiter looked surprised at JJ's remark. It was the first time he had noticed any friction between the normally loving couple.

The wine arrived first, which JJ immediately started downing. He sank two glasses before Francine's water and their pizzas arrived. He made another rude comment to her as the waiter served their meal. She tried not to look or feel hurt but JJ's remarks were upsetting as they referred to her having been in prison, 'A real jailbird' was the way he put it.

'Please don't be nasty, you knew all about me before we started our relationship and you said you didn't mind,' was all she could summon to try and stop his taunts.

He had greedily downed another glass of wine and poured another before replying, 'Once a jailbird, always a jailbird.' He was about to down another glass of his wine when Francine reached across the table and tried to take his hand. He pushed her hand away, spilling most of the wine he had just poured into his glass over the table. She lost her temper as planned and reached again across the table, not to offer comfort but to hit him open-handed around the face, first with her palm then backhanded. He staggered under the impact and nearly fell from his chair. She rose and stormed to the door. As she reached for the handle she turned and looked at him and, with tears running down her face she shouted, 'You stupid man I love you, and now I hate you!'

The door shook under the force of her departure as she slammed it shut behind her.

JJ was left sitting at their table feeling very satisfied with her performance and glad that the whole thing had been witnessed by the watching policeman, as well as a restaurant full of diners, who would be repeating the events of the evening thus far to anyone who would listen.

# Chapter Thirty Three

JJ left the restaurant shortly after Francine's heated departure and walked slowly home. He was regretting being so rude to her but pleased with her reaction. He thought, 'I'm glad she didn't have an Uzi or her skinning knife with her, otherwise she may not have been content with just hitting me.' He noticed the men in the police car – one of them was talking rapidly into his radio phone, obviously reporting the events in the restaurant to his superiors.

As he entered the house he noticed it was quiet. Going through into the bedroom he realized that Francine had been back there, after leaving the restaurant, to collect her clothes and personal belongings. He felt a mixture of loneliness and relief. Loneliness, on the one hand, at the loss of her and relief on the other, as he knew he would never be able to feel the same, or be able to relax with her, after seeing her covered in Abdul's blood with his mutilated body at her feet idly kicking it with her old suede boot, like the rest of her, caked in blood. He sighed and started to pack his own things for his move back to the Pera Palace.

He managed to find a taksi to take all of his assembled clutter back into Istanbul the following morning. He looked back at the house as they drove away, his mind drifting back to his wife Elizabeth. She was the reason he had rented the house in the first place. Then he thought of Francine, who had filled his house and life with love and excitement in a way that his wife never could have. *It was*, he thought, *not that she didn't want to but that she didn't know how to*!

JJ suddenly shouted out, to the surprise of the driver, 'What a damn mess.'

With the assistance of the hotel porters he managed to transfer all of his belongings to his suite. When he had made his reservation he had booked a suite instead of a room – well, Conrad was, in effect, still paying.

Needing to know how things were going at the training camp, JJ made his way to the hotel reception and booked a hire car for the afternoon. As he drove himself for the first time, along the route he remembered Abdul taking, to the training camp, he thought fondly of the man who had taught him so much of Turkish culture and way of life in this wonderful country. As he approached the old building he blew three blasts on the car horn, one long and two short. As he parked, he saw Lieutenant Ali and Ishmael trot around the building, both carrying Uzis. He waved to the two men as he got out of the hire car, Ali waved back and a huge smile burst out over his face, 'Hello, sir, great to see you.'

'Thanks, Ali, good to see you as well. I thought I had better come and have a chat with you and see how you are getting on without me.'

Ali and Ishmael escorted him around to the parade ground. JJ was pleased to see all the men actively engaged in unarmed combat training. JJ took Ali by the arm and walked him away from the rest of the men. 'Ali, I have some important news. Francine has killed Abdul and she and I have had a big fight and she has left Yesilcoy.'

'I can see her hand prints on your face, I am sorry that you have separated, you made a good team. I am not surprised that she has killed Abdul, it was her right after what he had done.'

'Are you managing OK without me?'

'Yes, sir, we are doing OK. Please let me show you.'

JJ followed him around the training camp, nodding agreement as Ali showed, or told, him about the training. Feeling relieved that he had made a good choice in making Ali his number two, he explained that he had to go to the UK for a few days but would be back before the raid.

Ali walked JJ back to his car and they shook hands and embraced each other like old friends. JJ waved as he drove away.

Ali stood to attention and saluted.

The following day, JJ made a trial journey to Sirkeci station. He started out at two o'clock and to his surprise he realized he was being followed. He had hoped that he would be followed, but today was only a trial, tomorrow was the start of the real thing. Would the watching and following continue? He set off down the hill, looking forward to a cold beer when he reached the station. It wasn't until he reached the bridge that he turned to check if he was still being followed. It took him a minute to identify his pursuer, shabby dark blue suit and a huge thick black moustache. He turned and continued his journey across the bridge's lower section, out onto the road, waited for the lights to change then he and, it seemed, half of Istanbul crossed the road together and he entered the station. It was a relief to enter the relative cool, to escape the heat of the early afternoon sun. He sat at a table outside the bar where he had first seen Francine and ordered two beers. The first he devoured in four huge swallows the other he poured and sipped at slowly. He was pleased to see his pursuer in obvious discomfort, in his thick dark blue suit, seated at a coffee shop a few hundred yards away drinking water and waiting for, JJ assumed, his coffee. *Well, my friend, you had better wear something cooler tomorrow otherwise you may suffer heat exhaustion*, JJ thought.

The following day dawned clear and sunny with no wind – a sure sign that the afternoon was going to be hot and humid. JJ breakfasted on the terrace, orange juice, coffee with bread and cheese and a few black olives. The waiters remembered him from his short stay earlier in the year and joked with him about the blonde belly dancer that he had obviously taken such a liking to…

It was only ten o'clock when he finished his breakfast and he was still sitting and pondering his afternoon journey and the prospect of seeing Francine again. He was finding that his body was missing her although he knew his head would never again allow his body to relish in the pleasures that he had so readily accepted as his right. He was still sitting at his breakfast table when a shadow passed across his face. It startled him for a moment, he had been deep in thought. He looked up to see what had cast the shadow and he found himself looking into the face of Ayşe, Francine's sister.

'JJ, what has happened between you and Francine?' she asked breathlessly. 'She is staying with me and is very sad. She must have cried most of last night but would say nothing except that you had had a big fight and had moved back here.'

'Did she tell you about Abdul?'

'Yes she did, she did what was right.'

'I guess I'll never understand how you all think,' JJ said wearily. 'Would you like breakfast?'

'Could I have just some coffee please?'

JJ signaled a passing waiter and ordered two more coffees. He leaned back in his chair and considered telling Ayşe the truth about the fight and that it was only a ploy to get the police thinking they were meeting at the station in some attempt at reconciliation, and that they were trying to set a pattern so that when the bridges went up and the authorities suspected them they would look for them at the station – but they would be driving out of the country in Conrad's car. He didn't say anything, suddenly unsure if he could trust her. Maybe both she and Conrad had been in the employ of Kemal? Conrad had made remarks about her love of money and possessions. He decided that he must warn Francine when they met that afternoon not to say too much to her.

They finished their coffee in silence. JJ stood. 'I have to go shopping at the Grand Bazaar,' he said, in an attempt to get her to leave.

'Yes and I must go home and see how my sister is, she really is very upset. I thought that if I came and explained how she is you would try and help.'

They shook hands as she left – she had never encouraged JJ to kiss.

JJ had no need to go shopping but he had over three hours before he need to start his journey to Sirkeci. He got a taksi to the bazaar and was surprised to see the policeman of yesterday, still wearing his blue suit, also get into a taksi that he must have had waiting in readiness. He settled back in his seat, pleased that things appeared to be working out as he had planned and hoped they would. He strolled around the main streets of the bazaar not really looking at anything, just killing time. He decided that it was time to return to the Pera Palace and have a cold beer before he started his real journey of the day.

As he left the hotel, he noticed the blue suit of his follower turn and pretend to look in a shop window. He strolled down the hill, content that the policeman in the blue suit would be feeling terrible discomfort. As he walked up to the little bar, he saw Francine sitting at a table with a coffee in front of her, her hands in her lap screwing up a handkerchief. She suddenly caught sight of him, and jumped up bestowing on him her most radiant smile. He responded with a little wave.

'Hello, darling, I'm so pleased to see you. I was very upset about hitting you and shouting.'

'You did fine, my face is only a little bruised. I hope you didn't hurt your hand.'

'No, I'm fine. Were you followed?'

'Yes, the blue suit over there.' JJ jerked his head in the direction of his pursuer. 'I did a practice yesterday and he followed then, also, I came down to the bazaar this morning and he followed then as well. Did you spot anyone tailing you?'

'No, I just needed to get here and see you. I've been so miserable without you.'

'OK, I'll see if you are followed when you leave, but first of all I need a cold beer. Would you like anything else?'

'Yes please. I would like you to hold me and tell me you love me like you used to do.'

'You know that I can't do that, it's too early, we can't make up so soon. Let's just sit and talk for about five minutes then you get up and go.'

'OK, say nice things to me then, he can't hear you over there.'

JJ occupied himself with his beer, not giving Francine much of his attention, trying to remain distant as if they had fought and he was not going to be coerced into a reunion. He ordered himself another beer and when the waiter had set down the glass, running with condensation, in front of him, he looked at her again and muttered, 'OK, it's time for you to go, see you tomorrow.'

She caressed his shoulder as she stood. 'Bye, darling. See you tomorrow, I love you.'

'I love you too.'

She walked away without a backward glance. JJ was looking to see who followed her. *Got you*, he thought. A tall, willowy, man dressed in jeans and sport shirt, his hair black with the almost obligatory huge moustache, tagged along about twenty paces behind her. As she walked she not only swung her thick blonde hair, but her superb hips as well. She was making sure she was being followed.

# Chapter Thirty Four

With the pattern set, Francine and JJ continued their now separate lives, coming together for a few minutes each day. For JJ, the worst part of the day was the journey to the station with the heat of the mid-afternoon, the noise the traffic and people, singularly clamoring for attention and jointly producing a cacophony of sound that he found difficult for his brain to process. The sixth day, when JJ arrived at the station, instead of seeing Francine sitting at what he had come to regard as their table; he saw a policeman sitting there, wearing those sinister reflector sunglasses. There was no sign of Francine. She suddenly appeared at his side, taking his hand and pulling him down in order to kiss him on the lips, before explaining, a little breathlessly, that she had been in a shop and that both he and the train were early that day.

Francine, on the other hand, only feared that JJ would not be at the station and that he had somehow gone to England and his wife without her knowing, and that she would never again see him or to feel the strength of his body against hers. She was well able to cope with life in this city of over ten million people all going about their daily lives at frantic speed and at full volume. Her mind was worrying about life without JJ. Her body ached for his caress. When would he next take her and transport her to that place beyond the clouds from where she just floated back into his arms? Why could her husband not have made her feel like that – her poor husband who was locked away in a living hell? She shook her head to try and clear it of all but the few minutes she was about to have with JJ.

She forced down a mouthful of the local brandy that he had ordered for her and before rushing to the toilet before he could see her tears, pushed her glass towards him, telling him to finish it and to relax. She was not sure who the tears were for, herself, her husband or JJ?

For the first time in almost a week JJ allowed her to walk with him to the station exit where she was hoping that he would embrace her. Instead, he said, rather sharply, 'Continue the fight, and please don't give in now.' Very much against her own instinct she did as he had asked.

'It's no good; I'm not interested in your excuses anymore,' she shouted, and stood with her hands on her hips and glared at him. JJ expected her to slap him again. Instead, she mouthed silently, 'I love you,' turned and marched off.

JJ noticed that the willowy man in jeans, sports shirt and huge black moustache followed her. She looked divine and he began to wish that he were following her.

He turned around in mock astonishment and noticed the man, who was still dressed in his blue suit, hovering near the station doorway. Smiling, he turned and perversely decided to walk back to the Pera Palace, knowing that his follower would be subjected to the sun's heat and the stifling humidity.

The following morning, JJ took off from Istanbul airport. He was dreading the prospect of seeing Elizabeth again. Not sure what his own reactions to her would be, now that he had decided that his affair with Francine was finished. Although he knew that he would never be able to make love with her again, after the barbaric way in which she had killed Abdul, he was still in love with her and had to do all he could to ensure the escape of both of them after the demolition of the bridges. He still could not believe that the mission could fail.

Elizabeth was dutifully waiting for him. As he came through customs control, she waved and managed a smile of welcome. As he walked over to her she stood waiting for him with her face raised to be kissed. They kissed! Well, what JJ would have to learn to expect as a kiss from now on. He put his arm around her waist and they walked together to the waiting Porsche that was wedged between a Range Rover and a huge BMW. JJ managed to wriggle down into the driver's seat and gently edged his car out and parked by the waiting Elizabeth. She slid into the passenger seat without the least trace of flashing thigh. JJ sighed at the thought of the delight that Francine had always given when she had got into the car in the past. He had a moment of guilt. Was he turning into a dirty old man?

The journey to Reading passed uneventfully. They were soon turning into the driveway of their home. JJ was feeling particularly desolate as he listened to Elizabeth explaining why she had had to buy new curtains for the sitting room. The usual thrill and exhilaration he felt driving the Porsche for once had failed to materialize. If he had been asked he couldn't explain why he felt as he did. It was caused by nothing, by nobody, it was just a feeling of despair.

Elizabeth was really trying to make JJ's visit a success. She had cooked him a special dinner, had bought him his favorite wine and whisky. She served dinner on the patio under the dying embers of the moon which made JJ think about the job he still had to do when he returned to Istanbul when the moon was at its darkest. She had dressed carefully and hadn't complained about JJ attacking the wine before dinner was served. JJ on his part was also trying – trying not to compare every move she made to what Francine would have done! At one point, when Elizabeth was serving him with vegetables, he had run his hand up her thigh and almost made her drop her spoon in surprise. Dinner was a great success. They were both trying very hard to make it a happy occasion. After the meal JJ offered to make coffee, which she accepted gracefully, asking for a small cognac as well. He reappeared about ten minutes later with a tray loaded with cups and coffee pot, glasses and bottle. He had put some music on the player, which was soft and romantic, the strains drifting out over the lawns to the relaxing couple. They sipped their coffee and brandy in companionable silence. Elizabeth, at one point, reached across to JJ and let her fingers trace the outline of his face. JJ found the gesture very exciting, it was something that she hadn't done for many years. He suddenly realized that he wanted to make love with her. He resisted the urge to grab her knowing that if he had he would have spoilt the moment.

The music ended, the coffee drunk and the brandy bottle half empty, Elizabeth stirred in her chair and asked, 'Would you like to go to bed and make love, it's been a long time?'

They both stood and arm in arm they walked to the house, ignoring the empty, dirty cups and glasses. They made love that night as they had years before without the inhibitions that had crept unnoticed into their lives over the years. The following morning JJ decided to make her breakfast as he had done a few months previously, hoping that he would not again incur her displeasure. He added to the breakfast tray a fresh red rose that he had picked while waiting for the coffee. Carrying his burden to the bedroom his sole thought was, *Not a row again please.*

As he entered the bedroom she roused and opened her eyes and smiled at him. 'Good morning JJ darling. Thank you for a wonderful night. I had forgotten how considerate and tender you can be.'

'It was my pleasure. Breakfast on the balcony?'

'That will be perfect, thank you.'

They sat eating their breakfast, bathing in the early morning sun, looking out over the gardens.

'Do you realize that I shall be finished in Istanbul in about two or three weeks?'

He didn't want to give a precise date just in case something went wrong and he was still unsure what he was going to do with Francine. It was turning out not as he had planned.

'Let's leave booking that holiday until I get back, it will be more fun to do it without a lot of planning.'

He was thinking back to his holiday with Francine and how they turned up the airport and just booked and went. Could it be as good again this time with Elizabeth? She reached across and took his hand, raising it to her mouth she kissed his fingers and murmured, 'Whatever you prefer is fine with me.'

'What shall we do today? I don't fly back until tomorrow morning.'

'I would be happy with the day in the garden, unless you want to go into town?'

'The garden sounds fine and I could do a bar-b-q for dinner like the old days.'

'In that case, first things first. You pop to the supermarket and get salad and meat while I shower and tidy up from last night.'

JJ rose to his feet, bent over and kissed her gently, then said, 'I would like to add my thanks to you for last night, it was very nice.'

She blushed slightly, as she remembered how she had let herself go the previous night, her inhibitions had been locked away. She hoped that they would remain so for the next day at least.

As JJ got into the Porsche to drive to the local superstore for the ingredients for that evenings bar-b-q he was feeling elated. He couldn't remember when making love with Elizabeth had been as enjoyable, not the frantic passion of Francine but none the less very pleasant. He also realized that they had both been trying very hard for it to be a success and he pondered when he had stopped trying. Probably about the same time that Elizabeth had. Who was to blame? He was still deep in thought when he parked his car. He suddenly understood neither of them were to blame, it was just one of those things that happen when two people become complacent about life together. He resolved not to stop trying again. With that thought firmly in his mind he went into the shop. He selected the meat and vegetables with care. His choice of wine was the type that he knew Elizabeth preferred and for good measure he added a box of her favorite chocolates to his trolley of goodies.

She was dressed when JJ arrived home. He contemplated

trying to persuade her to return to bed with him but decided that would be the best way of destroying their newly reformed relationship. The weather during the day was perfect. Elizabeth could be heard humming quietly as she busied herself. JJ actually whistled whilst mowing the lawns, something he would never normally do.

JJ's bar-b-q was a success, as had Elizabeth's dinner been the previous evening. After they had eaten, they again lingered over coffee and brandy each not wanting to rush the other. Eventually JJ at last took the initiative and announced that he ought to be thinking about some sleep as he had a fairly early start the following morning. Elizabeth declared, 'Let's leave the dirty plates and things, it will give me something to do when I get back home tomorrow.'

Hand in hand they walked to the house as the first rumble of thunder could be heard in the distance, accompanied by a spot of rain.

'Just in time,' they both said together, and laughed as they looked at each other.

She reached up and put her arms around his neck and pulled him down towards her. 'I love you, JJ.'

'And I love you as well.' Not sure whether he did or not. Time would tell.

# Chapter Thirty Five

After Elizabeth had driven sedately away from the airport terminal building, JJ stood for a few minutes, watching his car disappear into the distance, trying to rationalize his thoughts. Did he still love Francine? Yes. Could he ever forget what she had done to Abdul? No. Could he ever be intimate with her again, probably not? Did he love Elizabeth? Maybe. Had he enjoyed his few days with her? Yes. So did he love Elizabeth? Not sure. He shook his head to try and clear his mind when he suddenly remembered Marie and Prague. *Now, that's an interesting thought*, he mused.

He queued up with all the other passengers at the immigration desk in Istanbul airport, wondering if anyone would meet him. Oh Abdul, he could always be relied upon to be in the right place at the right time. No, no familiar face was in sight. He sighed.

JJ got a taksi outside the terminal building. He pushed his trolley, which was unwilling to go in the required direction, across the tarmac towards the taksi rank. Was it the same trolley that he had used that first day in Istanbul when he had pushed that overloaded and uncooperative trolley towards Abdul?

As the taksi passed Sirkeci station he looked at his watch. It was one-thirty, time enough to drop off his things at the hotel and be at the station in time for the arrival of the train. Would Francine be there? He wasn't sure if he wanted to see her or not. What about his follower – would he be waiting for him as usual?

At exactly two o'clock JJ emerged from the shade of the Pera Palace into the harsh sun of a summer afternoon. Before turning towards the sea he briefly looked up the road to where his follower had previously waited and, sure enough, he spotted the blue suit. He turned and started his journey, his mood considerably improved by the knowledge that his plan was working.

As he walked up to the café he spotted Francine at their usual table, she saw him and waved, he waved in return. Unable to contain her excitement she stood and ran towards him, her face showing the pent-up desire of her body. JJ wished he felt the same desire for her that he had only a few short days before. They embraced briefly, JJ holding her away as he said, 'Hang on a minute, let me get my breath back, it's hot out there.'

'Come and have a cold beer, it will make you feel better.'

He ordered a beer for himself and a coffee for Francine. He looked around and noticed her follower trying to find something of interest in the shop window he was looking in. Giving up the battle he strolled over to their café and flopped into a chair as far away from them as possible. JJ heard him order water and a coffee. Suddenly JJ grabbed Francine by the arm and whispered, 'Come on, let's go, I want to see what he does.'

They left money on the table for their drinks and rushed away. JJ had managed to get a few paces in front of her and, on the pretext of trying to hurry her along, he turned and managed to see the willowy follower of Francine trying to get change from the proffered note, the waiter thinking it was to be a tip. They continued to rush, burst out into the sun and flagged down a passing taksi. No sign of either pursuer could be seen as they roared away. 'Pera Palace,' ordered JJ.

Francine squeezed his arm and said, 'This is a surprise, I didn't think you'd want me today after your visit to your wife.'

JJ still had his room key so they didn't need to stop at the reception desk, which would have caused embarrassment for all of them, particularly Francine. JJ phoned down for coffee, helping himself to a cold beer from the mini bar fridge. They both fell into the deep chairs of the sitting room of JJ's suite. JJ drinking his beer from the bottle, needing a cold drink he hadn't bothered with a glass.

After the room-service waiter had served Francine her coffee, she rushed across the room and put her arms around JJ's neck, pulling her body into his, her mouth hungrily seeking his. JJ for his part was trying not to spill his beer and persuade Francine to slow down and relax a little, he needed to talk to her. That at least made her sit down and listen whilst JJ explained that he had got his wife's passport and had had it stamped with an entry visa. He had simply presented to the immigration official with his own passport and without bothering to check, he had simply stamped both passports and took the ten pounds from JJ, for two entry visas before moving on to the next waiting passenger. He threw the passport across to Francine and asked, 'Can you make yourself look like that?'

Francine pretended to study the passport photo before answering, and then suddenly jumped to her feet declaring, rather unkindly, 'Do you really want me to look so old? I didn't realize, she must be older than my mother.'

JJ was annoyed, after his few days with Elizabeth he had started to like her again and didn't like the idea of anyone insulting her. 'Just be grateful that you have the opportunity of escaping the country after we do the job and don't forget I'm older than your father,' he shouted.

'Well, she does look old, maybe it's not a very good photo?'

'OK,' JJ said. 'Let's forget about how old she looks. Can you make yourself look like her?'

'Yes, it's easier to look old. It's more difficult to look young, as your wife must know.'

'I said, drop the subject of how old she looks,' he shouted at her.

'I'm sorry JJ, I won't mention how old she looks again,' she said, making sure she had the last word on the subject.

Francine had moved over to his chair and was sitting on the arm then slid down onto his lap. He squirmed as she landed none too gently. He sat quietly for a few moments, savoring the prospect of her body, then suddenly seeing the image of Abdul laying in a pool of blood and Francine idly kicking at his body with her already blood soaked suede boot, he suddenly felt violently sick and had to push her away as he rushed to the bathroom. He returned to the sitting room some five minutes later, still feeling repulsion towards her. She was still sitting on the floor where she had landed from JJ's push. Looking up at him, she asked, 'What's wrong with you? Too much sun or a bad beer?'

'Must be the effects of the sun, it was very hot outside.'

She pushed herself up and once more perched herself on his knees. 'Well, aren't you going to at least put your arms around me and kiss me?'

'Just give me a few minutes please, I feel a little rough.'

'You never used to let that interfere with having me before,' she responded, a little sharply. 'Are you sure it's not an excuse as you've been with your wife and aren't interested in me anymore? I can't imagine why you would prefer an old woman instead of me though.'

'Please, Francine, don't start again. I feel rough and am not in the mood for either you or an argument with you.'

She got to her feet and walked towards the door. Opening it quietly and leaving the room, she slammed the door behind her. The room shook, the windows rattled and JJ feared the chandelier would fall from the ceiling. The silence after Francine left was almost suffocating. JJ was in a state of shock at her departure, not sure if he was pleased she had gone or sad at the prospect of a lonely night. If only she had shown some remorse at what she had done, but no, if anything she was proud at having killed Abdul.

He showered in hot then cold water and afterwards he felt refreshed and clean. He had resisted, Francine's advances and knew he was now free of the hold she had had on him.

As it was only five o'clock and dinner didn't start until eight, he decided on trying to get some sleep as it had been a long day so far and he did actually feel a little unwell. Lying on the bed he was soon in a deep sleep. Another nightmare was in progress.

Francine, with her skinning knife in hand, was stalking someone or something through what was obviously the African bush. He saw her pause and crouch down in an attacking pose, she leaped forward and then there were two bodies writhing in the dust. He couldn't believe what was happening, Francine was trying to kill Elizabeth! JJ tried to call out but no sound came from his mouth, he tried to move to break up what was obviously a stupid action on Francine's part. His legs would not move and he was compelled to watch as they fought. Elizabeth was no match for the younger, stronger, more agile, Francine who soon had her arm around Elizabeth's neck in a sleeper hold. Elizabeth was soon unconscious. Francine let go her hold on her and jumped to her feet holding her knife poised ready to strike. Turning to JJ she shouted, 'If you don't take me now, I will skin her. You know I can, I practiced on Abdul, remember.'

JJ was still unable to move as Francine reached down and sliced off a lock of Elizabeth's hair and held it aloft, for JJ to see. 'Next time it will be an ear or a finger!' she screamed, her voice indicating her deranged mind.

JJ woke from his nightmare and was violently sick, this time he never made the bathroom. He lay on his bed in a pool of vomit, that in his mind he thought was his own blood, it was warm and sticky. He retched again on an empty stomach and passed out.

# Chapter Thirty Six

He regained consciousness after a few minutes and had almost to crawl to the bathroom. He went into the shower fully dressed to try and remove the clammy vomit that had got everywhere on his clothes and body. Item by item he removed his clothes and threw them into the bath. Then he set about reviving his body, soaping and massaging his torso, legs and arms. Then, turning the shower onto cold, he forced himself to stand under the cascade for a full five minutes. Rubbing himself dry with a rough towel, he got the blood flowing again through his body which was feeling better by the second. Fastening the towel around his waist he headed for the sitting room and his bottle of whisky. Taking a mouthful, he remembered he had only picked at his food on the plane and had had nothing else to eat all day.

Looking at his watch he discovered he had slept for almost three hours and it was time for dinner in the hotel dining room. He placed his part full whisky glass on the table and dressed for dinner, grey slacks, white shirt, regimental tie and blazer. Arriving in the foyer he apologetically explained to the receptionist that he had messed his bedclothes and could the valet sort out his soggy clothes in the bath? He handed over a fifty dollar note with instructions that it was to be divided between the maid and valet as his thanks for their extra work.

Entering the opulent dining room he was met by the head waiter who showed him to a table next to the dance floor and in spite of JJ's protests he insisted it was the only table he had free. JJ sat and asked for a bottle of wine, Turkish red.

The wine arrived and the waiter took his order for dinner, steak and salad as he had had the first night he had been in the hotel. He had just started to eat when the room lights dimmed and the almost obligatory cloud of colored smoke appeared. As it dissolved he could see Francine in her short belly dancer costume, she was just standing in the center of the room, her body was shimmering, then the band started to play her signature tune. She started to dance, not for the assembled audience, but for him alone. The dance lasted about five minutes finally ending with her falling to the floor where she writhed and shook. The assembled audience were on their feet showing their appreciation with almost deafening applause. The lights were switched off and when they were turned on again she had vanished – the floor where she had laid was bare.

JJ was filled with excitement and wanted her very much and could hardly contain himself for her next dance. When the music started again, in place of the delightful, tantalizing Francine, a regular dancer appeared who went through her routine in a clinically professional manner, but without the fire and exuberance that Francine displayed. The applause at the end of her act lacked the enthusiasm which had been shown for Francine.

He did not see Francine again until he was sitting on the terrace having his breakfast. She just breezed up to his table and immediately tried to start an argument about his lack of interest in her the evening before, 'Had you used all your energy with your wife?' she shouted at him.

With a flick of her magnificent hair she turned and marched away. JJ was stunned by her verbal attack on him. His fellow diners were all quiet as if waiting for the next assault, which never happened. JJ left the table and tried following her out of the hotel, but by the time he reached the main lobby she had disappeared. He went to the door and looked both ways up and down the street. He asked the porter who said he had not seen anyone fitting her description leave the hotel. He didn't go back to his breakfast, instead he returned to the foyer and booked a hire car for the day, determined to find her.

He drove to the training camp and was met by Ali, who seemed pleased to see him. He escorted JJ on a tour of inspection.

JJ could find little to criticize so contented himself with words of praise for Ali's efforts in getting the troops ready. JJ asked if he had seen or heard from Francine. Ali confirmed that neither he nor his wife had any idea where she could be. He couldn't be any help in giving JJ the address of Ayşe. He had telephoned and she had told him she didn't know where Francine was. JJ returned to the Pera Palace and rebooked the car again for the following day. Noting the time, he decided to try the railway station. As he left the hotel he noted his blue-suited follower was in attendance. JJ was disappointed to find that Francine was not at their usual table, he asked the waiter, who claimed not to have seen her.

Feeling totally dejected he walked slowly back to his hotel. He walked slowly trying to analyze his feelings for her and his motives for trying to find her. Had he put the image of Abdul and his nightmare of yesterday out of his mind? Did he still love her? Did he still want her? Could he be intimate with her again?

He was completely at a loss to explain his actions and his thoughts. He was, however, determined to find her.

The following day was a repeat of the first day – telephone to Ayşe, visit to training camp, walk to the station. His follower was beginning to annoy him – at one point he almost stopped and attacked him. His better judgment prevailed and he decided that the last thing he needed at that point was to have the police his definite enemy.

The third day he varied his routine a little and after leaving the training camp drove down to Kadicoy and visited the restaurant where they had eaten on that first day. Again, a blank, it was as if she did not exist, nobody knew anything concerning her whereabouts.

He drove slowly back to the hotel and on entering the foyer he was given an envelope along with his room key. He put both in his pocket as he made his way up to his suite. He went immediately into the sitting room and poured himself a very large whisky. Sitting in one of the deep armchairs, he took the envelope from his pocket and carefully opened it. Pulling the folded piece of paper from the envelope, he took a sip of his drink before opening the letter. It simply read:

> *JJ,*
>
> *After your attitude towards me on your return from England and your wife I do not wish to see you again.*
>
> *Furthermore, the group has decided to cancel the attack on the bridges. We have decided that such a venture could never succeed and it could result in a futile waste of life. Neither of these items are open to any discussion whatsoever.*
>
> *Goodbye.*

JJ was absolutely devastated, the two most important things in his life had been snatched from his grasp with a few simple words on a piece of paper and he was powerless to do anything about it.

He decided that he would not go down for dinner that evening, instead, he ordered a steak and salad along with a bottle of red wine from room service and sat looking out over the Golden Horn eating, drinking and thinking. He didn't enjoy his food, the wine tasted sour. The whisky on the other hand had been going down well. He felt that there was no point feeling sorry for himself, as it was his own fault and decided that he would spend the next day visiting all the places that they had been, on the off chance of finding Francine.

# Chapter Thirty Seven

JJ spent a futile day searching all the places that he and Francine had ever visited. He didn't venture to the Black Sea, knowing that she couldn't have got there alone! When he arrived back at the hotel he was feeling exhausted and disappointed. He booked a table for dinner on the off chance that Francine would dance again. He had a miserable meal. The food, as usual, was excellent but he was finding it difficult to get over the loss of both Francine and his project. He decided that he had lost Francine and staying in Istanbul would not help. She had obviously decided that she was finished with him and staying around would only make his grief harder too hard to bear.

The following morning he booked a one-way way airline ticket to London and spent what time he had left in the city by shopping, hoping that he would see Francine, maybe in the bazaar or her other favorite shops. Not a sight. He phoned Ayşe again but she claimed to have no knowledge of her whereabouts. JJ was not completely satisfied that she was telling him the truth, but if Francine had gone to such lengths to disappear, he was not going to find her.

JJ sat in his first-class seat on the teatime Turkish Airways' flight to London, Heathrow. Gently sipping at his pre-flight gin & tonic, his mind dwelt more on his first flight to Istanbul and the subsequent passionate love affair with Francine, the beautiful belly dancer, and the adventure that subsequently followed. Then he felt sad at the thought of executing Conrad, who had betrayed them all. Then the sight of Francine covered in Abdul's blood from when she had tried to skin him and the nonchalant way she was idly kicking at his body with the toe of her suede boot, as she explained to him what had happened. The visit he had made to Prague and meeting his old Rhodesian army friends and Marie. His last visit to England and his time with Elizabeth, what was life going to be like being constantly at home? Should he go back to work in London? He had already spoken to his old boss, who had assured him that a job was always available for him. So, should he start at once or take Elizabeth on the promised holiday? He certainly didn't feel in the mood for a holiday. Then his mind returned to the week in Cyprus with Francine. Was he still in love with her or had it been pure lust on his part from the beginning, flattered by the attention of a beautiful young woman? Maybe he had never been in love with her, was it just his body saying, "I want you"?

He was roused from his thoughts by an announcement over the intercom system that they were about to start their descent into Heathrow, 'Would all passengers etc., etc.'

It was the beginning of September and England was starting to show the onset of autumn, sunny but with a chill in the air, the leaves were beginning to fall from the trees. He queued in the sun for a taxi to take him to Reading, home, the beautiful house, his beloved Porsche, the dogs and Elizabeth. He hadn't phoned to tell her he was coming home, it hadn't seemed worth the effort – she would be full of questions to which that he didn't know the answers. Soon enough when he got home and being face to face he hoped would make things easier to explain.

It was finally his turn for a taxi and as he put his luggage into the vehicle the driver looked over and noticed the Turkish Airways baggage labels, he asked, 'Have you heard the news? Some idiots have blown up half of Istanbul.'

'What happened, when, did they say if they caught anyone?' JJ was feeling frantic, why had they done it without him? He asked, 'Did it say if anyone was hurt?' He got into the taxi, *More functional, but not as much fun as Abdul's taksi*, he thought, as he settled into his seat.

The driver told him what he had heard on the radio ten minutes before. 'It appears that army trucks full of soldiers arrived at both sides of some big bridges. They took over and closed the bridges and made any traffic that was close move away about a mile, then sent the bridge employees home, tied up the few police on duty and put them into the trucks. They set explosives all over both the bridges and their supports and drove away down the coast road and met at a point about halfway between, and then one of them got out his mobile phone and pressed some buttons. Then an almighty explosion occurred, apparently, the ground shook like it does in an earthquake. The tops of the bridge supports had disappeared and a huge cloud of dust and smoke filled the air. The soldiers were jubilant cheering and hugging each other like footballers do. They then released the police and drove away.'

'Can you get any more news on the radio?' asked JJ.

The driver fiddled with the radio and gave up, leaving it on a news channel. 'We will hear if anything else comes through, why the big interest?'

'Just curious I suppose. I have been staying near one of the bridges.'

No further news came through on the journey to Reading. JJ had to wait nearly half an hour after arriving home before he could switch on the TV. Elizabeth needed to be kissed and the dogs patted, his luggage taken upstairs to the bedroom. He feigned exhaustion and pleaded for ten minutes in front of the TV with a large whisky to come round. He found a news channel on satellite that was making a huge splash on the events in Istanbul. As the driver had told him, it was carried out like a well-planned military exercise. But it wasn't his plan, not a daring daylight raid. His was to have been a silent night-time attack when everyone on the bridge was feeling weary. The TV presenter interrupted the previous report that was being rerun for about the fifth time, to announce that they had just received confirmation from Washington DC that two American frigates were trapped between the wreckage of both the bridges and that no-one had been injured.

Elizabeth came into the room at that point and interrupted the newscast to announce that she had ordered an Indian take away and she would drive and collect it.

'JJ, I'll only be ten minutes. Can you please set the table and find some wine, and do turn the TV off. Then maybe you can talk to me when I get back.'

He was once again JJ, the JJ of those months in Istanbul were something of the past and that he would never forget. He knew that he would always remember those events – Francine, Abdul, Conrad and Ali, who had undoubtedly masterminded the daylight raid. He realized that he hadn't been an essential part of the team except from perhaps organizing the explosives and weapons and maybe a bit of initial encouragement to the men. He pondered as to when Ali had taken over; probably around the time of Abdul's denouncement as a traitor.

Dutifully, he set the table for dinner and opened a bottle of crisp white wine and topped up his whisky glass, feeling that he would need all his fortitude for Elizabeth's interrogation. What was he going to tell her?

Should he explain what he had really been doing in Istanbul or should he maintain the story of teaching? He decided on the latter, no point getting her all upset when it was all over.

Dinner was a strange meal. He had been looking forward to a curry, something that was not readily available in Turkey. He had developed a taste for the dish whilst working in the Persian Gulf. Elizabeth didn't speak except to ask for something to be passed. JJ decided that attack was the best form of defense. 'Elizabeth, before you say anything, let me try and explain. I had to do something to escape the monotony of what I have been doing for the past fifteen years. I needed to try and get back some of the enthusiasm, ten years of catching the train and the hassle of working in the city. Or maybe take early retirement. The trouble is, I still don't know what I want to do with the rest of my working life. I enjoyed my time in Istanbul, but it's not somewhere I could live full time. Can I afford to retire? Yes, definitely, but I still need something to do with my time. I am not the type that can do charity work, I've always had a mercenary approach to working, people have to pay me a lot of money to gain my interest, except for Istanbul of course, that started out as a charity job, well charity money anyway. I managed to leave with much more, than if I had been working at the old job. I think that I would like to return to my old job and see how I feel in a few weeks. I know they will have me because I spoke to the office before I left Istanbul.'

'It's a pity you didn't bother to phone me and let me know you were coming home!' she managed to get in, as he paused for breath.

'If I had called you we would have spent an hour talking and not got anywhere. I think it was better to just arrive and discuss it like we are now.'

'Just tell me one thing, did you have anything to do with the explosions in Istanbul today?'

'How could I? I was on the plane home when the explosions happened.'

'JJ, we have been married for nearly twenty years and I think I know you well enough to know when something has your trademark on it. You are, in your own words, one of the country's experts in blowing anything up. I do not believe that you have been sitting around in a school when all of the planning and training for a raid like that was going on around you. I believe that you were in Istanbul as a soldier of fortune, not a teacher, and that you put your life and our marriage in danger for some quick adrenalin fix.'

She was starting to become a little hysterical and JJ tried to calm her down by talking to her in a relaxed manner, 'I left all of that kind of thing behind when we left Rhodesia. I know nothing about the explosions in Istanbul other than what I have seen on TV.'

Taking her hands in his he dropped onto his knees in front of her and continued gently, 'You know I would never do anything that would jeopardize our marriage and I don't want to get shot again, it hurt a lot.' He smiled up at her.

'I don't believe you and I never shall, it's got your name all over it, but if you maintain that you were not involved I will accept that. How much money did you say you got paid?' she added as an afterthought.

'Enough! I got paid enough. Now how about a drink and watch TV and see if I get a mention?'

'JJ, please don't joke about it. I started worrying about you when I first heard the news about what had happened out there, and I had had no news from you in days.'

JJ poured the drinks and they settled together on the settee and tuned into the news channel. They were still recapping on events from earlier in the day so he flicked through other channels and came across a channel that was declaring it had important news on the events in Istanbul. The newsreader had a sheaf of paper before him. He declared that his channel was the first TV channel to break the news. 'The police in Istanbul have just announced that they have in custody a retired army general who had admitted that he, with the help of a group of Libyan suicide bombers, had blown up the bridges as a protest about Turkey's slide into the hands of the imperialist West, and that they were fighting a Holy Jihad.'

The newsreader went on to announce that in addition to the two American frigates that were trapped in the Bosporus between the wreckage of the bridges, a Russian submarine was also trapped.

JJ turned to Elizabeth and said smugly, 'I told you I had had nothing to do with it didn't I?'

'Yes, JJ, you did, but I still don't believe you. Let's forget about it for tonight, I'm ready for bed.'

'Me too, I'll let the dogs out and lock up.' JJ needed time to reflect on what had happened and how Francine could be so cruel as to deny him his right to lead his men into the attack. He felt utterly devastated.

And so they quickly drifted back into a routine that they soon would both become bored with again. JJ started work in London two days later, old job, old desk and the same old faces. He quickly resumed his life. At the railway station for seven in the morning, at his desk by eight-thirty, down the pub for lunch by one, with part of the office for company, leave the office and be at the station again by six, home by seven-thirty.

# Chapter Thirty Eight

JJ had quickly returned to his old habit of stopping off at the pastry shop outside his office to pick up a Danish to eat with his morning coffee whilst he waded through his e-mails. JJ opened his personal e-mail inbox and was staggered to see a message with Francine's name on it. He immediately remembered that day in Istanbul when he had set up her account and the frustration of teaching her how to open, send and maintain her e-mail system. Clicking on her name he took a bite of his pastry and read.

*Darling,*

*I am sorry that I had to deceive you. I didn't want you to be involved any more in case something went wrong. I could not leave Turkey at the moment, this is my home. I want our son to be born in this beautiful place. I found out while you were with your wife in England that I was pregnant that was why I was so annoyed with you and it also gave me an excuse for not seeing you while we got you out of the country. I went to see my husband and told him that I am going to have your son.* JJ suddenly realized he had never known the name of Francine's husband. *I have told him every-thing. He was furious, I told him I had killed his father, as it was he that had betrayed us and caused him to be arrested. I told him about our baby. He went berserk if hadn't been for the razor wire between us I think he would have killed me, but I had to tell him. In his attempt to get to me he tried climbing the razor wire, his hands and body were cut to pieces, he seemed not to notice, a guard shot him twice in the back, he just hung on the wire like a piece of litter. I am pleased that it was quick rather than the long lingering death of another seven years in that filthy place! I am living with Ayşe until our son is born then I will decide what will be best for us.*

*Seni Seviyorum Jamison Bey*
*Francine.*

He just sat and looked at the message. He didn't believe what he had read. He wanted to cry, to scream. He just deleted the message and, putting on his jacket, went for a walk down the street to try and clear his thoughts. What was he going to do? Could he leave Francine alone as she appeared to want? On his way back to the office he stopped a bought a second Danish pastry. Was all she wanted was a baby and as her husband was in prison he could not assist in the matter? His mind was reeling with all kinds of stupid thoughts. Was she trying to get him to leave Elizabeth? Was she trying to get him back into Turkey? Maybe she had done a deal with the authorities, to get him back into the country and hand him over as the leader of the attack and for smuggling the weapons and explosives into Istanbul. 'No,' he said out loud, to the surprise of other shoppers in the pastry shop. He suddenly realized that Francine being pregnant was his own fault, he had never discussed the possibilities with her. He suddenly wished he hadn't deleted the message, he had no souvenir, no memento of their relationship.

He started to blame himself, he should have searched harder for her, somebody must have known where she was hiding, probably her sister.

By the time he had returned to his office he was thinking a little more rationally. She didn't want him and he hadn't wanted her, he had made that abundantly clear. He just felt very sad that things had turned out the way they had. Oh! Why had Francine killed Abdul so brutally? He could have forgiven and forgot it if she had simply shot him, but to be so callous as to take her knife to him in that way, to torture him. He again felt physically sick at the sight of her just standing there covered in Abdul's blood. Showing no sign of remorse.

His day in the office had been total hell. He had not been able to concentrate, lost his temper with junior staff that only really needed guidance to get a job done correctly. His journey home was even worse, two trains cancelled, that would mean he wouldn't get home until after eight. He had no sooner arrived home, looking forward to a glass of scotch and ten minutes in front of the TV to unwind, when Elizabeth started a row. It was as if he hadn't been away for nine months on his own. JJ announced, 'I have decided to retire, give it all up. With the money I made in Istanbul and our savings we shall be well off. I don't want the aggravation anymore. I'll find something to do locally.'

Elizabeth looked at him in a daze.

'Are you ok, what has happened?'

'I am fine. I've just had enough, the trains, the journey, the job, the people. I want to spend time with you now, get back to how we were when I came home last time.'

She reached over to him and took his hand. 'Thank you, I love you.'

'I love you too,' and he meant it.

Roundfire Books put simply, publish great stories. Whether it's literary or popular, a gentle tale or a pulsating thriller, the connecting theme in all Roundfire fiction titles is that once you pick them up you won't want to put them down.